BLIND JUSTICE

Also by David Mark

Novels

THE ZEALOT'S BONES *(as D.M. Mark)*
THE MAUSOLEUM *
A RUSH OF BLOOD *
BORROWED TIME *
SUSPICIOUS MINDS *
CAGES *

The DS Aector McAvoy series

DARK WINTER
ORIGINAL SKIN
SORROW BOUND
TAKING PITY
A BAD DEATH *(eBook only)*
DEAD PRETTY
CRUEL MERCY
SCORCHED EARTH
COLD BONES
PAST LIFE *

* *available from Severn House*

BLIND JUSTICE

David Mark

SEVERN
HOUSE

First world edition published in Great Britain and the USA in 2022
by Severn House, an imprint of Canongate Books Ltd,
14 High Street, Edinburgh EH1 1TE.

Trade paperback edition first published in Great Britain and the USA in 2022
by Severn House, an imprint of Canongate Books Ltd.

severnhouse.com

British Library Cataloguing-in-Publication Data
A CIP catalogue record for this title is available from the British Library.

ISBN-13: 978-0-7278-5054-6 (cased)
ISBN-13: 978-1-4483-0901-6 (trade paper)
ISBN-13: 978-1-4483-0902-3 (e-book)

All Severn House titles are printed on acid-free paper.

Typeset by Palimpsest Book Production Ltd.,
Falkirk, Stirlingshire, Scotland.
Printed and bound in Great Britain by
TJ Books, Padstow, Cornwall.

In Loving Memory of R Ashcroft, gentleman and scholar.

‘There is nothing proper about what you are doing, soldier, but do try to kill me properly.’

Cicero, at the moment of his execution

PROLOGUE

Don't move. Don't make a sound. You move and you're dead.

He starts to tremble. Grips himself wherever he can find purchase. Wills himself still. Shivers, as if icy breath were caressing the nape of his neck. He pleads with his own disloyal bones.

Stay still. Be a fake corpse now or a real one later.

The cold is leaching into his skeleton now. His jeans are soaked with rain and piss; mud on the knees, blood on the cuffs. His T-shirt clings to his outline like a second skin. He feels his teeth rattling inside his head. Bites down until his mouth fills with the iron reek of keys and coins.

Keep your head down, dickhead. Be the earth. Be the bloody floor!

He raises his head in tiny increments. Opens his eyes as if expecting the hinges to squeak. Stares into darkness and rain.

He blinks some detail into the static fuzz in front of his face. Makes a picture of the long grass and tangled wildflowers; sees black whorls and snarled stems. Sees headless dandelions: bodies bent double by the gale.

His nostrils fill with the stench of damp earth; of mildew and bog weed; the sweet reek of horse shit and potato peelings; the static tingle of the gathering storm.

His eyes adjust; pupils opening like bullet holes.

Slowly, the darkness delineates into palpable shapes. The murky columns become tall trees; bark shimmering like fish skin as the rain and the wind turn the air into a million prisms – moonlight splintering in a chaos of silvery iridescence.

He raises his head another inch. Glimpses the great oblong of inky dark that pokes through the maze of trees. Thinks his way inside it. *Remembers.* Sees himself wriggling in through the sash window, scraping his belly on the sill, clattering down on the sawdust and metal filings of the workshop floor. The glitter of metal and oil. The cordite. The sulphur. The blood and the gold.

It was supposed to have been so damn easy. Straight in and out. A chance to make serious money for minimal risk. Even split three ways it was going to set him up for life. All he had to do was follow his new pal through the dark of the cramped little outbuilding and into the poky dampness of the pit beneath the floor. The treasures would be inside. He already had the code for the safe. Had a buyer lined up. They were doing something important, something noble, and it was going to make them rich. It was sheer serendipity. Two momentous things happening at once. Trudy's news, and the immediate chance to put things right. He just had to keep his nerve, and help him carry the stash. There would be nobody there. The dad was away at sea, the mum on a course – the lad long gone. It would be criminal not to help themselves.

Seventy miles east. An hour and a half in the silly little car. Dark roads, and black trees and the storm becoming tempest overhead. They had found the place eventually, just where he'd said it would be – found the strange house a little way back from the silent road; shielded by the kind of trees that harbour wolves and witches in fairy stories. He had kept his nerve. Followed his pal. Climbed through the window and kept himself silent as the grave.

Then came the great flare of blinding light, a roaring blaze of unbearable whiteness: bulbs blowing out and spraying tiny daggers of glass; filaments burning with their hot metal tang; bulbs bright as a nuclear dawn. He had fallen. Stumbled into the place below the floor, his senses reeling from the sounds of planes taking off inside his head. He had felt his bones coming apart inside his skin.

He closes his eyes again. Sees his companion. Looks again at a memory so fresh that the colours still haven't dried. Sees *him*. Sees the flash bastard who thought he was too clever to get caught. Prone, in the pit. Starfished: a Vitruvian man, gulping and bleeding; eyes like pickled eggs. He's making strange shapes with his mouth, gasping soundlessly, his hands opening and closing as if an anatomist were pulling at the tendons in his wrist. There's blood leaking from the ugly trench in his shin. Blood puddling on the floor.

He had moved to help him. Stumbled blindly forward through the shards, feeling for the edges of the place beneath the ground.

Then absolute blackness. Dark like the inside of a coffin; the centre of a skull.

He had turned away. Fumbled his way to the open window. Slid back into the cold of the hard December air.

Shouts followed. Pleas. Desperate screeches for help, scything down from somewhere behind him; a discordant screech against the song of the gale. He had felt himself pursued. Heard footsteps echoing his own. Thrown himself down into the mud and the leaves and wrapped his hands around his head, pain singing inside the marrow of his ruined leg.

Here he lays.

Don't move. Don't raise your head. Wait until dawn. Get back to the car, back to your friends. He'll be OK. It was his idea. His damn plan. You don't know him. Not really. The other one doesn't even need to know. Cut your losses, save your life . . .

He catches a whiff of something incongruous. Smells roasting meat. Feels his tongue and stomach respond to the momentary scent of burnt pork. Pushes his face back down into the grass and feels sharp little pebbles digging into his skin.

An animal sound from somewhere nearby. The shriek of a creature in pain. Goose pimples rise all over his body as some ancient sense memory takes hold of his synapses and sinews. He feels himself shake as adrenaline floods him. Knows, suddenly, that if he doesn't get out of here right now, something terrible is going to happen.

He wriggles through the damp grass. Slides and slithers over tree roots and thistles, sodden branches and the mulch of dead grass. Moves like a snake emerging from dead skin.

Another scream. A cry of absolute horror; as if somebody were looking at parts of themselves that they were never meant to see.

He shakes his head. Refuses to allow his thoughts to take the shape they want to.

No. Don't. You're not a hero. Don't be a fool.

He reaffirms his decision. Tells himself that the howl is that of a fox or a frightened cat. Tells himself that this has all been a big mistake. He shouldn't be here. Shouldn't be shivering against the cold wet earth in this little patch of woodland in some secluded little pocket of East Yorkshire. They got carried away with themselves. Talked themselves into attempting something they weren't cut out for. He's learned his lesson now. He's had his scare. He's going to change his ways. Going to work harder; get his grades up to scratch, take his studies seriously, lay off the fags and the booze.

He pulls himself into a crouch. Holds himself like a sprinter in the blocks. Looks up, rain pummelling his features, and sees the great rotunda of bone-grey stone. Glimpses the name carved into the marble tablet. Flashes his eyes over the inscription.

Mortui Vivos Docent

The Crypt. The house of bones at the edge of the woods, where mortal remains lay in their silken coffins and stare sightlessly at the curved dome far above. Tries to make sense of the words, to remember their meaning, but his mind is all storm and blood.

Another scream. The gale upon his skin. The sound of branches snapping far overhead as the elements clash in the dark sky. Feels his feet sliding on mud. Feels spindly branches whipping at his face, his chest, grabbing at his ankles like the hands of the dead.

Running now. Through the woods, slipping and stumbling as the rain lashes down and the ground seems to tear itself apart beneath his feet. A roll of thunder, out there, past the village and the motorway to where the storm gathers above the deep, dangerous waters of the Humber.

A crash, somewhere nearby. Tree roots rising from the earth as if some long-buried monster were emerging from its slumber. Trunks splitting; earth and stones cascading down from the maggoty whiteness of exposed roots.

Headlights, just beyond the fence. The car, back where they had left it. His companions. His friends. Safety, warmth. He lets out a ragged breath, fixing his gaze upon the big yellow eyes of the little Fiesta, illuminating the billions of raindrops that tumble from the demented sky.

Don't stop. Keep going. You're nearly there. Don't say a word. Say he abandoned you. Say he did a runner. Say anything.

But don't let them know. Don't let them know what you saw, or heard, or smelled. Don't . . .

He doesn't even feel the teeth of the metal trap crunch shut around his leg. Has taken two desperate steps towards sanctuary before he looks down and sees the gruesome steel contraption chewing into the bone of his shin. Tumbles down with such force that the tibia rips clean in two – spears of bloody whiteness skewering the tattered meat beneath his knee.

The pain, when it comes, is beyond endurance. It is as if red-hot knives and shards of glass were being pushed directly into the marrow beneath his shattered bones. He opens his mouth to scream and feels mud and earth spill onto his tongue, down his throat, flooding his gullet. Tries to turn right way up, to focus himself upon the lights of the car; the nearness of escape.

A shadow falls across him. An outline of rippling silk. Bare feet. Exposed shins. Robe flapping and billowing around defined well-muscled flesh.

I'm sorry. So sorry . . .

The words never leave his mouth. His desperate pleas spill bloodily into the sodden earth. Hears a faint whisper, an insinuation of words muttered wetly at his ear.

'*Sic gorgiamus allos subjectatos nunc.*'

He cannot reply. Cannot turn the phrase into words he comprehends. Cannot cry out as he feels the hands upon him. He does not make a sound until he has been flipped, deftly, upon his back and the ropes are being fastened around his wrists. He experiences a hazy, far-off moment of separation; of disconnection. Makes out the gristly crunch and snap as bone and sinew and tendon disarticulate and come sloppily apart around the jaws of the trap.

And then he is being dragged upon his back, moving through the wet earth and the tangled roots and the smashed branches; stones in his flesh, earth in his ears and nose; dragged like a felled stag bound for the fire.

Before the dawn, he will remember this moment with something like fondness.

For there is so much worse to come.

PART ONE

ONE

Hessle Foreshore, East Yorkshire
Tuesday, April 8th
6.04 a.m.

He's halfway down the stairs before his brain wakes up. Muscle memory and instinct have conspired to get him out of the warm softness of the marital bed. He was still asleep when he pulled on T-shirt and shorts and placed a delicate kiss on his wife's damp, sleep-scented cheek.

He stops on the squeaky stair and permits himself an extravagant yawn, stretching his arms as high as he can. At six foot six, he rarely gets such an opportunity. The little, white-painted cottage on the waterfront is cosy and snug, but the ceilings are low and each doorframe has been introduced to his forehead enough times to warrant a CT scan. He's not a clumsy man – just big. He's got the build of a heavyweight boxer: eighteen stone of muscle and scars. His huge, cracked hands dangle from dauntingly solid arms. There are white lines scored into his face, half lost in the tangle of his beard. He has the look of a berserker not yet roused from sleep. And yet Detective Sergeant Aector McAvoy would blush to be thought of as a hard man. He's painfully shy. A softie, according to those who love him. A family man. A doting husband and father. A big lumbering bear of a man, with a greying red beard and a shock of unmanageable auburn hair.

He listens again for the sound that roused him. Hears the *tink* of a teaspoon against the lip of a china cup. Hears the soft rumble of the washing machine. He'd nearly mistaken it for the storm. The winds were crazy last night, blowing in off the river as if seeking shelter from the blackness above the sea. The rain had pummelled the glass with such ferocity that he had put down his book and crossed to the window, staring out through his own reflection at the tempest taking place above and beyond.

It's blown itself out now but he has little doubt this will be a difficult day for the area. Trees will have blown down; chimney stacks will have tumbled; power lines will be dangling in wet gutters. Roads will be blocked; commuters will get stuck in static traffic. Tempers will flare. There will be violence. There will be crime.

He opens the door to the kitchen and his face folds into a warm smile. His teenage son, Fin, is sitting at the kitchen table, blowing on a mug of hot chocolate. His red hair is still damp from the shower and sticks up in places. His broad, freckled face is pale and there are dark smudges beneath his eyes. He is his father in miniature – right down to the unfathomable sadness that seems to radiate from his brown eyes. He's wearing a dressing gown and the set of his shoulders speaks of a troubled sleep, and painful bones.

'Did I wake you?' asks Fin, quietly. 'I tried to be quiet. Is Mum . . .?'

McAvoy squeezes his son's shoulder. Feels the tension in the muscles. Bends down to give him a kiss on his crown and stops himself, unsure what today's rules are. Fin is thirteen, and though he remains in many ways the sweet and thoughtful boy of his childhood, he's very nearly man-sized and sometimes flinches at displays of affection.

'I was awake anyway,' says McAvoy, in his soft Scottish brogue. 'And your mother can sleep through an earthquake.'

Fin nods, satisfied. 'There's more hot chocolate in the pan,' he says, pointing at the cooker. 'I was going to give it to Lilah, but first come, first served.'

McAvoy smiles at his boy. Lilah, seven, won't wake for at least another hour and even then it will be amid serious protest. She doesn't mind school, but has serious misgivings about the curriculum and has a tendency to get annoyed when her teachers don't treat her objections seriously. She has the personality of a single mum in their mid-forties: somebody who has seen it all and punched some of it. Her teachers are slightly afraid of her. McAvoy has yet to win an argument with Lilah. He feels slightly nervous about the potential consequences of his actions as he pours the sludgy hot chocolate into his big mug and sits down at the table next to his boy.

'Happen again, did it?'

Fin looks down into his mug. Nods. 'Sorry.'

'We all wet the bed now and again,' says McAvoy. 'Auntie Trish most nights. And you didn't need to wash them yourself, son. I'm here for that stuff. And Mum . . .'

'Mum gets so sad about it,' he says, and his hands turn white around the mug. 'I don't know if I want to talk about it or forget it forever. It's like it happened in a nightmare or something but then I get sleepy and lose control of myself and it feels like it's happening again. The man's got me and he's tying me up and hurting me, but how do I tell her that? She can't help it – her eyes just fill up like there's a tap running inside her head. And you . . .'

'What about me?' asks McAvoy, gently. 'I'm here for you. Here for whatever you need.'

Fin leans over and gives him a nudge with his elbow, managing a smile. 'You don't even know how to use the washing machine.'

McAvoy opens his mouth to protest then closes it again, gently chastened. He can't really object to the gentle character assassination. The last time he tried to help out around the house he ended up shrinking all the school uniforms and ladling half a bottle of fabric softener into the tumble drier. The children still refer to it as The Day of The Suds. So do some of the neighbours. His wife, Roisin, is a proud Traveller woman and will not allow him to perform any task that falls under the banner of 'housework'. She has been firm about this throughout their fourteen-year marriage. He is expected to provide a wage and to be equal to whatever challenges life throws at them. She, in return, sets herself the task of keeping their little home sparkling and the bellies of her loved ones full. She is dismissive of her own contributions to the family purse – operating a 'don't-ask-don't-tell' policy whenever Aector raises an eyebrow about the origins of some new piece of furniture or finds a rolled-up sock full of banknotes down the back of the sofa. McAvoy has long since stopped trying to alter her outlook. He's a modern man who wants to do his bit to lighten her load but Roisin resists his every entreaty. Only when it comes to parenthood does she relent. He is a hands-on dad: great at story time, play time, bath time. He hasn't ever really got the hang of discipline, but Roisin makes up for his shortcomings. Her love for her children is fierce. So is her temper.

'It was the same dream,' says Fin, quietly. 'The water. The place. Him.'

McAvoy reaches out and rubs his son's back. His chest gives a painful flutter; his fingers and toes prickling with pins and needles as the sheer weight of feeling floods through him. He would give his life if it meant Fin could forget what happened to him six months ago. He can feel his heart being squeezed within a pitiless fist as he considers what his son has endured – the things he has seen his father do to save him. The ordeal has left him with night terrors. At first he would wake screaming and lashing out at the darkness. Now he barely makes a sound. Just wets the bed and wakes in sodden clothing and with sweat drying on his skin. He bears it with fortitude. Showers, and washes his sheets. Gets himself ready for school and does his bit to get his little sister ready for the day. He doesn't talk about it unless he's asked. McAvoy has encouraged him to visit a trauma specialist but as yet he has resisted. He just wants to be left alone to work through it all. His school has been good about it. He's not got many friends but he's not somebody that the bullies are likely to target. He just plods on: sad and tired and fearing closing his eyes.

'Did you hear the storm?' asks McAvoy, wiping chocolate off his moustache. 'I thought the window was going to come in.'

Fin nods. 'I heard Lilah shouting at it,' he smiles. 'Telling the wind that if it didn't shut up she was going to kick its head in.'

McAvoy winces. 'Maybe better not relay that to your mother.'

'They're as bad as each other. When they argue it's like they're both having a fight with their reflection.'

McAvoy feels a blush of pride. His son expresses himself with a certain degree of poetry. He's a bookish lad, like his father. Reads adventure stories and history textbooks. Sometimes he writes a journal or dashes off a few lines of thoughtful prose. He does it for himself rather than for anybody else, but McAvoy delights in seeing his boy express himself. He's envious, in a way. Wishes he had found the way to channel his feelings when he was still an adolescent. Perhaps then he wouldn't still be so bloody hopeless at forty-two.

'PE this morning isn't it?' asks McAvoy. 'Field will be soaking. If you don't fancy it I can write you a note.'

'Not wanting to do something is not a good enough reason not to do it,' says Fin, adopting his father's accent. 'A wise man said that, I think.'

McAvoy grins and screws up his face in embarrassment. 'He sounds like a bit of a pain.'

'He means well,' says Fin, and looks at his father with eyes that have seen too much.

On the wall by the door, the landline chirrups into life. McAvoy winces and jumps up, knocking his chair to the floor and growling in frustration at himself. He grabs for it and bangs against the table, causing Fin's mug to clatter onto its side and spill a gloopy sludge of chocolate onto the white lace cloth.

'Oh, for the love of God,' mutters McAvoy, whipping off his T-shirt and blotting uselessly at the stain. Fin looks at him, half a smile on his face, then gets up and plucks the phone from the cradle.

'Morning Auntie Trish,' he says, by way of greeting. He looks back to his father: huge and feckless in his shorts; a great map of scars beneath the grey hair of his broad chest. 'Yes. No, he's up but his mobile will be upstairs. No. No, I don't want to tell him that, it would make him sad and Mammy would give me grief. Yeah. About twenty minutes, probably, though you might have to get him breakfast on the way. Thanks. No, it will go away, I know it will. I know that. I do know, yes. OK, I'll tell him. Yep. See you then. Bye.'

Fin hangs up and turns back to his father. 'Auntie Trish says there's been a body found in the woods out at Brantingham. Doesn't know much more but she's stuck with it and she's already got so much to do that she thinks she might have a stroke before lunch. So you've got it, because that's what you're for, and if you look all sad and put-upon then I'm to take a picture and send it to her so she can add it to the pile. Detective Constable Two-Shits will be picking you up in twenty minutes and you're not to forget your wellies.'

McAvoy pushes his hair back from his face, smearing perspiration into his temples. His boss, Detective Superintendent Trish Pharaoh, is his closest friend. She knows him and his family better than anybody. But sometimes, just sometimes, he'd like her to respect protocol and social boundaries, and not treat his children like civilian staff in the Serious and Organized Unit of Humberside Police.

'Oh,' says McAvoy. 'Right.'

Fin makes a rectangle out of his fingers and thumbs and points the imaginary phone at his dad. 'There,' he says, smiling. 'That's the expression. Click.'

TWO

Twenty-five minutes later, McAvoy is sitting in the passenger seat of a Subaru WRX STi. He knows the make, model, specifications and cubic capacity because Detective Constable Berco Fusek talks about little else. He loves his fast, ultra-shiny blue car in the same way that small children love unicorns. McAvoy is drinking tea from an insulated travel-mug and knows from past experience that it is impossible to complete such an action without dribbling at least three sips into the general vicinity. He's endeavouring to make sure that any errant drips land upon his own blue suit or his green-and-gold tie, rather than onto the cream leather seats of Fusek's pride and joy. Pharaoh, who has sent him three text messages in the past five minutes, is encouraging him to unscrew the lid and pour the remaining contents into the footwell. Her latest missive, offered as a direct order, included the instruction to 'do a shit and stamp in it'. She rates the junior officer as a detective but is very much a person who likes to poke somebody in the nostril just to see how they will react.

McAvoy glances at his colleague, who appears to still be talking about the car. He's in his early thirties and though his family are Czech, he speaks with a Manchester accent that is pure Britpop. He's got the right hairstyle for the gig too: dark locks brushed forward and clippered into a severe fringe. With his slim frame and silver-grey suit, his pinstriped shirt and floral tie, McAvoy senses that he would quit the police service in a moment if he had the chance to work as a roadie for Paul Weller.

They're heading west: fifty miles per hour on the A63 – sending great waves of standing water splashing onto the hard shoulder. The sky above still throws down the occasional handful of rain but the worst of the storm has blown itself out. The road is quieter than usual, even given the hour. Fusek is enjoying the ride, pulling in behind fat-bottomed wagons, then racing out into the middle lane as if trying to avoid detection. McAvoy has the distinct sensation that the young man is pretending to be a spy in a high-speed chase. He feels horribly uncomfortable in the bucket-style seats: his knees up by his shoulders and his hands splayed on his thighs.

'That were a lass driving that wagon – d'you see that? She was all right too, though I think she might have been eating a Scotch egg. Hard bit of food to eat elegantly, the Scotch egg, don't you think? They really Scotch, or is that, like, marketing speak? I mean, do you actually eat 'em up in Jock-land? I remember hearing that you all tell the tourists that haggis are little wild creatures, running around in the heather. That true? I couldn't eat one – looks bloody awful. Salute them, don't you? Say poems? Each Burns Night? Bit fucking weird some of you lot – no offence meant. And that Burns – he were mad for it, weren't he? Proper shagger, though I reckon I could give him a run for his money . . .'

McAvoy feels a drip of tea fall from his lower lip. Feels momentarily conflicted.

'Almost got a place there when I moved,' says Fusek, nodding towards the village to their left. 'North Ferriby, isn't it? I heard they had a decent non-league side. Might have given football a go myself if it wasn't for the cruciate ligament. Doctor said he'd never seen a CL so badly damaged. Said it was a miracle I was even walking, let alone that I stayed on until full-time and put through the pass that led to the winner. Beautiful ball, it was. Curled it in and he took it on the volley. Neat daisy-clipper into the bottom corner. I've got a video of it on my phone, I can show you when we stop . . .'

McAvoy wonders whether DC Fusek is aware of his nickname . . . DC Two-Shits. It was the newly promoted Detective Sergeant Ben Neilsen who had come up with it. Fusek has always done more than everybody else. Whatever story is being told, he has done the same, and more besides. Got a headache? Fusek has overcome a brain tumour. Run the marathon? Fusek's won it. Got a commendation for bravery? Fusek has a letter from the Queen, counter-signed by the Pope, declaring him Global King of Courage. And if you've just done a shit, Fusek's done two. McAvoy isn't a fan of coarse humour and tends to grimace at the mention of bodily functions, but he has to admit that as far as nicknames go, this one is rather apt.

'Do you think you could tell me what we have?' asks McAvoy, when a gap finally emerges in the monologue. 'A "body in the woods" is all I've got.'

Fusek glances at his boss. Gives him a second look when he notices the tiny embroidered figure on his lapel. 'Sweet threads, sarge. Is that Hackett? Yeah, I know a bloke back home who can get you Tom Ford at a third of the price. Only gives them to people he knows, of course. I modelled a few for him – ended up in the style mag, as it goes – so he gave me the pick of the rack. Don't wear them for work, of course, but they're spot-on for a meal out. That coat – cashmere and wool, is it? Lining works with the dark blue. Your missus must have an eye, does she?'

McAvoy counts backwards from ten. They're passing the little village of Welton. He knows it well, from the rusty sailing boat that's been parked in a driveway for the past two decades, to the pretty valley beyond the pub and the duck pond where he and Roisin used to picnic when the kids were small.

'We're nearly there,' mutters McAvoy. 'I'd really appreciate some information.'

'Rattling on, aren't I?' laughs Fusek, changing down through the gears and roaring into the outside lane with enough force to push McAvoy into the leather. 'Had two Red Bulls and a double espresso when Pharaoh called so I'm wired as fuck.'

'The boss,' mumbles McAvoy. 'It's her full name and rank, or *the boss*.'

Fusek doesn't hear the rebuke over the roar of the engine. 'Walker called it in this morning – early enough that it's still more or less night-time. Name of Mappleton. First name begins with a D. Doris? Maybe Denise. Or Alison. Did the decent thing and called 999. Blues-and-twos were straight there. She was good enough to wait, even though she must have been piss-wet through. Uniform lads had a job finding her but we're good on that score as we've got the grid ref in the satnav. Oh shit, there's the turn . . .'

McAvoy feels his guts contract as Fusek swings the car onto the slip road to their left and zooms across the crossroads in a spray of dirty rain. This is the road to Brough: a fair-sized town that's home to aerospace giant BAE Systems. It's a respectable postcode, although the other nearby villages routinely add a zero on to the asking price for being a bit further away from the busy motorway. Little places like Elloughton, Welton and Riplingham are where the serious money lives, though there are some pleasant little houses scattered in and around the more palatial homes. McAvoy has investigated murders here as often as he has been called to suspicious deaths on the sink estates in nearby Hull. He knows that murder doesn't respect county lines.

'PC Zara Carver was the one who confirmed it as a suspicious death,' continues Fusek. 'Straight on the blower to CID. DCI on call didn't get the message because the storm had bollocksed the power lines nearby and he was busy bailing out his hallway in his jim-jams. So it went to Serious and Organized. Pharaoh bagged it. Called me. Called you. And here we are.'

McAvoy winces as the Subaru skids around to the right, bouncing over potholes in a shower of grit. They pass an impressive bungalow with decorative eaves and neat gardens, shielded from the road by a screen of tall shrubs. A little up ahead the road starts to climb and the forest creeps gingerly down the flanks of the hill, thickening on both sides of the road until the branches meet overhead and the Subaru's lights switch automatically to full beam.

McAvoy glances at his phone. There's not much of a signal here but he's able to receive texts and emails without too much delay. Roisin has woken in the half hour since he left home and has taken it upon herself to tell him that she's warm and naked and enjoying the smell of him on the bedsheets. He has to fight the urge to smile like a schoolboy. He is very much in love with his wife and their long years of marriage have done nothing to dull their passion for one another. He sends her back a trio of kisses. He would like to tell her about Fin's nightmares and the bed-wetting incident but he wants her passage into the day to be a gentle, lovely thing. He has no doubt that within the hour, she and Lilah will be screaming at one another like sisters arguing over use of the hairdryer. He'd rather let her enjoy a few more moments of relative calm.

'Oh, here's the party,' says Fusek, brightly. Up ahead are two patrol cars, an ambulance and a forensics vehicle. There's a civilian car on the other side of the road. Fifty yards away, a uniformed officer in a fluorescent jacket is putting out cones while another, wincing in the face of the rain-speckled gale, is winding police tape around the trunk of a tree.

A young, bright-eyed PC emerges from the patrol car, jamming her hat down on her tightly pulled-back hair. She looks no more than twenty-five and McAvoy doesn't recognize her. He doesn't really recognize anybody from uniform any more. He's heard it said that you know you're getting old when the police start looking like teenagers. If that's true, he feels positively geriatric. The last time he commanded a door-to-door he felt as though he were marshalling a group of adolescents on a school trip.

'Hard to tell, innit?' mutters Fusek, slowing to a halt and casting a critical eye over the approaching officer. 'The coat and the trousers, you don't know if they're worth a punt.'

McAvoy's temper snaps like a twig. He turns in his chair and glares at the driver: his sad brown eyes suddenly dark; his features chiselled in granite. He puts all of his size and reputation into the glare and Fusek visibly shrinks beneath it. He doesn't need to say anything. He can tell that Fusek is running the past few moments back in his mind and trying to work out what he has done to cause offence.

'Sorry, sarge,' he mutters. 'Red Bull, innit? Carried away . . .'

McAvoy climbs out of the car, his hiking Wellingtons disappearing straight into a muddy puddle. He's glad he took the time to tuck his suit trousers into the legs. The cursing from the driver's side suggests that Fusek wasn't so well prepared and his two-tone brogues are currently ankle deep in muddy sludge.

'McAvoy,' says the officer coming to a halt in front of him. She pulls a little face, half unsure of herself. Despite the cold he feels the blush starting to spread across his cheeks. Those who know him well would recognize what they lovingly refer to as 'the McAvoy effect'. Over the past ten years he has received three Chief Constable Commendations and a Queen's Police Medal for bravery. He's suffered life-threatening wounds in the line of duty and brought down the crooked Head of CID. On top of that he's handsome, in a shy sort of a way, and looks as though he's never quite sure whether to smash through a wall or burst into tears. Some of the younger officers go a little silly around him, much to the enjoyment of Trish Pharaoh.

'You'll be Police Constable Carver, will you?' asks McAvoy, smoothing himself down and stretching out as much as decorum will allow. He feels as though his spine has been jarred loose on the journey. 'Zara, as I recall.'

The young officer preens. Nods. Gets a hold of herself and switches to professional mode. 'Yes, sarge. Busy setting up. Held fire until somebody from your unit could come and get things under control, but we've preserved the scene and done the necessary. We've let Mrs Mappleton go home for a cup of tea and a bit of a rest, but she's happy to provide a statement. She was up at the crack of dawn. Into the old speed-walking, if you know it. Not the slimmest lady, our Mrs Mappleton. Trying to get some pounds off for a wedding in July and the speed-walking is doing the business for her, but in her words, she "feels a right silly twat" wiggling her arse this close to home so she does it under cover of darkness. Five miles a day. Same route, give or take. Wasn't sure she would get out today what with last night's storm, but she put the old fell boots on and went for it. Pure luck that she saw what she saw.'

McAvoy holds her gaze as she talks. The information slips into his head like coins into a slot. He appreciates the frankness of the briefing. Doesn't want to stop her in full flow.

'She was more interested in the tree, you see,' continues PC Carver. 'Big great ash maybe twenty yards into the forest over the fence there. She does the walk every day, like I said, and she spotted the gap in the tree cover as she waddled past. Tree had blown down, you see. You heard the gales last night, trees down all over the bloody area. This one must have made a bloody racket. She couldn't help popping into the woods for a bit of a peek. Thought she might get a picture snapped off for BBC Look North or Facebook. Must have been a hell of a fright in the half-light.'

'Are you going to lead the way?' asks McAvoy. 'I can suit up . . .'

'CSI have laid a trail,' she says, and gestures to the little wooden fence at the edge of the wood. It's low and sagging in places but beyond it are a series of metal footplates. McAvoy steps over the fence, Fusek silent to his rear, and follows the young officer as she steps lightly between the trees. McAvoy grimaces as rain falls between the branches and down his collar. Shivers as he remembers another day, another case: looking up through the kaleidoscope of branches and blood as the life dribbled out of him. Has to shake away the memories before they overwhelm him.

'Yonder,' says PC Carver and there's a touch of rural Cheshire to her accent. McAvoy moves past her and slips beneath a broken branch, ducking under a great spray of sodden branches. Ahead is a tall ash tree, laid out on its side. At its base stands a wall of roots: a tangle of mud-soaked serpents standing at least twelve feet from the ground. McAvoy thinks of a peacock displaying its splendour: considers a thick spiderweb across the mouth of a dark cave. Nothing seems to quite fit. The exposed roots look like nothing but themselves: so many maggoty, tuberous twists dripping peat and dirt and rain upon the forest floor.

McAvoy moves forward. Steps around the curve of the fan. Catches the smell of the exposed underbelly of the forest: the loam and mulch and fungus of the world beneath his feet.

Stops short as he sees what dangles from the roots of the fallen tree.

'Jesus,' mutters McAvoy, wiping the rain from his face.

Fusek appears beside him. Blasphemes, similarly, under his breath. PC Carver joins them and together they stare for a moment at the rotten corpse, dangling from the roots in a messy tangle of tattered meat and exposed bone.

McAvoy refuses to look away. Focuses on the mud-spattered face. Strips of rotten meat hanging in places from the sunken cheekbones. The teeth grin yellowly from a gap in the covering of dirt. McAvoy stares. *Sees.*

'Yes,' whispers PC Carver. 'You see . . .?'

Fusek narrows his eyes. Sees the glint of metal; the nail heads protruding from the sightless eyes.

McAvoy looks down at the forest floor. Looks at the

collection of bones that protrude from the gaping hole in the earth. Looks back to the body: the ribcage and skull; the arm caught on a lengthy root and seeming to point at a place deep within the wood.

'He's in two bits,' whispers McAvoy, mostly to himself. 'The roots have grown through him. He could have been there for an age. Could even be centuries old. It may be something for an archaeologist . . .'

'No more than thirty years,' comes a voice from behind.

McAvoy turns to see Dr Pippa Salmond picking her way across the boards. She's Sally, to her friends. She's wagging a finger at him and wincing into the wind.

'Sorry?' he asks, gently removing PC Carver from his line of sight and glaring at Fusek until he makes himself less visible. 'Thirty years?'

Dr Salmond gives him a proper grin. 'Say what you want about early man but I don't think they wore Adidas Gazelles.'

McAvoy spins back to look at the ruined human being that dangles from the tree. Looks down again to the dark brown earth. Sees the tattered running shoe. Sees the mess of meat and bone that protrudes from within.

'Oh,' says Fusek. 'Oh fuck.'

All things considered, McAvoy can find nothing in the statement to contradict.

THREE

McAvoy has wriggled himself inside a white forensics suit and pulled on a pair of blue booties. From behind, he looks like a snowman built with a tractor. He's standing on a metal footboard halfway up the length of the fallen tree, examining a strange scar in the trunk. It's a deep groove, long since healed over: an abraded ridge around three feet long. McAvoy cocks his head, trying to get a better view. In his ear, Detective Superintendent Pharaoh is insisting he tell her everything he can see, including if he knows how quickly he will have an ID and whether or not the body was found with a note pinned to its chest with the name and address of whoever put them in the ground.

'Ash tree,' mumbles McAvoy. '*Fraxinus excelsior*. Deep roots. Deep Pagan symbolism, from what I can recall. Representations of solidity in some cultures, fertility in others. Certain supernatural aspects, if you've got the time. Pliny said that snakes were afraid of it – that a snake would throw itself into a fire rather than enter a circle made of branches of the ash tree . . .'

'For Christ's sake,' growls Pharaoh, in his ear. 'No Pliny, Aector. Not today.'

McAvoy turns away from the tree to where the science officers are erecting a tent around the exposed corpse. Dr Salmond is squatting down at the open entrance; bulbs are flashing on big chunky cameras – each flare setting off a new chirping and fluttering in the branches above.

'It's not quite private land,' says McAvoy, watching as DC Fusek looks disconsolately at his ruined shoes and places them in a paper evidence bag. One of the CSIs saw him step from the footplates and decided his footwear would need to be seized to avoid any accusation of cross-contamination.

'Go on,' says Pharaoh, sounding harassed. She's in her office, smoking out of the open window trying to manage a case load that sent her predecessor mad. She's currently Acting Head of

CID having left McAvoy in nominal charge of the rapidly depleting Serious and Organized Unit. As Acting Detective Inspector he commands two sergeants, five constables and three civilian staff. He has a softer management style than Pharaoh: finding it impossible to say no to any reasonable request and preferring to do everything himself rather than give an order that might be questioned or ignored.

'We're sort of halfway between Brantingham and Welton,' he continues. 'Brantingham Dale is just beyond the ridge and this little copse of trees is next to the road that leads up towards Walkington. Do you know where I mean?'

'I'm not even listening,' grumbles Pharaoh, her teeth clamped around the butt of her long black cigarette. 'I'm just hearing a kind a buzz of static interspersed with made-up words.'

'There are three houses nearby,' replies McAvoy hurriedly. 'Quarter of a mile or so between each one. We'll get them door-knocked as soon as we know what we're asking. There's the remains of a fence a little way into the wood and beyond that is a bungalow with a couple of outbuildings. We'll go there first.'

'ID, Hector,' says Pharaoh. 'I need more than their trainers. If the deputy chief asks what resources we'll need, I don't want to have to fall back on some interesting trivia about Pliny.'

'Dr Salmond has only just got herself set up. The CSIs are working hard. I'll see what I can do to hurry things on.'

'Fine, fine,' says Pharaoh impatiently. She pauses, grinding out her cigarette. Her tone changes as she transforms from his boss to his friend. 'How's Fin?'

McAvoy gives a little grunt: a bear stung by a bee. 'He's trying,' he says, softly. 'Breaks my heart.'

'He'll get there,' says Pharaoh. 'He's tough.'

'I don't know what to teach him,' says McAvoy, softly. 'Is toughness what he needs? Bury it all down for somewhere in the future? Help him work through it? Paint his feelings? There's so many books giving contradictory advice . . .'

'Just be you,' says Pharaoh, gently. 'Do your best. You, Roisin, Lilah – he's got a good team around. And if all else fails I'll get him pissed and let him punch a drug-pusher in the cells for an hour.'

McAvoy doesn't laugh but there's a smile in his voice as he thanks her and hangs up. He makes his way back to Dr Salmond who is crouched down in front of the dangling human remains. She looks up at him through a pair of protective goggles: strands of hair somehow conspiring to create a mesh within.

'Ah, Aector,' says Salmond, brightly. 'You have the look of a well-groomed yeti, if you'll pardon my saying so. I sense from the colour of you that you've been speaking to Trish. Swamped, isn't she? Don't you find that one's reward for being good at something means more and more opportunities to do that thing? Something of a disincentive, I've always found . . .'

McAvoy stands still, waiting for her to tell him something he can use. He used to always have a notepad in his hand: scribbling Teeline shorthand at 100 words per minute. He rarely uses it now. He still takes detailed notes but he does so entirely in his head. He has an unnerving memory and his recall of obscure facts is a cause of awe and mirth among his colleagues.

'So, we have ourselves a young male,' says Salmond, chattily. 'I'm going to put the age at somewhere between eighteen and twenty-two, but I can probably narrow that down for you. Caucasian. Brown hair. Brown eyes . . .'

'You've found his wallet then,' says McAvoy, who is no stranger to what passes for humour among forensic pathologists.

'Spoilsport,' replies Salmond with a smile. She hands him a clear plastic evidence bag. 'University of Bradford. Ian Musson.' She holds up another three bags each containing a rectangle of faded plastic. 'Bradford and Bingley account, so that gives you a start on dates. And this is a video card for Ahmed's on Great Horton Road. The other is a phone card. Remember them?'

McAvoy gives her a grateful smile. 'Jacket pocket or the back of his jeans?'

'Left sock, as it happens,' says Dr Salmond, straightening up. She moves past McAvoy and directs a pocket torch through the damp air to focus on the assemblage of leather and bones in the sodden crater beneath the tree. 'I'll give you what I have when I feel able to, but at first glance I'd say he went into the ground naked. We've found a scrap of leather twine that might have been a bracelet or a necklace. But the sock and the trainer were in decent condition – unlike the bones they concealed.'

McAvoy follows the light. Angles his head and makes sense of what the doctor is explaining. 'The leg had been cut off? Still in the shoe?'

Dr Salmond nods. 'Tossed in after him, I suspect.'

McAvoy licks his dry lips. Looks up past the canopy to where a smudge of white cloud has been daubed on the low grey sky. Nods to himself as he comes up with a scenario that makes something like sense. 'Lads do that,' he says, with a shrug. 'If you don't carry a wallet but you need a fiver and your identification, just tuck it in your sock. Used to do it myself when I still went jogging.'

Dr Salmond gently moves McAvoy back, keeping a close eye where he plants his feet. She stops him a few paces away from the hole in the ground and waves expansively towards the scene.

'He hasn't been there long enough for the roots to have grown through him. It's not my area but this is an old tree and for the roots to have gone through him like that he would have had to be planted around the same time it was a sapling and I doubt very much that anybody in the nineteenth century carried a video card.'

McAvoy follows her reasoning. 'There's a scar in the tree. Deep.' He looks around the little copse, staring straight towards the sky and trying to make sense of the geography. There are two tall oaks either side of the ash. Beside him, Dr Salmond does the same. 'There,' he says, pointing into the tangle of branches. A twist of material dangles in the breeze, swaying like a snapped noose.

Dr Salmond calls for one of the white-suited technicians and gives a series of instructions. McAvoy, unbidden, steps further away from the scene, moving back before Dr Salmond gives the inevitable instruction to widen the scene.

'Nails?' asks McAvoy, quietly, when Dr Salmond gives him her attention once more.

'Still in situ. We'll have the whole lot snapped and wrapped and I'll have answers for Her Highness as soon as. I know that's not going to satisfy her so I will say this – the nails are older than the body. Much older. We're talking big heavy crucifixion nails. And they've been driven right in through two heavy metal discs.'

McAvoy opens his hands, asking for a little more. 'I'm not saying they're coins. You can await my written report on that score. But if you were to acquaint yourself with a certain type of *antoninianus* – a small denomination Roman coin bearing the good lady Aequitas – it probably wouldn't do any harm.'

McAvoy thanks her. Screws up his face as a memory scratches for his attention. 'Aequitas? Equity, yes? Justice, conformity, balance – the scales of justice. She carries a scale in most of the images. A blindfold. Our whole notion of blind justice . . .' He trails off. Thinks of the nails through the eyes.

'Rather you than me,' says Dr Salmond, sympathetically.

Takes another look at the body before he turns away. What remains of Ian Musson glares eyelessly, toothily down from his position among the tree roots. Flesh hangs from his yellowed ribs. One of the science officers is delicately brushing away loose earth from the broken cage of his ribs. McAvoy gives the merest of nods: offering up the same pledge that he always makes on behalf of the dead.

I will find answers.

You will know justice.

Feels the cold air leach into his scars and the old wounds start to throb.

FOUR

Newland Avenue, Hull
1.34 p.m.

Neither Aector McAvoy nor Trish Pharaoh are built to feel at ease in beanbag chairs. McAvoy looks like a giant toddler at a soft play area, sinking into the rolls of sagging upholstery and floundering around as if trying to bail out a sinking ship. Nearby, Pharaoh attempts to recline like some size sixteen Cleopatra but keeps over-balancing and rolling off sideways onto the Aztec rug. Both are trying not to laugh at each other but the upper floor of the cosy coffee shop tends to be favoured by students and yoga enthusiasts who can sit in such appliances without injury. Pharaoh and McAvoy are not similarly blessed but have no intention of leaving until they have devoured today's specialist hot chocolate. As such, the setting for their meeting will simply have to remain incongruous. They have serious business to discuss and treat their duties to the dead with genuine solemnity. They also like the spectacular drinks served at Planet Coffee on Newland Avenue and are willing to put up with looking ridiculous in order to boost their daily calorie intake by a hefty dollop.

'This is fucking ridiculous,' mutters Pharaoh, picking herself up and brushing muffin crumbs off her spotty dress. She tugs her leather jacket around herself and glares at the beanbag as if it were a violent criminal needing to be subdued.

McAvoy coughs to disguise his smile, grinning into his hand as he gives up and makes himself comfortable on the floor, leaning against the windowsill and leaning his head against the glass. It's miserable beyond the glass: a fine mizzling rain blown in diagonally by a hard wind. Even so, McAvoy likes this studenty, multicultural neighbourhood. Real butchers, greengrocers, sandwich bars serving most of a pig's backside in greasy white bread rolls. There's something honest about the area. Just two streets away the postcode speaks of Victorian townhouses and well-off, two-car families: of people with names like Mindy and Myles, who like their coffee ethically sourced and put their empty wine bottles into other people's recycling bins. Newland Avenue has more of an edge. The university isn't far away. Neither is Clough Road Police Station, or Pharaoh's flat. As such, Better Latte Than Never has become a regular place for a debrief.

'Are you settled?' asks Pharaoh, snappily, as she shuffles her beanbag back against the wall and returns her attention to her phone. She's still wearing her sunglasses and looks more like an ageing rocker on a comeback tour than the acting boss of Humberside Police CID. McAvoy, with his long coat, scarred features and massive frame, could well be her bodyguard, though anybody suggesting such a thing to Pharaoh would soon regret it. She's keeping score and remains convinced she has saved his skin more often than he has saved hers.

'Press release is through from Gemma,' she says, tapping at the phone screen and glaring at her own reflection. 'Going out in the next half an hour. You're happy?'

'Makes sense,' confirms McAvoy. He has his vast mug halfway to his lips; a giant confection of whipped cream, marshmallows, flakes, chocolate biscuits and a flavouring that might well be some type of marzipan. 'The cards in his pocket don't prove anything and until we get a proper ID we're just running the risk of steering ourselves into what might turn out to be a cul de sac. Better to keep it vague first time out and see what we get.'

Pharaoh flicks her long dark hair behind her ears and gives a theatrical wink. 'Talking like a detective inspector, Hector. You make me glow inside.'

McAvoy looks back out of the window refusing to rise to it. She still teases him as much as she used to but he is much better at not rising to it, or exploding in crimson blushes.

'*Hull Mail* have run with the basics already,' continues Pharaoh. 'Body found, no idea who, Humberside Police utterly hopeless at everything other than dishing out speeding fines, that kind of thing. The crazy fish at the *Yorkshire Post* got a quote from a local councillor about it not being the usual sort of thing to happen out there, but nothing of any real worth. Radio Humberside sent Amanda to the scene and she's no doubt freezing her arse off as we speak. No national interest as yet.'

'There will be,' predicts McAvoy. 'When the details of how he was found leak out, things will explode.'

'The nails, you mean? The coins on the eyes? The foot hacked off at the shin? Yeah, it might entice a hack or two.'

'Especially if it is Ian Musson,' broods McAvoy. His sergeant, Ben Neilsen, has been working the databases and trying to acquaint himself with everything the police files and the internet might have to offer on the man in the ground. It has quickly become apparent that West Yorkshire Police has done precious little to follow up on a solitary missing persons report filed in 1998.

'Family?' asks Pharaoh, pushing her glasses to the top of her head and correcting a spelling mistake on the press release with a stern 'tssk' of irritation. 'Who's been looking for him?'

'Reported missing by student services at Bradford University,' says McAvoy. 'Completed one year and one semester of a three-year degree. Archaeology. Went off for the Christmas break and didn't return. His aunt eventually contacted the university and he was listed as missing, but it doesn't seem like it was anybody's priority. West Yorkshire took the basics, uploaded him into the database. No mention since.'

'So you'll be speaking to friends, tutors, trying to get some sense of his last movements . . .'

McAvoy nods and Pharaoh mimes zipping her lips shut. She taught him most of what he knows and is trying to let him stand on his own two feet. She knows he's got good instincts and will follow the evidence wherever it leads. He has the scars to prove it.

'These coins,' she says. 'This is going to be weird, isn't it. As soon as you mentioned archaeology I just bloody knew we were going to be up to our eyes in cider drinkers and beards . . .'

McAvoy takes a discreet slurp of his hot chocolate and glances at his phone. He has a message from his trusted detective constable, asking him to call when he has a moment. McAvoy gives his attention to Pharaoh first. 'Ben's dipping a toe in as we speak,' he says. 'He's already been on a couple of dealer websites trying to find out what he can about the particular type of coin. Suffice to say, they're pretty rare but not overly expensive. I should have some sense on it all by the six p.m. briefing by which point the incident room will hopefully have had some calls and Dr Salmond will have a clearer picture.'

Pharaoh looks at him, exuding pride. 'Are you enjoying your hot chocolate?' she asks, like a mum who wants to know whether her son's poorly tummy is feeling better. 'And don't go thinking I didn't see you put the extra sugar in. Honestly, you're like a seven foot wasp.'

'I'm six foot six,' mumbles McAvoy.

'That's gone up an inch since I first met you. Isn't that just like a man, eh?'

McAvoy looks down, embarrassed, and sees his phone has started ringing in his hand. Pharaoh gives him a gracious nod and he answers quietly. 'Andy?'

Detective Constable Andy Daniells sounds a little breathless. A strong wind is gusting around him and McAvoy fancies he can hear cars swishing by. 'You free, sarge?'

'Sure,' says McAvoy, warmly. 'How's the house-to-house?'

'Perfect job for a plump chap,' laughs Daniells, into his mobile. 'Three houses? Even I can handle that. Anyways, the site is on the edge of land that belongs to one Professor Dodds-Wynne. It actually listed her as professor, can you credit it? I've knocked on the door but no answer. Posted a card through the door. Old-fashioned place with a couple of outbuildings, all tucked away behind a big wall of woods. No car in the driveway. Next house over belongs to Ray and Eileen Smethurst. Lovely old couple. He's eighty-two and a retired architect. She's late seventies and loves a chat. None the wiser about any suspicious activity in the woods but did mention in passing that the last time trees had blown down in any number was Christmas 1997. She remembered the year as they were staying with family down south – her first grandson had just been born – and the fallen trees made it hard to get home in time for the New Year celebrations.'

'Good work,' says McAvoy, chewing his cheek. 'The other house?'

'Little bungalow just after the turn that takes you back to civilization. Jill Nicholson, fifty-eight. She was on her way out when I caught her. Saw the lanyard and the ID and thought I was with the archaeologists.'

'The archaeologists?' repeats McAvoy.

'Throw a skull in the air and it will hit an archaeologist around this area at the moment, sarge. All part of the Petuaria Project.'

McAvoy is familiar with the huge volume of work that has been done in digging into the Roman origins of the East Yorkshire town of Brough, known by the Romans as Petuaria. Archaeologists have uncovered endless fascinating artefacts and claim to be moving closer to unearthing a fabled villa mentioned in an ancient text. McAvoy, a former Classics scholar and a keen historian, has followed the project with interest and briefly hoped to volunteer to take part in one of the digs. Fin was very much on board with the idea and even Lilah started asking whether there was such a thing as a cubic zirconia trowel. The opportunity never arose. Even so, he's looking forward to seeing whether Petuaria becomes a recognized part of Britain's Roman landscape and has been mercilessly mocked by Pharaoh for spending his 'pocket money' on dusty pamphlets and textbooks detailing past excavations.

'I was chatting with Ben and he mentioned what we have on the victim,' explains Daniells. 'Bradford Uni, the archaeology degree. So when Jill Nicholson brought up the subject, I let her run with it. Archaeologists, I mean. Anyway, she's been in that house for thirty-years plus and remembers a couple of enthusiastic young lads coming to knock on her door some time in the mid-nineties. They were part of some dig or other and were looking at locations for some fancy tests they had the funding to carry out. She said it was all very *Time Team* but they seemed such nice lads that she let them in to her little patch of garden. They turned up a bit of pottery and some old cat bones but it came to nothing in the end . . .'

'Oh,' says McAvoy, trying not to sound too disappointed.

'. . . that's when she sent them up the road to Mrs Dodds-Wynne. Said they could learn a thing or two from her because she was fascinated with history and had been to Oxford or

Cambridge – she couldn't remember which – but her son was just about to go off to university and might appreciate tagging along . . .'

'Slow down, Andy,' says McAvoy. 'Remember what we talked about.'

He hears Daniells stop and take a breath. Compose himself. Line up his salient facts in order of importance and deliver them as if handing out envelopes. He takes every piece of advice dispensed by McAvoy as if it were chiselled into tablets of rock and handed down from a mountain top.

'Mrs Dodds-Wynne of Lepidus House – that's the old place that looks over the murder site. She has a son who went to Bradford University. Studied archaeology. Moved away after the storm in 1997. Antique dealer now, last she heard. The dad is "a massive chap", by all accounts. She doesn't know the family intimately but she's been to the house a few times. Told me I should take the time to look around the gardens where they disappear into the trees.'

'That's a weird instruction Andy.'

'That's what I said. So she told me. Said that's the family mausoleum. Private crypt.'

McAvoy reaches down and picks up the remains of his hot chocolate. Stirs the sludge and cream, thinking hard. 'You heading back?' he asks, catching Pharaoh's eye and giving her a nod that suggests her press release may need to be rewritten. 'I don't want us diving in. Let's try and make a bit of sense of what we know, yes?'

'Why do we always get the weird ones, eh, sarge?' asks Daniells, cheerfully.

McAvoy pauses, not quite standing up. Looks at Pharaoh as she nonchalantly slides off the beanbag and a lipstick rolls out of her leather biker boot. Shakes his head.

'It's the job we were born for,' says McAvoy.

'Not a fucking word,' mutters Pharaoh, from the floor.

FIVE

Claremont Terrace, Bradford
January 8th, 1997

Four young women are gamely attempting to make themselves comfortable in the high-ceilinged, damp-walled living room of this big Victorian house, affecting positions that are a cross between diners at a Roman banquet, and sea lions relaxing on a beach. There is no furniture, but they still seat themselves in the places it should be.

Two nineteen-year-olds, both called Sarah, are idling with their backs to the wood-chipped, tobacco-stained wall, both dressed in a baggy mishmash of nightwear and loungewear: shapeless vests and loose-kneed jogging bottoms beneath bedraggled dressing gowns. One of the women is a redhead with broad shoulders; the other, slimmer, has long purple braids and an eyebrow ring. They are the best of friends. Between them, positioned on an upturned plastic crate, are two bottles of supermarket cola and an American football helmet filled with corn chips. Neither of them know where the helmet came from, but they both agree that filling it with snacks is one of the best ideas anybody has ever had.

In the place where an armchair used to be sits Julie, her back straight. She's sensibly dressed and her hair is still wet from the shower, legs out straight in front of her and hands upon her knees. There are textbooks by her side and a mug of some malty drink. By the far wall is Eliska, wearing a Miami Dolphins top, her brown face turned beetroot red from the effort of half inflating the plastic armchair that now lies disconsolately at her side, air leaking from a dozen different puncture holes. The focal point in the room is the small boxy TV and video recorder, mounted on a stand of lever-arch folders and surrounded by empty video boxes. The carpet, horribly stained, still carries the imprint of the three-piece suite, coffee table and bookcase that still filled the room last term. In their absence, the dust devils in the corners look like a procession of rodents.

A friendship of necessity unites these four university acquaintances. Three are on the same archaeology course at the University of Bradford. The fourth is studying public administration and hating it to the point of madness. She has little or no interest in archaeology, but her friends have told her this is no impediment to studying it to degree level. They stopped caring after the first semester.

On the boxy TV screen, tonight's movie is on pause. Eliska keeps flicking pointed looks at the remote control, waiting for the other three to shut up. This is only their second day back after the Christmas holidays and they've done little else but talk. Now, with *Crash* tantalizingly close to the opening credits, the Sarahs and Julie have decided to start nattering on about their absent housemate. They were markedly more concerned about the missing furniture. Mo, the landlord's nephew and their own occasional houseguest, had been quite candid about its disappearance. He had, he explained a little sheepishly, simply taken it to another house owned by his uncle. The new students there had been promised fully furnished accommodation and Mo had dutifully provided it, just as he had promised it to the Sarahs, Eliska, Julie and Ian when they filled out their tenancy agreements five months earlier. The new intake of tenants will get to enjoy it for a full term before it is moved on to impress potential occupants at another house owned by Mr Laghera. Eventually he will have to purchase enough sofas and bookcases to furnish his entire portfolio, but he will keep putting it off for as long as he can. Most of his tenants are transient types and he sees no reason why his furniture should not be similarly temporary in nature.

'I heard he'd gone to Bali,' says Sarah, spraying crumbs. 'That's right, isn't it? He once asked me if you could surf in Bali.'

'You can, yeah,' replies her namesake. 'Or in wheat. And you can get lost in a maize.'

'What?'

'A-maiz-ing. Do you get it? Keep up. Honestly, you haven't got a clue.'

'What?'

'Do you mean "pardon"?' interjects Julie, blowing softly on her Horlicks. 'You speak like that in job interviews and they'll just send you out.'

'Sorry, Mam,' laughs Sarah. She is well used to being corrected by her prim, proper friend. 'We can't all sound like we've got the Prince of Wales's plums in our mouths.'

'I'm only saying,' protests Julie. 'And you are gross.'

'He's gone, that's the point,' sprays Sarah. 'Skedaddled. Offski. Pootled off.'

'What about Whatsherface though?' says the other Sarah, eating nachos from her palm like a horse consuming oats. 'Trudy-kins. I mean, isn't she . . .?'

'Preggers? Worst nightmare, isn't it?' sighs Eliska, feeling she should probably contribute. She's feeling the pressure of having selected this evening's viewing. She's the one with family in America and a subscription to a monthly movie magazine. As such, she's the Barry Norman of their little group, having cemented her reputation early on in their friendship by recommending a double-bill of *Starship Troopers* and *Rocky Horror. Crash* is very much a departure. She's heard that it's a dark drama about people who get turned on by crashing cars. Given how often she dings her own Peugeot, she's hoping that some of the kink might rub off on her.

'No,' says Sarah, pulling a face. 'I have nightmares about big weird squares appearing in the universe and trying to eat me.'

'That's really weird, Sarah,' chimes in Julie. 'That's something to talk to a therapist about.'

Eliska flashes another glance at the TV screen. Moves her thumb, cautiously towards 'play'.

'He'll come back when he's worked out what the decent thing to do is. Maybe he's got to get whatever it is out of his system,' says Sarah. 'I don't think he was really into her any more anyway.'

'Into what? The course. Who's into the course?'

'Well, he was, at first.'

Eliska considers her absent housemates. Whatsherface left last term. Ian isn't coming back, at least according to Mo. Off to see the world, or at least, the parts of it where he can drink, smoke and work on his tan. She'll miss him, truth be told. He was quiet and studious and though he went a bit awry last term, she was pretty sure he was going to get himself together once the winter break was over. He was one of the few on the course with a genuine interest in archaeology. She hopes he finds his way back to it. Wishes she'd actually told him that she had a bit of a crush on him, truth be told. He looked a bit like the guitarist from Suede, if the guitarist from Suede wore Woolworth's jeans and round-neck knitwear.

On the TV screen, the opening credits flicker on pause. Eliska grinds her teeth as the others continue to prattle. She decides that the best way to end the conversation is to insert herself into it. She throws in a little grenade of new information, hoping that it will ensure they all either shut up, or that the chat becomes as entertaining as the film.

She stretches, extravagantly. Lobs her gossip into the circle. 'Mo said DT is taking Ian's stuff back to his auntie – not that there's much to take.'

The Sarahs open their mouths in unison. 'Is he? That's like, nice . . .'

'Why would he do that?'

'And Mo said he'll pay the rest of his rent – up until summer.'

The Sarahs high-five, laughing as they miss one another's hands. One of them rummages in her cleavage for something edible. The other takes her glasses off and cleans the lenses with her hair.

'I didn't think DT did stuff like that,' mutters Sarah, repositioning her glasses. Above her, a poster of a naked Bjork stares down, happily, shielding her dignity with a large green leaf.

'Like what?' asks Eliska.

'You know. For other people, and that.'

Julie decides to make a contribution. 'Ian was good at Tekken. And he was the tidiest of the boys.'

Eliska shoots her a look of pure scorn. 'He's not dead. That's like a whatsit – a eulogy, or whatever. Don't talk like he's dead, Julie.'

Julie bristles. She's good at bristling. 'I know that. I just don't like people not being where they're supposed to be.'

One of the Sarahs has found a dead moth stuck to some of the fluff on the carpet. She's holding it up by the wings, staring at the pattern, lost in thought. 'Mo will miss him,' she muses, wiggling the moth so that it appears to fly. 'DT will too, though he's been a right pain in the bumhole since he hurt his leg.'

'I reckon DT will quit the department soon,' says the other Sarah. 'Kent will bin him off. He can't keep turning up in that state.'

'He smokes way too much,' adds Julie. 'And it wasn't nice, the way he treated the weirdo.' She pauses, displeased by something. 'I don't like saying that, actually. It's mean, isn't it?'

'Not compared to what we call some people,' laughs Sarah. 'And you can call me what you like.'

Julie goes into full librarian mode, pulling in her elbows to her waist and giving a piercing stare. She's in a particularly judgmental mood this evening. Her boyfriend recently decided that a year of waiting is too much for anybody to endure and used their brief separation over the Christmas break to finally lose his virginity, hooking up at a family gathering with some distant cousin he's known since childhood. Julie is willing to overlook the frisson of incest inherent in the coupling, but is far from happy about the infidelity. She has made the pragmatic decision to forgive him, certain that his guilty conscience will ensure he is faithful and diligent in all relationship matters henceforth.

'He owes money,' says Julie. 'DT, I mean. It makes no sense. He takes a big cut of what we pay in rent and he hasn't got any outgoings . . .'

Eliska gives her a look that is mostly nostrils. 'That's the thing about addictive drugs, Julie, they're quite moreish.'

'I'm just saying.'

'Dropping like flies though, aren't we?' says Sarah, tossing the moth. 'Whatshername, and Ian.'

'Beardo?' asks Eliska. She mimes a shudder. 'I won't miss him.'

'Him and DT were cute, I thought,' mutters the other Sarah. She's braiding her bushy red hair with her fingers and inserting the resulting tassle underneath her nose like a moustache. 'Look, I've got a moustache . . .'

'He was broken-hearted when DT gave him the cold shoulder, so Ian said,' chimes in Julie, ignoring her silly, immature friend, who is three weeks older than she is.

'He was already messed up,' says Sarah, unbraiding her hair. 'Those eyes. He always looked at you as if he's imagining seeing you on fire.'

'Woah, that was mental.'

'He *is* mental,' laughs Sarah. 'I doubt Kent will miss him. I swear, if he told him one more time that he'd got a fact wrong or named the wrong emperor or something, he was going to do him damage.'

The conversation rattles on. Outside, a persistent rain is slowly turning the mounded-up takeaway boxes and discarded essay notes into a perfect mulch. Occasionally a car swishes by. There's a party going on at a nearby house, but nobody from this one is invited. They're not really partygoers. They like their movies and their snacks and they'll down the occasional shot when the bottles of cheap French lager are exhausted, but they're good girls really. Bookish, sensible, well-raised. In years to come they will each wish that they had thrown themselves more fulsomely into their university lives. They will wish that they studied harder too. Most of all, they will wish they asked more questions about what happened to their friends.

'I don't know why the weirdo even came to Bradford,' mutters Julie. 'I mean, with his connections, he could have gone to one of the posh ones. Dreaming spires, and all that . . .'

'Maybe just for the beautiful scenery. Or he really liked rats.'

Eliska's patience finally snaps. 'Are we watching this or not? The video's been on pause for like, twenty minutes . . .'

Sarah ignores her. Takes a final handful of nachos from the football helmet and devours them. 'Did they even get their big score?'

'Get you, sounding like a gangster,' laughs the other Sarah, trying to take her sock off with her foot and pulling a face that suggests an absolute determination to see the job through. 'What big score?'

'That was what they were talking about before the Christmas break,' says Sarah, reaching over to tug her friend's sock off for her. 'Ian, DT, Mo – they asked to borrow my Peugeot but there was no way . . .'

'I'm pressing "play",' snaps Eliska. 'You can watch it or not.'

'You're so stroppy,' laughs Sarah, whirling the sock around in her hand.

'Shush,' grumbles Eliska. 'Have you eaten, like, all the nachos?'

'There's an old box of Frosties in Ian's room. I can fill the helmet . . .'

'Yeah, go on then.'

SIX

The Serious and Organized Unit has gathered in the incident room for the six p.m. briefing. It sits on the first floor of the Police HQ on Hull's Clough Road: a peculiar, multi-coloured slab of a place that McAvoy finds horribly soulless compared to the crumbling monstrosity that used to house the elite CID teams. The Queens Gardens facility housed many bad memories for him but it did at least have a little character. It had known violence, known grief; the stench of cigarette smoke and unwashed clothes had seeped into the walls. The new building, by contrast, feels temporary – as if it's only a matter of time until the coppers move out, and the accountants and web designers move in.

Pharaoh has perched herself on a desk next to a pull-down projection screen and is tapping away at her phone: jaw locked at the hinge like a bull terrier refusing to let go of a meaty bone. Detective Sergeant Ben Neilsen lounges by the door, hands in the pockets of his expensive suit and with his tie pulled down just enough to suggest he has had a trying day. He's late thirties. Handsome. Local. He hadn't expected to be able to stay part of the unit after his promotion to sergeant but Pharaoh moved things around to accommodate him; and allowing McAvoy to continue what he was already doing but under the nominal title of Acting Detective Inspector. For a man who has answered to the name of 'sarge' for the past decade it's taking some getting used to.

DC Andy Daniells looks windswept and manic as he swings on his chair; anorak hanging damply from his shoulders to expose a suit that has taken on the appearance of blue camouflage gear thanks to the pummelling of the rain. He's a talkative, ebullient detective but the elements have briefly silenced him. Even so, he's found the wherewithal to heat up a microwave lasagne and is currently spooning it into his mouth with a Costa coffee loyalty card.

McAvoy, seated beside Pharaoh, gives a subtle cough when he notices some of the civilian staff looking at the clock on the wall or glancing out of the window at the rain-speckled darkness. They've worked hard and would like to go home. McAvoy understands the urge. He wants to spend some time with Fin before the lad falls asleep. Wants to fill his head with pleasing thoughts and good memories before he succumbs to the terrors of sleep.

'Right, lords and ladies,' says Pharaoh, clapping her palms together and giving a rictus grin to the assembled officers. She has been using this greeting ever since a disgruntled junior officer complained to HR about her use of the phrase 'boys and girls'. 'What a busy day we've all had. Has everybody said thank you to Hector? No? Right, do it now.'

All eyes swivel to McAvoy, who blushes at once. There are smiles and a few little chuckles in his honour. Everybody in the unit would give their life for the sarge, but all enjoy watching him squirm under the hot light of attention.

'How's it my fault?' asks McAvoy, sullenly.

'You found him, didn't you? You were first there . . .'

'No, I wasn't!'

'Apology accepted,' says Pharaoh, waving her hand dismissively. 'Now, thanks to Hector, we have ourselves a suspicious death to investigate. Early indications are that we have found the remains of one Ian Musson, nineteen years old, archaeology student at the University of Bradford. I've sent DC Two-Shits to the north east to see his maternal auntie and enquire after any possessions and, most importantly, a DNA sample. As you know, it's a lot easier finding a needle in a haystack if you're armed with a metal detector. A blood relative, or better yet something containing genetic material from Ian himself, will speed things up considerably on the ID. Ben – can you tell these marvellous people what you've found on Ian in the world of databases and social media.'

Neilsen gives a polite smile from his position by the door. 'Nadine and Sarah have done a bang-up job, boss,' says Pharaoh, to grateful nods of thanks from two of the civilian administrators. 'Pieced together the skeleton of his life. Born June fifth, 1978. Mother was Evelyn Musson, aged twenty at the time of his birth. Home was a town called Consett, midway between Durham and Hexham, for those of you who know your geography. Mum died when the lad was ten years old and Dad wasn't on the scene. Went to live with aunt and cousins in a town called Stanhope, about eight miles away. Went to secondary school in a place called Frosterley and was a good student. Interest in history, bookish kid, good exam results, not very sporty. Got the grades he needed for the course he wanted and went to university with a spring in his step. First year spent in halls. This was before tuition fees, of course, but he paid his own way anyhow, working part-time at a newsagents and doing some moped deliveries for a takeaway. Dropped out after the first term of the second year and it would be fair to say that nobody seems to have thought about him since.'

'The aunt just presumed he'd vanished, did she?' asks DC Sophie Kirkland, pulling a face.

'Hard to credit but it happens all the time,' said Pharaoh with a shrug. 'In '97 mobile phones were something yuppies and wankers had and the internet was still borderline *Star Trek*. We don't know anything about their relationship and maybe this kid was somebody who'd spoken about big plans, big ambitions, a desire to see the world. Maybe the auntie couldn't stand having raised her sister's kid. Let's not prejudge, eh?'

McAvoy swivels in his seat and looks at Neilsen. 'Social media?' he asks.

Neilsen gives a wry smile. 'There's a group on Facebook for those who were part of the "D Floor Posse" between '95 and '98. It's only got twenty-one members and my request to join hasn't been approved yet, but I've got the name of the admin and messaged her direct. It's a start.'

'And his tutors? Pastoral care? What's the university come back with?'

Neilsen spreads his hands, apologetically. 'I think they're probably consulting their legal department. Done nothing wrong but the administrator I spoke to almost swallowed her own teeth when I mentioned it was a potential murder enquiry and insisted I go straight to her boss. That being said, I've tracked down the name of one of the course leaders at the time Ian Musson was there. Dr Kent Bromley. His LinkedIn page suggests he's slightly more impressive an archaeologist than Indiana Jones . . .'

'Bromley?' asks McAvoy, sitting up. He knows the name. 'He's the head of the Petuaria dig. The search for the villa in Brough. Private firm, working in association with the university and Humber Field Archaeology.'

Pharaoh smiles at him. 'Do you have his poster on your wall?' she asks.

'I just like history,' he mumbles, glancing at DC Daniells, who seems to be coming back to life.

'The neighbour mentioned that name too,' says Daniells, raising his hand. 'When she talked about the archaeologists working at the dig in Brough, she referred to "Bromley and his lot". Don't know if it's relevant.'

'Everything's relevant,' says Pharaoh and McAvoy, in unison. They each wince at the other.

'I'm intrigued by this Calpurnia Dodds-Wynne woman,' says Pharaoh pushing her hair behind her ears. 'She hasn't called you back yet, Andy, no? OK, Hector, could you pop out there again and see if you can persuade her to take an interest in the body in her grounds? Maybe she's just had a busy day, maybe she's on her hols, but I don't like that many maybes and would feel happier if we'd ticked that box. I may not know my Pliny from my Aristotle, but the name Calpurnia makes me want to arrest her.'

'I knew him,' says Daniells, wiping lasagna from his chin. He grins, guilelessly, as all eyes turn.

'Who?' asks Pharaoh, confused. At the door, Neilsen closes his eyes, already embarrassed on his friend's behalf.

'Harry Stottle. Ran a fruit and veg stall at our market. Nice bloke.'

'Somebody shoot him,' mutters Pharaoh. 'Somewhere non-fatal, but painful.'

'Report's pinging through from Dr Salmond,' says McAvoy, leaning over to look at Pharaoh's screen. She snatches up her phone and squints at the glass. Pulls a face. Slips down from the edge of the desk and walks from the room keying a number into the pad.

McAvoy, momentarily in charge, removes his own phone from his pocket and looks at the cover note from Dr Salmond, attached to the post-mortem report. McAvoy is halfway through reading it when Pharaoh bangs back into the room.

'You're going on loudspeaker,' says Pharaoh into the mobile, and slides it into the centre of the table. Slightly tinny, Dr Salmond confirms that she has heard the instruction and says hello to the group as if she were the new kid in class.

'Say it again, please,' urges Pharaoh. 'Keep it simple. We're a mixed ability group.'

'He suffered,' says Dr Salmond, simply. 'Suffered horribly. The lower leg that was hacked through – there's evidence suggesting a tourniquet was applied to stop the bleeding. I would say that might have been the act of a medical professional were it not for the fact that he was the victim of sustained violence in the hours before his death.'

'Somebody saved his life so they could keep hurting him?' asks McAvoy.

Dr Salmond pauses. 'I know better than to offer a hypothesis, Aector. But one thing is unequivocal. The flesh that remains on his back, shoulders and thighs was ruptured repeatedly in the time immediately preceding his death. Our forensic anthropologist is still seeking any further tissue or materials that might be at the site, but just from what we gathered from the initial site, it's clear that he was beaten repeatedly and that the epidermis was shredded down to the bone. There's also trauma to the mandible mental foramen and mental tubercle . . .'

'Chin and neck,' say McAvoy and Pharaoh in unison.

'Puncture wounds to the soft flesh beneath the chin, if you will,' continues Dr Salmond. 'Abrasions to the wrist: tissue torn down to the bone.'

Nobody speaks for a moment. Each is briefly somewhere else, imagining the agony endured by the young man before he was given the sweet mercy of death.

'The coins?' asks McAvoy, quietly.

'The report will give you it all in detail but suffice to say the coins indeed show representations of Aequitas. Minted as and when we discussed. Hard to say whether they are new finds or a part of a collection with registered provenance. But there is trauma to the ocular cavities that, coupled with the presence of earth in what remains of the lungs . . .'

'Jesus wept,' mutters Sophie Kirkland, as she joins the dots. 'He was alive? He was put into the ground alive?'

'And the nails were driven in while he was conscious and struggling,' says Pharaoh. 'I think it might be a really good idea if whoever did this was in a prison cell, don't you?'

McAvoy chews on his lower lip. He's thinking of the pattern of injuries. Of the ash tree. Of a half-remembered passage from a book he read in his teens.

'The wounds to the back,' says McAvoy. 'A distinctive pattern?'

'Quite the opposite,' says Dr Salmond. 'It's more than one cord. More than one weapon, I think. I've tested some of the material we picked out of the open wound to his back, but that turned out to be a flake of oxidized iron so may have entered the cavity post-mortem. I wondered whether a whip or a cord might have been responsible but the pattern of the injuries is more erratic. There are lesions and tears, as if the skin has been punctured and then the implement torn free . . .'

'Flagrum,' says McAvoy under his breath. 'A Roman torture device. A cat-o'-nine-tails studded with anything nasty that you can get your hands on. Nails, animal bones, little barbs of wire . . .'

'A scourge?' asks Dr Salmond. She pauses, and they can hear her tapping away at a nearby keyboard. 'Yes. Yes, that would certainly fit the pattern. It would have worrying biblical connotations certainly.'

Pharaoh looks at McAvoy, comprehending. 'Before the crucifixion,' she says, her tone sombre. 'Before the crown of thorns. Before the walk to Golgotha. Jesus was scourged. I mean, we don't have any reliable witnesses but that's very much the accepted version of events.'

'I remember that,' says Daniells, aghast. 'I mean, I saw the film . . .'

McAvoy takes a pen from his inside pocket. The pad in front of him is blank save for a name and a date. He makes a series of deft strokes on the page and then takes a picture of the stick man he has sketched out.

'Sending you something,' he mutters, and in-boxes ring out in unison as the picture arrives in the pathologist's email. She doesn't reply at first. When she does, her voice is grave.

'Yes,' she says. 'The position would fit the wounds.'

McAvoy looks down at the drawing. It shows a man with his hands bound at the wrists, kneeling down and with a sharp double-pronged fork pressing into the skin of his neck. His back is exposed awaiting the kiss of the whip.

'No jumping to conclusions,' says Pharaoh, warningly, and gives each of the troops a stern look. 'We still don't know who he is, still need confirmation . . .'

'Yeah, and perhaps there's a really good reason why he had coins nailed through his eyes,' chips in Daniells, eager to help. 'Accidents happen.'

Nobody speaks. The members of the unit fold in upon themselves for a moment: staring into their own laps or out through the glass. Each experiences a moment's fleeting communion with the dead man; experiences a heartbeat's kinship with the youngster whose suffering was truly biblical. McAvoy, who has looked into truly evil eyes, feels his skin prickle and the puckered edges of his scars start to throb. He knows, already, that they are searching for somebody capable of truly monstrous deeds.

'Go do your best,' says Pharaoh.

It takes a few moments before anybody finds the strength to move.

SEVEN

McAvoy is grimacing as he makes his way down the wide stairs towards reception, listening with a sense of mounting anguish as DC Two-Shits does battle with the elements and his car's speaker system and explains that his day trip to the north east has been 'mad, banging proper smart'.

'. . . she was all right, like. Sort of knew it was coming, you know? Didn't give the game away but she could read between the lines. Said the lad was a good boy but always a bit distant, never really any closeness between them. One of those relationships built on politeness, yeah? It was ovarian cancer did for his mum and his aunt just kind of felt obligated and he didn't cause her any trouble. He was a big reader, so she says, and she's a load of his books out in the garage. I don't think she's sentimental or anything because she dumped a lot of his stuff when she downsized. Still in Stanhope though – nice little place by the river. Full of old biddies but there are some good driving roads. Proper put the foot down coming over the fell – thought the beast was going to take off . . .'

'Concentrate please, detective constable,' growls McAvoy, arriving in reception and smiling to see Roisin and the children waiting for him. 'In fact, I can wait for the written version.'

McAvoy looks fondly at his family, delighted to see the impish smile on his wife's face. Out of an innate desire to irritate authority, Roisin has dressed in a fashion that is part Traveller, part table dancer. She's wearing fur-lined boots, a short denim skirt and a clingy leopard-print top with vents up the side. She has four necklaces descending into her sparkly cleavage and her hooped earrings disappear into a mass of dark hair. With her fake-tan over a real tan and her overwhelming odour of Silk Cut cigarettes and fruity perfume, she has succeeded in baffling the new desk sergeant who had simply told McAvoy that there was 'a person' waiting in reception to see him.

'You've got the swab, yes?' asks McAvoy, as Lilah, still in

school uniform beneath her hooded red coat, points at an imaginary watch and scowls at him – making it clear that she's got places to be and no time for his shenanigans.

'Belting, like I said,' says DC Fusek. 'Got an old jacket of his in the evidence bag too. Thought there might be a useful hair or dandruff or whatnot. I'll give you chapter and verse in a bit, but if I don't stop for a piss I'm going to drown.'

McAvoy almost tells him that he's done a good job and not to drive too swiftly on the way back to Hull, but a sudden burst of Morrissey from the speakers convinces him that DC Fusek is very much his own man when it comes to decision-making. He hangs up, and wills himself not to blush as Roisin grabs his beard and pulls him down for a kiss. She's a whisper over five foot tall and ten years his junior, but somehow they look right together. Lilah mimes being sick as her mum smears lip gloss in Daddy's beard, while Fin, lingering by the doorway, gives a shy smile.

'By Christ but you look good coming down those stairs,' whispers Roisin. 'Is the desk sergeant a friendly? There must be a spare cell we could pop to for six and a half minutes, eh?'

McAvoy subtly wipes the lip gloss off his face and bends down to say hello to Lilah. 'How was school? Teach anybody anything?'

'I'm oppressed,' says Lilah, with a sigh. 'She's a dictator, that supply teacher. She won't listen to reason. Why do we have to conform to these Victorian rules? They're preparing us for a workplace that doesn't exist! And the muffin today only had three blackberries and one of them might have been a spider, and . . .'

McAvoy stands up to hide his smile. Gives a nod to Fin. 'OK, son?'

Fin shrugs. 'Rugby match on Saturday. I thought I might go back.'

'He barely touched his meal,' says Roisin, quietly. 'Does he look peaky to you? He looks peaky to me. Fin, show your father your peakiness . . .'

McAvoy feels his phone tremble in his pocket. Apologizes, feeling like the worst kind of husband, and turns his back to take the call. 'Ben?'

'Couldn't find you, sarge,' says Neilsen. 'Just a quick one. I managed to get an answer at the house. Somebody picked up the landline. I didn't get more than half a dozen words out when they said "not today" and hung up. Woman's voice. I tried again and no answer but it means there's somebody there if you want to go and give them a shake. Meantime, I've done a little digging and she's got quite the impressive CV. Real scholar. King's College, couple of doctorates, published some real weighty text-books. Not a lot on her in the mainstream, but if you get yourself into a loop of academics then she's quite the name. Not as much on the other chap registered as living there. Isaac Plummer. No pictures of him in the *Hull Mail* archive after 1991, though the one I'm looking at is enough to stick in the memory. Massive chap. Bigger than you, if you don't mind being a yardstick. Took part in a charity motorcycle trail with some other local enthusiasts and you can tell from the photo that the snapper had to go way back to get him in the picture. I don't know if that's remotely important he's just very much in "bloody hell he's massive" territory, which might mean that you have to be all the other people if there's ever an ID line-up . . .'

'Thanks, Ben,' says McAvoy. 'I'll go directly. Just taking care of something urgent.'

'I know,' laughs Neilsen, drily. 'I saw them coming in. By goodness but you are a lucky man.'

McAvoy colours at once, hanging up rather than have to hear a ladies' man like Ben Neilsen sing the praises of his young, beautiful wife. He turns back to Roisin, who has an unlit cigar-ette between her teeth and is looking at the desk sergeant with an attitude of outright provocation.

'Sorry,' he mutters. 'Now, where was I?'

'Parents evening is next Tuesday, and your repeat prescrip-tions need to be changed from tablet to capsule at the pharmacy, but they can't do that until you see the doctor for a medication appraisal, and if we're wanting that new tumble drier from Valentine then we need to tell him now because he's got another taker, so you need to decide whether you want to pronounce life extinct on the old one or still pretend to be capable of fixing it. And I did the big shop at Sainsbury's so couldn't get those cookies you like but I think I know the recipe so . . .'

McAvoy strokes his wife's hair back behind her ear as she

briefs him on the endless tasks she undertakes without complaint and for which he can never truly express his gratitude. Whenever he tells her he feels as though he takes more than he gives, she laughs in his face and calls him an eejit.

'Hector!'

McAvoy hears his name being bellowed down the stairs. Roisin winces, stopping mid-flow. 'Her Majesty?'

McAvoy nods. 'It's a bad one,' he says, quietly. 'I'll be late.'

'And I'll be waiting,' replies Roisin with a smile, handing over a canvas bag full of Tupperware dishes. She refuses to let him eat the food from the canteen and has brought him some lamb casserole and a huge hunk of pineapple upside-down cake, together with a few scones for anybody who might be working alongside her husband and not being properly looked after by their significant other.

'There's a bowl for her too,' says Roisin, wrinkling her nose. 'But I want it back. And the soda bread didn't turn out right so don't go giving her any or she'll just offer advice, and I'm way too pretty for prison.'

McAvoy pulls her close and kisses her forehead. Feels her whispered 'I love you' against his chest. He gives Fin another glance and sees the boy staring through the glass towards the road. The rush-hour traffic is becoming more sporadic but there are still dozens of headlights casting mazy circles into the wet evening air. 'I'll come say goodnight,' he says to Fin. 'Whatever the hour, I'll come say goodnight.'

Fin gives a little smile. His eyes seem sad and far away. Roisin, pulling away, gives her husband a look he recognizes. She's concerned for him. She knows that he is on the trail of somebody bad and that he will do whatever it takes to catch them. Experience has taught her that 'whatever it takes' leaves him bloodied and bed-bound. 'Be safe,' she tells him, and it's as much a prayer as an instruction. 'We need you in one piece.'

McAvoy watches them leave. Wonders whether it will always be like this. Wonders if it is some kind of sin to be so loved when a young man lies unmourned and brutalized on a slab.

'Hector, I am fucking starving!'

He turns and hurries back up the stairs.

EIGHT

The tarmac feels dangerously greasy beneath the worn tyres of the old saloon. The steering pulls to the left, and there is a disquieting flicker to the light emanating from the headlamps, as though a child is making shadow puppets with nimble fingers against the bulbs.

The rain is still drifting in off the water, but it is disappearing into nothingness upon the black tarmac of the winding country road, while the tops of the bare hedgerows that edge this unlit lane are too skeletal to support anything more than the most inconsequential covering.

'Christ!'

Two wheels in a ditch. A patch of wet road. A sudden, inelegant swerve. Strong hands white-knuckled on the wheel, steering into the slue; boot pressing gently on the accelerator; a change of gear, a squeal of protest from the rubber, and the car rights itself, leaving the driver breathless and sweating, eyes glimpsing the towering, bare-branched oak that he would have ploughed into had he tried to slam on the brakes.

McAvoy, a headache suddenly gnawing at his temples, makes a mental note to alert the desk sergeant to its inadequacies when he returns the pool car to the compound. The desk sergeant will nod. Take the keys. Hang them up. Forget about it. Life will continue as before.

He's heading towards Brantingham by the back roads, giving himself a little private time to think. It's pitch dark and the trees that line the curving road remind him of rival football fans, leaning forward trying to reach one another across the divide. There aren't many houses on the road. He passed a splendid old place half a mile back and he seems to recall reading about a converted church somewhere nearby, but almost this whole section of the map is either woodland or farmland or both. It comes as a surprise when the darkness to his left suddenly takes on the shape of a low, solid-looking building set back from the road behind a line of trees and an iron fence. He comes to a halt in the little patch of gravel and damp grass outside the gates and switches off the engine. Sits in the absolute blackness for a second. He can't see any lights coming from the property but he knows he will need to take a look rather than just driving away and coming back in the morning.

He steps out into cold, dark air. Five hundred yards down the hill is the edge of the crime scene. He knows there will still be uniformed constables guarding the site; science officers hard at work under the orders of the forensic anthropologist. By torchlight, men and women in big white suits will be painstakingly working their way through the earth and the leaves and the broken trees, sifting for scraps of clothing, scraps of leather, scraps of skin.

The wrought iron gates make a suitably Gothic creak as his hand closes around the damp metal of the handle. A white security light flares into life overhead. McAvoy, feeling as though he has been caught breaking out of a high security prison, raises a hand to shield his eyes, watching as his shadow lengthens and disappears into the mass of black trees that encircle the property. Grimacing, he lets his eyes adapt to the harsh glare. Stands in the driveway and stares admiringly at the big old property. Lepidus House is an old coaching inn and although it's been renovated and updated, it still carries much of the ramshackle splendour of its Georgian heyday. The slate roof hangs low; greasily black with moss and rain. The mullioned windows are black as pitch and dead-headed rosebushes cling to trellises mounted on the cream-coloured walls. To his right are what he presumes to be the old stables: three arches with great old coaching wheels nailed to the brickwork; big double wooden doors chained shut across the openings.

'Lepidus,' mutters McAvoy, looking at the nameplate on the wall. He recalls a line from Shakespeare, referring to the Roman general as a 'slight, unmeritable man, meant to be sent on errands'. He looks at his own reflection in the dark surface of the wooden nameplate, and tries not to draw any unfavourable comparisons.

McAvoy bangs as politely as he can on the red front door, tapping on the wood rather than the multi-coloured glass panels.

There's no reply. He stands for a spell on the little porch, hoping for a sound from within. The curtains aren't yet drawn across the darkened windows either side of the door and he peers in through his own reflection trying to make out any signs of life within. There's a letterbox set perpendicular in the door and McAvoy cannot resist the urge to softly tease it open with the cuff of his coat. He feels warm air drift out from within. Takes a deep breath and tastes something appetizing: the whiff of bacon fat and slow-roasted meat. He wonders whether it's worth heading to the back of the property in search of the occupants. There's no car in the driveway but the family might well use the stables as a garage. They could well be home, hunkered down in some cosy room at the rear of the building and entirely oblivious to the big, damp police officer on their doorstep.

'No,' he says to himself, making up his mind. 'No, leave it . . .'

He hears himself speak and curses under his breath. He has begun giving voice to his thoughts of late: muttering under his breath when he is unsure of himself and giving himself full motivational speeches when alone in the car. He remembers it as something his father used to do: rarely silent; always whistling or clicking or muttering as he went about the chores on the family croft. McAvoy hasn't been called out on it yet but he's noticed Roisin looking at him with a half smile on her face whenever she catches him softly criticizing the politicians on *Newsnight* or telling the broken toy that he's trying to fix that he will have it right in a jiffy.

He turns his back on the property and stares for a moment into the dark tangle of woodland beyond the little area of neatly-ordered grass. He walks briskly across his own shadow, leaving a trail of big boot prints on the damp lawn, putting a good forty paces between himself and the harshly lit house. With his back to the property he stares into the trees, trying to work out how far away he is from the site of the fallen tree. He can just see a soft white light, rising like a halo above the rising ground. He looks down at his feet, to where the grass becomes the woods. He fancies he can smell anemone in the air. Crouches down and looks for the pretty white flower but can't find it amid the mulch of the forest floor. When he breathes again it is gone, overcome by wild garlic and the general fungal whiff of the woods. As he straightens his back he spies the outline of the bow-topped building that Daniells had spoken of. It's set back among the trees and, in the gathering darkness, McAvoy feels no compulsion to move closer to it. He is not a fearful man but he treats the dead with a certain reverence and cannot see the benefits to poking around a bricked-up family mausoleum when he could be somewhere else. He turns back to the house, irritated at having wasted his time and still unsure whether it mightn't be worth calling the landline and telling whoever answered previously that they have a caller at the front door.

He catches the scent again. Hears the rustle of air moving through the skeletal trees: their spring leaves only just beginning to bud. He fancies he can hear a nuthatch in the branches somewhere nearby. Reaches out and touches the smooth bark of a silver birch, taking his time, breathing in and out like a bear testing the air for spilled fruit and fresh meat. He doesn't think he's ever told Roisin and the kids the myths associated with the dainty flower: sprung from the tears of Venus as she wept for her slain Adonis. He knows better than to pick any as a gift – the flower's romantic origins spoiled somewhat by the ammonia-heavy aroma and the poison milked from its petals. The song again, from above. The rustle of the trees.

The sound from nearby: the soft footfall of a figure moving somewhere off to his right.

McAvoy, barely breathing, slips into the cover of the woods, pressing himself against the bark. It's instinct really. He may have a badge and a good reason for being here but he suddenly doesn't want to have to explain his presence at the bottom of the garden. He peers out from behind the makeshift hiding place, feeling like a fool, wondering if he should announce himself or turn and hurry back to the car with whatever dignity he can muster.

Jesus, Aector, you're meant to be a police officer . . .

Then he sees him. Sees the colossal figure that Ben Nielsen had told him about. He's moving between the trees: a great bald dome surrounded by a straggle of grey hair, tumbling down into a silver beard that twists and turns like hissing snakes. He's a monster of a man: six foot eight at least, and his shoulders are as broad as McAvoy's. He wears a simple cotton shirt and what look like motorcycle leathers. Wears black gauntlets too. And in his hand . . .

McAvoy slips his hand into his pocket and takes out his phone, activating the video recorder. He isn't sure whether he will be able to make anything out but he tells his junior officers that it's good practice to record anything that may have even a whiff of relevance. Most importantly, he wants to be able to have what he is witnessing confirmed by a second set of eyes. He's pretty sure that the big man is carrying something in his right hand: something shiny and metal and catching the light of the moon.

McAvoy watches as the big man stops in front of a tall silver birch. He puts his big hands on the trunk, tapping at the bark as if trying to find a secret door. Then in one fluid arc he swings the object in his hand towards the tree. There is the sound of metal on wood: a sudden fluttering from overhead. Then the big man is leaning in, taking something from a pocket and pushing it into the hole he has hacked in the trunk. He bends down again, rummaging around at the foot of the tree, and retrieves a glass demijohn and a length of tubing from beneath a tangle of fallen branches and raised roots. McAvoy finds himself breathing out, so utterly relieved that he feels a bizarre urge to laugh. The big man is simply tapping the birch tree: siphoning the sap. It's an old country practice: a way to make a potent, honeyed wine. Correctly done, the demijohn will be full by morning.

McAvoy feels a flash of irritation with himself. For a moment he had thought himself witness to some bizarre Pagan ceremony: had pictured the big man unearthing a stone altar and setting about some hideous ritual. He wonders whether he will speak of this to anyone, whether he will admit to being frightened out of his skin by a man who looms like an ogre in the raven-dark woods.

Only as he is preparing to end the recording does McAvoy see that the big man has not yet finished. He kneels down, rummaging afresh in the forest floor. There is a sudden sound of scuffling: the desperate sound of something small and terrified fighting for its life. And then the man is standing straight up, the ears of a rabbit clutched in his fist; the body jerking helplessly beneath. There is a moment when McAvoy feels like shouting out; to stop the cruelty to which he is witness. But he says nothing as the big man draws the knife from his leathers and slices it through the fur and sinew of the wriggling creature, stripping it from the animal in one perfect, practised motion.

McAvoy shrinks down into the shadow of the tree, watching in horror as the man drapes the glistening carcass over one of the branches then steps back to admire his handiwork. Slowly, his gaze travels upwards. McAvoy, too, finds himself staring into the branches.

As the big man turns and strides back to the house, McAvoy moves silently around the base of the tree, watching as he trudges silently back to the house, disappearing into the absolute blackness near the stables. Only when he is sure he is alone does McAvoy approach the birch. He cannot help himself. He switches on the torch on his phone and points it up into the branches. He needs to be sure.

His gorge rises as he sees that the rabbit still twitches, even as its skin dangles from its swaying feet. He catches the scent of fresh meat and spilled sap. Looks down at the filling demijohn. Steps back and hears the crunch. Looks down at the great graveyard of animal bones: skulls and ribs and meat and fur, all forming a grisly carpet around the base of the tree.

Looks down, and sees the pretty little wood anemones – their pungent aroma now lost amid the gore; their petals stark against the black, black blood.

NINE

It's springtime, 1989. It rained last night but the sun is causing the damp earth to steam and there is a heady pungency to the aroma that encircles this old, low house at the edge of the woods. Steam coils around the trunks of the encroaching woodland: a fine gauze punctuated here and there by the dark spears of fallen trees and errant branches.

Beyond the stable block, directly opposite the big ash tree, a blond-haired adolescent is reaching up to touch the places that were just beyond his reach last time they spent any time here. He's tall, and big across the shoulders. Already he can cultivate a moustache and there is an adult definition to his frame. He eats what he is told to: oats and honey one day; raw bovine testicles the next. He trusts that it is all to help him become that which he was created to be. And it's working. He's getting bigger. Becoming a man to revere. He has been away for a few weeks; travelling, learning, visiting the places that will some day welcome him back as if he were a conquering emperor. It pleases him that he has grown while absent from this place – reassuring him that the power from such transformation resides within him, and not the soil and stones and roots of the place where he was made.

He looks up, again, at the thick, rain-soaked block of timber above the front door. Elevates himself on tiptoes and squints at the wood. There are scratches in the grain. Strange, deliberate striations. He rubs his fingertips against the grooves. There is a power in these symbols. Power like that within him. A power both ancient and new: a source of strength that once painted half the world red.

'Protection,' comes the voice from behind him. 'Like your amulet. Your charms. Your torque.'

He bows before her. Admires the way the folds of fabric spill about her curves; the way the light seems to make her hair into a corona of gold.

'A minor goddess,' she says – her bare feet speckled with dirt and pollen from her walk across the little field before the woods. 'Potent, in her age. No Junio Lucina. We have spoken of her, have we not? Her name derives from Latin *lux*, *lucis*, light. She also presided at weddings, to bless the union with children. Her temple was on the Esquiline Hill in Rome, and nobody with knots in their clothing could enter. I was made welcome. To be with child, in such a sacred place – truly, it was to feel the light of her love within me. For the first time I knew the prayer had been heard.'

'It looks old,' he says, his voice soft, his eyes catching the light. Nods again at the symbol. 'Is it old?'

'As old as the house,' she replies. 'Many different ages have come and gone since the last true power fed this earth. Those marks are the gift of a witch. Four centuries ago, perhaps. Explore the eaves – you will find more amusements.'

Intrigued, he darts back into the house and manhandles one of the kitchen chairs out onto the front step. He climbs up, pushing his hand into the twists of thatch and slate. High up in the eaves, wedged into the gap in the roof joints above the doorframe, he can make out a flash of green. He wriggles further up, seizing something solid and dangling in mid-air, his bare feet wriggling above the lip of the chair. The space smells of feathers and rain. There's a slight whiff of sanded wood and burnt meat.

He grimaces and leans further into the recess, her face against timber and cold brick. The bottle is wedged into a space where a brick should be. Dust and a net of spider silk create patterns in the dark air. He thinks of fog hanging in the rigging of old ships. Steels himself and reaches in.

He lowers himself down and stares at the vial. It's shaped like an old light bulb and there is an etching of a bearded face staring up at him through a film of dust. He gives a theatrical shiver, as if a spider has run up his leg. He holds up the glass. Makes out liquid. Long, twisted iron nails.

'A charm,' she explains, in answer to his question. 'Long after the protagonists are forgotten, a story remains. This place knew blood. There are people who can feel when a place has known sadness. When it has known grief and tragedy. Such people try and control the environment with trinkets like these. Some well-meaning hag no doubt made money promising the first owner that they could be protected from the harm that lingers beneath the dirt.'

'Perhaps she believed it,' he ventures. 'Perhaps it worked.'

She shakes her head. 'We prayed to many before you came to us. Gods and goddesses of all shapes and sizes ignored our pleas and sacrifices. Only Juno gave us what we sought. It took offerings beyond what we thought we could spare, but the reward was greater than our inconveniences. We were chosen. I was the vessel into which the goddess's almighty strength was poured.'

He smiles at her as he always does when her eyes gleam like this. It pleases him to see her happy. He knows his own reflection to be occasionally transformed thus. When he is allowed to read the rabbits, he feels a thrill that is beyond sexual. When he holds a heart in his hands and watches it stop, he has felt himself climax, involuntarily, without the need to touch himself at all.

'Thank you,' he says. He repeats it in Latin, Greek and Etruscan, to show he has been paying attention to her teachings. It pleases her, as he had known it would.

'A gift,' she says, brightly. 'A pleb's weapon, but effective. Easily concealed. Lethal.'

She tosses an oval stone at his feet. He squats down. Watches as a gnat lands upon his skin and starts to feed upon the sweat and grease. Does not slap it away. Lets it slake its thirst upon his divine blood.

She tosses down a twist of soft cord. He wonders whether he is to witness a scourging; whether she will take pleasure today in the pain of her servant. She reads the questions in his face. Shakes her head, indulgently.

'A weapon of terror,' she explains, in her teacherly voice. 'Whistling bullets, guaranteed to terrify the barbarians; the simple, the superstitious. They can kill, if used correctly. They will penetrate flesh, smash bone.'

'The hole,' he says, rubbing his fingers around the rim of the little aperture in the pale stone.

'It screams,' she says with a smile. 'As the wind moves across the hole it makes a noise like a screaming demon. I want you to practise. This is as important as your other studies. Your people used something called a *fustibalus*, a stick sling. The largest stones it hurled were the size of lemons and the smallest, presumably used for a scattering effect in close quarters, were the size of acorns. You might be intrigued to learn that slingers were recruited from the Balearic Islands, where parents would force their children to earn food by knocking it over with a sling first. There will be reward when you are competent.'

He feels his skin prickle with excitement. It is a feeling he is coming to understand more and more. There is always reward for some new achievement; always a gift or a token or some sensual new act that he is permitted whenever he conquers a new milestone. He's on the verge of adulthood now. Almost a man. Already she has initiated him into some of the delights of maturity. He is a willing, enthusiastic pupil.

'When?' he asks, looking towards the treeline, where the big man is tending to the white, delicate bones. 'When will we . . .?'

She smiles, delighted with his hunger. He is vital, muscular, eager for any human contact. She will not have to wield the whip with this one. There will be a beautiful coupling, a union between mortal flesh and the divine.

He slips the stone into the leather thong. Wriggles, breathing heavily, as she takes her place behind him and runs her fingers over his bare arm.

'Like this,' she whispers. 'I learned this from my own father.'

He feels the cord tighten against his fingers. Feels the heft of the stone in his palm. Whips it and hears the scream.

'This way,' she says, again, as she presses herself against him. 'Feel the strength of it. Feel it against your skin . . .'

And then there is nought but the screaming of the stones, and the thunderous calling of his blood.

TEN

Wednesday, April 9th
8.34 a.m.

The liquid dispensed from the vending machine in the canteen of Police HQ is known as Soylent Brown. Most of the officers at the station have never seen the similarly-titled Charlton Heston movie and don't get the gag, but most are past-masters at covering up their own lack of knowledge by laughing heartily at those who know even less. The beverage in question is a broiling sludge, iced with a rim of spitty froth, and it tastes like a combination of tea, coffee, hot chocolate and gravy.

McAvoy takes a sip. It's like sucking a pedestal mat in a student house. He grimaces and flares his nostrils, raising the plastic beaker to his nose.

'Don't sniff it, for God's sake,' comes a voice from behind him. 'There'll be people in yellow suits bursting through the window to hose you down.'

McAvoy spins. The deputy chief constable is having an argument with the chocolate machine. The DCC's name is Callum McVeigh. He's bald and squat with a thick neck that oozes over the collar of his uniform like rising bread. He's a Glaswegian, and though McAvoy is from the remote Western Highlands and has only been to Glasgow twice, McVeigh treats him as if they are from the same neighbourhood and have dealt with the same anti-Caledonian prejudices. He's also, in Pharaoh's opinion, 'a fucking arsehole' who can't engage her in conversation without questioning her on any plans for retirement or whether she would consider reducing her hours, or increasing her workload for less money. He's been with Humberside Police for almost a year and is rumoured to be a personal friend of the commissioner. He's been brought in to help the service do more with less and has managed to replace a dozen experienced officers with cut-price civilians and a fleet of accountants; all going through the books looking for any funds that could have been better spent on something other than catching murderers, rapists and thieves. McAvoy is surprised to see him in this early. He presumed he would still be at home in Kirk Ella, trying to ascertain whether or not the refrigerator light really does go off when he closes the door.

'Please use exact change,' growls McVeigh, as he stoops to pick a returned fifty-pence piece from the slot. 'I'm bloody trying.'

'I'll see if I've got some change,' says McAvoy, politely, reaching into his pocket. He pulls out a handful of coins and walks to the other machine. 'May I?'

'Be my guest. I'm about fifteen seconds from an act of vandalism.'

McAvoy feeds pennies and silvers into the machine and keys in the right number. An instant later, a chocolate bar rattles into the tray at the bottom.

'You're a bloody superstar, son.'

'Not a problem.'

McVeigh attempts to hand him the fifty-pence piece, but McAvoy waves it away. 'Get me next time.'

McVeigh raises his eyebrows, clearly surprised. 'You sure?'

'Of course,' says McAvoy, wishing he'd just taken the fifty pence. He wonders whether he's about to be accused of bribing an officer.

'Much obliged to you.'

McAvoy turns away, raising the cup to his lips again. The smell hits his nostrils and he lowers the beaker.

'How do you drink this stuff?' he asks, doing his best to make conversation and wishing to goodness that he had the strength of character to run for the exit.

'Oh I don't,' says McVeigh. 'One of the traffic lads reckons it's good if you spread it on your allotment, but other than that, it serves more as what you'd call a last resort. When the options are to go without, or drink that stuff, you go without. We tried to get the forensics lads to test it once but it melted the test tube.'

They're standing by the window at the edge of the canteen;

crammed together in an alcove full of machines that dispense various drinks and snacks. It's a feast of chocolate bars, crisps and hermetically sealed sausage rolls. One of the revolving drawers is full of fruit, but it looks like it's been there for weeks, and appears to be only a few steps away from becoming punch. McAvoy wonders if somebody is cultivating a cure for cancer, or at the very least, hoping that it will evolve into something more interesting such as a Twix.

'Morning briefing went well?' asks McVeigh, chattily. 'The Unholy Terror is briefing me as soon as she bloody well gets the chance. That's an exact quote, by the way.'

McAvoy smiles. Manages a mouthful of sludge. He's bone-tired. He didn't get much sleep last night and was up before six a.m.: Lilah having woken him to inform him that Fin was in the shower and she thought he might be crying. McAvoy sat with him for half an hour, lounging on the doorstep and watching the sun come up, sipping hot chocolate and chatting about nothing and everything. He wishes he could take it all from him: all the bad memories, all the fear – wishes he could take it all in and carry the burden for him.

'I heard on the grapevine that we might have a suspect,' says McVeigh, under his breath.

'We barely have an ID,' says McAvoy, who knows from experience that the top brass has a tendency to get carried away. 'We've got some background on the owners of the house near where the body was found, and we should be able to positively identify the remains as Ian Musson by mid-morning. We've got a DNA swab that will narrow things down.' He stops, aware that he might be stealing Pharaoh's thunder. 'I've no doubt the boss will do a better job of briefing you.'

'Too modest by half,' says McVeigh, with a shake of his head. 'It's not in your nature to put yourself forward, I know that, but there are plenty bastards who'll be glad to ride your coat-tails and it's no shame to point out you've got a record that shows you should be doing a damn sight more than carrying Pharaoh's bags for her at this stage in your career.'

McAvoy doesn't know how to respond so just gives what Pharaoh refers to as his 'simpleton smile'. 'Will that be all, sir?'

'The couple,' says McVeigh, opening his Snickers and taking a large bite. 'Save me the drama and the earache. What have we got?'

McAvoy realizes he has no choice but to give McVeigh what he wants to know. He tells himself that he's sparing Pharaoh an unpleasant task but he still feels like a cad as he gives the deputy chief constable the bare bones.

'Isaac Plummer and Calpurnia Dodds-Wynne,' says McAvoy, in a rush. 'He's 64. She's three years older. She's lived there since she was small, judging from the electoral roll. He's got some minor convictions in his youth. Theft, stealing protected eggs; a bit of trespass here and there . . .'

'I heard he's a big chap.'

'Huge, sir,' says McAvoy.

'Bigger than you?'

McAvoy nods, wondering whether he would be used as a similar yardstick if he were four feet tall or thirty stone. People seem remarkably interested in the fact that the man he saw in the woods is so physically imposing. Pharaoh had been too drunk to take in much of what he said when he called last night to inform her about what he had witnessed in the grounds of Lepidus House, but she had been bright-eyed and full of energy at the eight a.m. briefing, telling the team that thanks to their favourite acting detective inspector, they may well be in hot pursuit of an ogre who spends his leisure time feeding a tree. She'd fallen silent when she watched the video. Neilsen had recognized the act of sap-tapping for what it was, but could offer no explanation for the skinning of the rabbit or the evidence of innumerable other small creatures killed and threaded on the branches of the silver birch. It was, they all concurred, weird and fucking horrible.

'And her?' asks McVeigh, growing irritated at having to keep asking questions.

'Academic, author, quite the celebrated thinker in her field.'

'And which field is that?' asks McVeigh, crumpling up his chocolate wrapper and stuffing it in the pocket of his navy blue uniform.

'A classicist, sir,' says McAvoy, and leaves a pause, unsure whether he need explain.

'And that is . . .?' asks McVeigh, with a sigh.

'An expert in Classics,' says McAvoy, unsure what level to pitch his explanation.

McVeigh clicks his fingers several times as he racks his brains. 'What, Dickens, Hardy, those whingeing Bronte women, you mean?'

McAvoy keeps his face neutral. 'The study of Classical antiquity sir. Romans. Greeks. It's the foundation of the humanities.'

'Oh,' says McVeigh, full of bluster. 'Oh, of course. The foundation of the humanities. You're going mob-handed this morning, are you? They've had twenty-four hours to acknowledge us. Maybe time to be a bit less deferential.'

'Whatever Detective Superintendent Pharaoh instructs, sir,' says McAvoy.

McVeigh picks his teeth with a stubby finger. 'Classics, eh?' he muses. 'Your field, all that, is it? The ex-wife wanted us to go to Herculaneum when we were on Capri. I left her to it. Not my thing.'

'There was an elective module at university,' says McAvoy, eager to end this excruciating exchange and get back to the incident room. 'I know some basics. It might come in handy, though we need a genuine expert if the Roman coins are relevant to the investigation.'

'They'd be relevant to me if they'd been hammered through my eyes,' muses McVeigh. 'Not the sort of thing many people have just lying around.'

'I'll see what Professor Bromley has to say,' mutters McAvoy. 'He taught Ian Musson, you see. Archaeology. There are connections, but it's all very tenuous.'

'This is what I mean,' says McVeigh, clapping McAvoy on the arm and keeping his face studiedly neutral as he feels the strength beneath his shirt sleeves. 'We could do so much with you, Hector.'

McAvoy looks at the floor. He'll accept a mispronunciation of his name from a lass from South Yorkshire, but from a Scotsman it's unforgivable. He wonders whether McVeigh is one of those Scots who gives shortbread tins and little Loch Ness monsters to people for Christmas: emphasizing his Scottishness at every opportunity.

McVeigh breathes out: a rattly sound at the back of his throat and a look of annoyance in his eyes. 'What is your plan, long-term, Sergeant McAvoy? What is it you think you might do next?'

It's a question McAvoy tries not to ask himself. He knows that if he had followed a different route he could be the same rank as the man who stands before him. He could be on double the wages and face none of the dangers that have so marked his skin. He also knows that he wouldn't be half the police officer that he is if not for Trish Pharaoh and he would rather quit the service and re-train as a primary school teacher than be disloyal to his mentor and friend.

'Plan, sir?' he asks, quietly. 'I'm seeing Dr Kent Bromley this morning. Archaeologist. Taught Ian Musson—'

'Yes, yes,' he says, waving a hand. 'She'll give me all that, I've no doubt.'

McAvoy pinches the bridge of his nose. Rubs his forehead. 'She, sir?'

'It's not beyond the realms of possibility, you know,' says McVeigh, lowering his voice. 'A smaller unit, a specialized team – fewer resources, of course, but a man of your learning could do more with less, I'm sure. A detective inspector, that would be you. A couple of constables, maybe a couple of retirees looking to come back on civilian terms. Who knows, maybe Pharaoh would be game for that, eh? Might keep her off the drink . . .'

McAvoy looks around at the empty canteen. Tables and chairs are askew and covered in empty cans, sandwich wrappers and half-eaten chocolate bars. The floor is an abstract of crumbs and trodden-in food. It puts him in mind of an apocalypse movie. The place seems abandoned. He half expects the shadows of hundreds of zombies to suddenly loom on the far, lilac-painted wall. He focuses on these things so as to drown out the overwhelming impulse to grab McVeigh by the head and put him through the wall.

McAvoy rubs his hand over his face. Smooths his beard. 'Very good, sir,' he says, looking past McVeigh towards the door. He flicks his eyes to the right and gives a smile. 'Ah, good morning, boss.'

McVeigh turns on his heel as if standing on ice, the colour draining from his face as he spins, expecting to look into the furious face of Detective Superintendent Trish Pharaoh. There's nobody there. He turns back, embarrassed and smoothing himself down. McAvoy glares down at him, eyes hard.

'Fifty pence,' he says. Then, pointedly: 'I won't forget.'

ELEVEN

Professor Kent Bromley has an office in Hull's recently redeveloped Fruit Market, down by the waterfront. This is the neighbourhood where the city's marketing and regeneration bigwigs bring first-time visitors to Hull – using words like 'renaissance' and 'cultural hub' and trying not to look at the occasional passing drunk as they fight with the seagulls for a scrap of discarded sourdough bread. It's billed as a modern, vibrant and unique cultural quarter and there's no doubting that when the sun shines, it's a nice place to sit and watch the boats and sip fruity cider through a straw. On bleak, windswept days like this, when the smell of fishmeal and petrol blow in off the Humber, it's pretty much deserted. McAvoy, in his rare moments of cynicism, wonders whether the future regeneration specialists will try and maintain some of the area's modern vibrancy when they come back to regenerate it again in twenty years.

Professor Bromley's office is on the first floor of a bright new building that looks out across a muddy stretch of the River Hull to Sammy's Point. The whole area is a strange mix of the ultra-modern and restored Victorian grandeur and the cars that take up spaces on the patch of nearby waste ground are similarly divergent. There are new-plate Fiat 500s and hybrid hatchbacks aplenty but in among them are several big, gas-guzzling beasts: long-bonneted Jaguars, Mercedes and even a well-preserved Rolls Royce. McAvoy's got the family car today: a tiny little Kia Picanto that looks like a silvery jacket around his broad frame. He felt almost embarrassed pulling up next to a Range Rover and hoped nobody saw that the chassis rose half a foot once he eased himself out of the driver's seat.

He gazes out through the panoramic windows, watching the rain and the dense grey air drift towards the grey-brown mass of the city. The cheerful, bright-smiled receptionist has told him to make himself comfortable; that the professor will be right down, and directed him to a little waiting area with two uncomfortable sofas and a great flask of water with cucumber floating in it. McAvoy, unsure whether it's a drink, a soup or a piece of modern art, has resisted the urge to sample it.

'McAvoy, is it? So sorry, so blasted sorry – I'm having a morning straight from Hades' backside, I'm afraid . . . are you well, catered for, ready to rock and roll?'

Professor Bromley is a spry, energetic man in his early fifties; his accent pure Home Counties. His handshake is firm and politician-like: both hands clasping McAvoy's big fist and his blue eyes never leaving McAvoy's own. He wears a round-neck pullover over a pink shirt, comfortable-looking brown corduroys and the kind of suede slip-ons that might be moccasins, deck shoes or slippers.

'Professor Bromley,' begins McAvoy. 'Good of you to see me. Is there somewhere we can go for a wee chat?'

Bromley looks around at the deserted reception and waves his hands expansively. 'I can't see us being disturbed,' he says, and points to the chairs. 'Shall we? Bloody uncomfortable but very ergonomic. I'd offer you some cucumber water but I'm not a total bastard.'

McAvoy smiles, trying to make himself comfortable. He finds himself liking Professor Bromley and feels a sudden stab of guilt at having to bring his good mood down with such unpleasant tidings. Sometimes, he realizes, he really is heartily sick of being a police officer.

'So, what have I done?' asks Bromley, hitching up his trouser legs to reveal an inch of pale skin between his cuff and his gaudy socks. 'I promise, whatever I said, I was probably trying to be funny.'

McAvoy gives him a sideways look, encouraging him to elaborate. 'Sorry?'

'Oh, we live in that age, don't we?' sighs the archaeologist. 'Compliment somebody on their hairstyle or tell somebody they're a delight and the next thing you're in the papers and in the dock. If anybody's saying I've made a pass at them, I can promise you nothing south of the equator has worked in at least ten years and I tend to be as surprised as anybody at the words that come out of my mouth.'

McAvoy isn't sure what to say so brushes over the exchange and pulls his notebook and mobile phone from the pocket of his coat. 'Might I ask you whether you remember a student by the name of Ian Musson?'

Bromley looks momentarily startled, as if he was expecting something entirely different. 'Musson?' he asks, scratching at his jaw. 'I teach him now, do I? I have to say, I'm not massively involved – it's more guest lectures and placements, you see . . .'

'This is a student from some years ago,' continues McAvoy. 'When you were at the University of Bradford.'

Professor Bromley slaps one hand against the other, sitting forward and back in his chair as if riding a rodeo bull. He's positively manic with energy, but McAvoy doesn't know whether this is his normal state, or the result of being interviewed by the police. 'Yes, yes,' he says, pleased with himself. ''97, '98, sort of time. Those were the days, eh? Cider and blackcurrant in plastic beakers and a cigarette behind one's ear. Yes, I was wet behind the ears myself, but I do like to think I gave them the best of what I knew, however limited that was. Yes, Musson was the boy from the north east, wasn't he? Quiet lad. I don't think he finished the course, did he? Wasn't there . . .?' He tails off, losing his ebullience, as he makes the connections. 'I take it the news isn't good?'

'Human remains have been discovered in woodland near Brantingham,' says McAvoy, as gently as he can. 'We have reason to believe they belong to Ian Musson.'

Professor Bromley looks thoroughly crestfallen. 'Brantingham, is it? My, that's a pretty spot. Not far from our dig and certainly a site of some interest. My, however did the poor lad end up there?'

McAvoy looks at his phone for a moment, considering Professor Bromley with his peripheral vision. The professor looks genuinely saddened to hear the news. There is nothing in his body language to suggest that he expected to ever hear Ian Musson's name again.

'What can you tell me about Ian?' asks McAvoy, kindly. 'I understand you were his personal tutor.'

'Was I?' exclaims Bromley. 'Perhaps I was. Quarter of a century ago though and I've had hundreds of students pass through my care so you'll forgive me if I don't have absolute recall . . .'

'Anything at all,' says McAvoy. 'The university has already been very helpful. I just thought I would take an hour to come and speak to you personally, given your nearness.'

'Grasping at straws, are you?' asks Bromley, sympathetically. 'Is it recent? Do you know where he went after quitting the course? I do hope it wasn't anything to do with the teaching methods – I'm pretty sure we provided value for money even before students started paying their own way . . .'

'The evidence suggests he has been there since 1997,' says McAvoy. 'That's why he left your course, professor. He'd been murdered and buried.'

'Good God,' says Bromley, standing up. He crosses to the window and back again then grabs a plastic cup and scoops up a beaker of water, downing it in one. 'Good God,' he repeats. 'Poor Ian! Solitary boy, wasn't he? I recall we had a few loud-mouths in that particular group. Some good minds, but always a few of the boisterous types who just want to get out into the field and look for treasure with a JCB. He was a collector now I think about it? Studious, certainly. I seem to recall he got off to a flying start academically but rather lost his way. Have you spoken to his friends? He shared a house with some girls from the course. Was rather chummy with one of the students from the lower year group . . . yes, it's coming back now I think on it. Yes . . .' He stops himself, his mind a few paces ahead of his words. 'Brantingham, you say?'

McAvoy nods, making sure to hold the older man's gaze. 'Significant?'

'Yes and no,' says Bromley, sitting down and promptly standing back up again. 'Just thinking back. There's a lovely walk up that way. And you'll know about the patio, of course.'

'The patio?' asks McAvoy.

'One of the great local legends,' says Bromley, looking distinctly more comfortable as he slips into professorial mode. 'You'll know of the Petuaria Project of course – even the gentleman from whom I buy my *Big Issue* seems familiar with what we're up to in Brough. But we have a fine body of men and women to thank for the information we're endeavouring to add to. Brantingham, Outgang

– that's the little wooded area between South Cave and Elloughton – the remains of a Roman villa were found there in 1941. Wonderful mosaics, the remnants of a heating system. Definite links to the main settlement. The finds were properly reported, of course, and there was an excavation a few years later. A group of well-meaning archaeologists from the Hull and East Riding Museum excavated the pavements and prepared them for transportation. They were to go on display. Anyway, they got one safely back but left the other on site overnight. Came back the next day and somebody had nabbed it. Never been seen again. There was a book written about it, I think. Quite the loss. I'm sure somebody is resting their feet on it right now, not knowing what they've got. It would be worth good money if you could find the right broker. The trade in antiquities is nothing if not lucrative, though it attracts some very nasty people in among those history buffs who are willing to bypass a few ethical concerns in order to hold something that was once gripped in the hand of somebody from antiquity.'

McAvoy makes a show of jotting down some notes, just to help Professor Bromley feel helpful. He isn't sure how much to give away. Isn't sure if he's getting useful background information, or a load of pointless historical trivia.

'I do know a family at Brantingham, as it happens,' says Bromley, cautiously. 'Classics professor. Calpurnia, if you'll credit any parent with giving a child that name. Her son was briefly one of my students. Very bookish but not really cut out for academia. Mother rather spoiled him, if you can keep that between us. Dad was a giant of a chap, if I recall. Merchant Navy, I think. She must have gone for the bit of tough, eh? Can't say she's my favourite person but she certainly knows her subject. I've tried to tempt her onto the lecture circuit, but she's a little high and mighty for that. Prefers to write the sort of papers that only half a dozen academics will ever read. Fun when she's had a glass of the home-made vino, of course. Their son – Magnus, was it? Yes, I think it was Magnus. He was meek as a lamb despite having his father's stature. Only came on one dig and broke three trowels, as I recall. He was quite chummy with one of our departmental rogues, as it happens. Dieter Something-or-other. My, there's a name.' He stops, giving McAvoy his full attention. 'Sorry, inspector. World of my own.'

McAvoy jots it all down. On the table he can see that his mobile is ringing but he makes a point of not answering and giving Bromley his full attention instead. 'Ian's body was found on land at the edge of woodland owned by Professor Dodds-Wynne,' confides McAvoy, neutrally. 'We've been trying to speak to her but there's no answer at the home address. You mentioned her son? Might you have a way of contacting him?'

Professor Bromley looks past McAvoy for a moment, his eyes seeming to blur. He snaps back with a smile that doesn't reach his eyes. 'I can find one, I'm sure. I do believe Cally has a place she stays when she is writing, though I wouldn't be able to tell you where. As for Magnus, well, a man of learning doesn't like to use the phrase "blast from the past", but he really isn't the sort that I keep in contact with. It was all a little awkward when we ran into one another at his mother's little tête-à-tête . . .'

McAvoy looks at his phone again as it rings for a third time. He apologizes and snatches it up, looking at the text message from Pharaoh's number that accompanies the missed calls. It demands he answer the bloody phone.

McAvoy apologizes and does as he is told. 'Trish, I'm with Professor Bromley, can I call you back in—'

'Shush,' says Pharaoh, cutting him off. 'Dr Salmond has heard back about the DNA swabs. And she can say with absolute certainty that the body in the ground is Ian Musson.'

McAvoy gives a grunt of acknowledgement. 'OK, well, at least we know which direction we're heading—'

'There's more,' continues Pharaoh, testily. 'Some of the samples of tissue – they came back as unknown.'

'Sorry, boss?' asks McAvoy, unsure if he's heard right. He stands up, whispering a thank you to Professor Bromley, quiet and static on the edge of the chair.

'There's more than one body down there,' says Pharaoh. 'Two different sets of tissue. Bones.'

'Bones?'

Pharaoh sounds genuinely worn out as she tells him something she knows will hurt him. 'Infants, Aector. Two babies at least.'

Beyond the glass, the sky fills with the static of the gathering storm.

TWELVE

Detective Sergeant Ben Neilsen holds his phone in one fist and an adjustable hand grip in the other. He's squeezing them both with equal fervor, feeling the resistance against his fingers and revelling in the flood of endorphins. Neilsen never misses an opportunity to work out and has only recently stopped trying to get his daily step-count up by marching on the spot while seated at his desk. Pharaoh had pointed out, with her usual tact, that it made him look 'a bit of a dickhead'. The hand grips are a decent compromise and have added even more definition to his biceps and triceps, resulting in a physique that looks as though it has been digitally enhanced. Today he fancies that he is seriously putting his muscles through the wringer. The man on the other end of the phone has the most boring voice he has ever subjected himself to. He was, until a decade ago, a detective constable with Sussex CID. Now he's listed on the police database as the chap to talk to regarding all matters to do with historical artefacts and the provenance of questionable objet d'art. He is, according to the spreadsheet, a 'numismatist'. Neilsen had required a quick Google search to make sure he wasn't letting himself in for anything untoward before calling him. A numismatist, as he has just found out, is a collector of, and expert in, rare coins.

Ex DC George Hepwell is doing little to alter Neilsen's mental image of devout hobbyists everywhere. He strikes Neilsen as being typical of anybody who spends their retirement obsessing over anything from koi carp to stamp collecting. He presumes it to be the preserve of those with a long-suffering wife, a fondness for real ale, and who keep tins of boiled sweets and a variety of ordnance survey maps in the glovebox of their pristine Volvo. His voice is so monotonous that Neilsen is starting to consider driving to Eastbourne and punching him in the face, just to see whether he can inject some colour into the word 'ouch'.

Hepwell, who has already told Neilsen about the exact dimensions of his two-bed dormer bungalow and the type of creosote he is using for the roof of the shed, is using the conversation as an opportunity to get some matters off his chest regarding the authorities' approach to safeguarding the nation's heritage. It would be interesting, if not so soporific. Not for the first time, Neilsen wonders how McAvoy manages to seem so interested in everybody he talks to. He has a horrible suspicion that it's not an act – that McAvoy really does go through life eager to learn more, and to put that knowledge to some worthy application.

'. . . as you'll no doubt already have ascertained, the unit in question was disbanded years ago and there was no real successor, which I flatter myself was down to the fact that nobody else could do what I did or know what I know and it was easier to stop looking for the criminals than to try and catch them. I said as much in my leaving speech, which wasn't greeted with universal acclaim, but was a good point that deserved to be made . . .'

Neilsen releases the hand grip. It twangs out of his hand and clatters off onto the desk of one of the civilian staff, who gives him a thumbs up. He drops his head to his hand. Tries again.

'As I say, it's an area in which we don't have a great deal of expertise . . .'

'Well, it says it all, doesn't it?' asks Hepwell. 'Eight years retired and I'm the only person you have on hand to ring? I don't blame you, inspector, but it does show how little the powers-that-be care about the nation's heritage. Of course, the Met has a similar unit, I believe, but these days they will be more focused on organized criminality and by goodness they have their hands full with that. There is a lot of money to be made trading in artefacts. One fears that we almost have a "loot-to-order" service. All an interested buyer has to do is make the right contacts and soon private collections or museum pieces are being pilfered and disappearing into the murk. Is anybody trying particularly hard to retrieve them – to bring the perpetrators to justice? It's worse now we've left the EU. Cross-border co-operation is even more minimal than hitherto, and there's barely a numismatist of note who can secure insurance for their collections or feels confident donating to museums being protected by poor CCTV or a solitary guard . . .'

Neilsen hears himself talking but it is quickly eclipsed by the bland utterances of the man at the end of the phone.

'. . . you'll be aware, of course, and do forgive me if I start sounding frightfully didactic but police in general have to be very fastidious, one might almost say pernickety, about what to pursue and what to try and turn away from. Their main focus is reducing threat, harm and risk. To me it's a national scandal that there's nobody proactively seeking out the black market dealers, but then I do of course have a great passion for history. More times than not when black market skulduggery does come to the attention of a force, some reluctant non-specialist detective is allocated and off they go, blundering about trying to cram a lifetime's learning into half a phone call. I mean, where does one start? I had this same situation last year when those metal detectorists decided to try and sell a colossal hoard of coins and jewellery on the black market. They would have got away with it had they not chosen to go to a museum to request a valuation first.'

'I just wondered about these coins in particular,' interjects Neilsen, wondering whether it will be morning, evening or the anniversary of some distant apocalypse by the time he finishes the call. 'I mean, I don't know . . . not just the worth, but where they might have come from – why they might be significant to somebody . . .'

'Sounds to me like you don't even really know what you're asking,' says Hepwell, in the tone of a geography teacher whose pupils have failed to find the classroom. 'This is the issue time and again. People dabble, you see. People learn just enough to get started but don't delve into the craft with the love of a purist. One decides to take up a new hobby, buys a metal detector or a textbook on ancient coins. One may be lucky enough to find something of value and then one learns about how damnably slow the proper channels are. One can spend a decade waiting to be told whether the find belongs to the finder, as it were. One can understand why people turn to alternative means of making some money from their finds, even if one does find the notion truly deplorable. It doesn't take long to find an interested buyer – somebody who doesn't care too much about provenance – that's basically having the correct paperwork about the item or items in question. There are brokers for such deals, men with contacts. It's quite a lucrative market, though one does come across some very nasty characters—'

'These coins,' butts in Neilsen. 'Just these ones.'

There is a sigh down the line. 'Silver denarius,' he says, and Neilsen pictures him peering at some ancient computer through jam-jar spectacles. 'Minted Rome, 125-128 CE. Laureate head, Aequitas herself on the reverse. Scales and cornucopia, naturally. Hadrian, looking rather well. A class B denarii. One wouldn't pay more than eighty pounds, though one does wonder about the hole through the centre. I see some mottling too . . .'

Neilsen doesn't let himself get drawn in. He doesn't want to start a conversation about crucifixion nails or how hard it was to blur out the brownish staining left by the dead man's blood.

'Hadrian?' asks Neilsen. 'As in "the wall".'

'Good God,' sighs Hepwell, making no effort to disguise his contempt. 'Yes, as in "the wall". A fascinating era for this fair isle. Hadrian – gladdened to be associated with her ladyship, I'll be bound.'

Neilsen drops his head to the desk. Considers emailing Andy Daniells and asking him if he will do him the favour of coming up behind him and euthanizing him with a shoe.

'Her ladyship?' he asks, brain spinning.

'Aequitas,' says Hepwell, and takes a slurp of some unseen liquid, moistening his mouth for what Neilsen fears will be a barrage. 'The symbol for equity, of course. What one thinks of as "fair play". The concept of conformity, symmetry . . . fairness. In Ancient Rome it could refer to either the legal concept of equity, or the dealings between two individuals. Cicero himself defined *aequitas* as tripartite: the first, he said, pertained to the gods above (*ad superos deos*) and is equivalent to *pietas*, or religious obligation; the second, to the *manes*, the underworld spirits or spirits of the dead, and was *sanctitas*, that which is sacred; and the third pertaining to us mere mortals – human beings (*homines*) was *iustitia*, or justice, if you will . . .'

Neilsen sits up. 'Justice? They're a symbol of justice?'

'One shouldn't be too literal,' says Hepwell, dripping scorn.

'Aequitas as a, well, one might say a "divine personification" was very much a part of the religious propaganda of the emperor, or a series of emperors, under the name *Aequitas Augusti* . . .'

Neilsen nudges the mouse by his computer and the screen-saver vanishes. He looks again at the crime scene photographs. Looks at the nails driven through the dead man's eyes.

'Would we be able to source them?' he asks. 'I mean, how rare are they?'

'Have you not been paying attention?' asks Hepwell. 'I speak here as a proud numismatist – the market for coins is absolutely wide open. The nighthawks with their metal detectors; private archaeologists, even members of the heritage organizations – they feather their own nests. People care less and less about provenance. Tracing an individual coin back through the ages is a near impossibility. Of course, you have the advantage geographically speaking – I do recall there was quite the Roman presence at Petuaria – Brough, as you would know it today – and the dates would match, but these things have had 1700 years to move around. I'm afraid it's a needle in a multitude of haystacks.'

Neilsen spins in his chair, slouching and staring at the sky, wondering how he's going to break this down for Pharaoh. Decides his best bet is to pass it through his translation service. As soon as the call is over, he's definitely ringing McAvoy.

THIRTEEN

McAvoy is the only person Pharaoh permits to drive her little Mercedes. He always feels ridiculous in the driving seat and never more so than when the top is down and passers-by have the opportunity to tell him he looks like Noddy. Mercifully, the swirling rain is ensuring that the roof stays up, and all McAvoy has to contend with as they head west is the cramps in both his legs, and the fact that he has to keep his head at an angle if he doesn't want to leave a dint in the fabric of the roof.

'They'll bloody answer the door this time,' growls Pharaoh, in the passenger seat. 'They'll answer it or you're putting your foot through it.'

McAvoy doesn't reply. He stayed virtually mute throughout the lunchtime briefing. Most of the team did. There were a few exhalations and some muttered curses as the big screen filled with images of tiny white bones and ragged scraps of clothing, but nobody felt the need to offer up anything witty to break the tension. No police officer can remain emotionally uninvolved when kids are involved and Pharaoh, a mum of four and recent grandmother, is giving off rage in waves. She's absented herself from an important meeting with the budget committee in order to make herself useful this afternoon. With no obvious leads to follow and having digested the little that McAvoy picked up from Bromley, her instincts are telling her that she will find answers at Lepidus House. McAvoy knows better than to argue. He feels happier as her subordinate than he does making decisions on his own. He trusts her completely, and rarely disagrees about how to proceed.

'Did I tell you that Sophie heard back from the Met Office?' asks Pharaoh lighting a black cigarette and looking across at him. Her sunglasses are on top of her head and he can see the darkness and broken blood vessels beneath her eyes. He wishes he could convince her to take better care of herself, even while he respects her freedom to treat her body like an ashtray.

'Your Sophia?' asks McAvoy, turning off at North Ferriby and seeing the smudge of river disappear in his wing mirror.

'No, you plank,' snaps Pharaoh. 'Sophie Kirkland, the only DC I'd trust not to balls it up. I had her chasing up with a friendly meteorologist. Turns out the last serious weather that was seen in this area was December 24th 1997. If our ash tree was toppled back then it would have created a nice hole.'

'Healthy trees don't tend to blow over,' muses McAvoy. 'And I don't know if they can be saved if they get re-planted.'

'The scars in the trunk,' points out Pharaoh. 'You saw. And if it was lashed to another tree it could have survived if the roots had access to the soil. It's possible. Would fit with the dates.'

McAvoy nods, chewing on his lower lip. Pharaoh pulls her phone from her leather jacket and sends a brief message. 'Thor,' she mutters, by way of explanation. She has a burgeoning friendship with an Icelandic police officer of similar size and temperament to McAvoy. Roisin finds the whole thing deeply creepy but would far rather Pharaoh was involved with her husband's doppelganger than McAvoy himself. The two women have an intensely complex relationship: admiring and loathing one another in equal measure, even as they thread themselves in and out of one another's lives and make plans to steer the good ship McAvoy into whatever harbour best suits their own needs. McAvoy stays out of it. He loves them both, albeit in markedly different ways.

'Dead lamb,' mutters Pharaoh, nodding out of the passenger window at a sad white shape on a slope of green field. 'Poor sod. What do you think happened?'

McAvoy doesn't see it. Doesn't know what to say. Wonders what it says about Pharaoh that her first question is about the 'how' of the little creature's demise. He knows from experience that this is how she sees the world and her place within it. Some people are shepherds, protecting the flock. Others come along when the shepherds fail, determined to do justice by the dead and to slap cuffs on whoever or whatever snuffed its life out.

'How did he sleep last night?' asks Pharaoh, turning towards him and giving him her full attention. She idolizes his son and it is no surprise to McAvoy that he is as much a part of her thoughts as the murder investigation.

McAvoy shakes his head. 'Every night now. Nightmares. Real terror, Trish – the kind of fear you only know when somebody's put a blade to your neck. It's hard enough being a teenager; hard enough having a mum who's a Traveller and a dad who's a copper. Hard enough being big and red-haired and blushing all the bloody time. But what he went through . . . what he saw . . .'

'He'll come through it,' says Pharaoh. 'I know his type. It'll always be there, but he won't let it define him. He's too good a person to hide away from life. Whatever he does with himself, he'll do with his whole heart.'

McAvoy, ignoring the obvious comparisons to his own sweet nature, gives an awkward shrug. 'I just want him to feel safe again.'

Pharaoh finishes her cigarette and throws the filter out of the open window, buzzing the glass all the way down and putting her face in the cold, wet air. She revels in the slap of the breeze; her black hair streaming out and the pinkness receding from her cheeks. She leaves the window down as McAvoy parks on the gravel outside Lepidus House, convinced that in so doing she is giving the vehicle a thorough airing that will remove the scent of nicotine and wine. She's entirely wrong, but nobody is brave enough to tell her.

'Nice enough,' mutters Pharaoh, fishing her ID out of her cleavage and disentangling her hair from her earrings and collar. 'Very Poldark.'

'Have you got to season three yet?' asks McAvoy, opening the gate.

'I don't know for sure,' says Pharaoh, leading them up to the door. 'I watch the scene with his shirt off quite a lot. Apparently there are other people in it, and a plot of sorts, but I can't say I've noticed.'

This time it's Pharaoh who bangs on the door: three hard blows with her fist. She gives it five seconds then flicks open the letterbox and yells into the warm air. 'Hello. Humberside Police. I really need you to answer this door.'

McAvoy leans with his back against the brickwork staring out towards the woods. He can just make out the outline of the mausoleum and from there he's pretty sure he could identify which tree it was that the big man tapped for its syrup, and where the rabbit met its end. He closes his eyes for a moment, feeling the rain on his face. Wonders whether Pharaoh was serious about having him kick in the door.

'Bugger this,' mutters Pharaoh and stomps down the steps, trudging over the gravel of the driveway towards the far side of the property. She stops to press her face against the glass and when she can make out nothing of interest keeps trudging. McAvoy dutifully tags along behind following as she disappears around the far edge of the property and tracking the low wall to the rear of the house. She stops short, surprised to see that the rear of the house looks out onto fine landscaped gardens. It's laid out in concentric circles: well-maintained grasses and border plants rising up to a central terrace of tasteful little statues and a series of mossy statues situated on ivy-wreathed plinths. At the highest point is a small wooden building: a summer house of sorts, though McAvoy can tell from the heft of the timbers that it has been hand-sawn and hand-built, rather than following some flat-pack design. The doors of the little wooden house are swinging open and a small woman is reclining in the entrance, sitting in a saggy floral deckchair and with her feet propped up on a vintage beer crate. She's reading a colossal textbook and has shown no signs of registering the intruders.

'Knew she'd be in,' says Pharaoh, smugly. 'That's her, yes?'

McAvoy only knows Calpurnia Dodds-Wynne from a grainy author photo he found on a publisher's website, but the slight figure fifty yards away certainly looks a likely suspect. She has unkempt blonde hair, darker and greyer at the roots, and there's something a little pinched and wan about her features, as if she may be recuperating from an illness. She has a blanket around her shoulders and her spindly ankles poke out of the bottom of a pair of baggy, dark-blue trousers. The book on her lap is nearly as big as she is. McAvoy watches as she licks the finger of her left hand and turns the page, shivering slightly as a fresh gust of wind assaults her. He sees a little wisp of smoke rising from behind the cover of the book. Sees her take her right hand in her left, and raise it, directing her cigarette to her mouth. Only then does she notice the two intruders in her garden. If she is surprised, she doesn't show it. Just peers at them both, curious to know what they might want.

'Professor Dodds-Wynne, is it?' asks Pharaoh, following the mazy footpath as it meanders in circles towards the summit.

A half smile creases the woman's lips as she watches the two officers draw closer, round in circles as if climbing a helter-skelter. When they are two circles away, Pharaoh comes to the obvious conclusion that she looks like a dickhead, and stretches her legs: taking half a dozen steps up and over the little walls and managing to step on some pretty purple flowers along the way. She arrives at the summer house slightly out of breath.

'That was acrobatic,' says the woman, again using her left hand to raise her right. 'Did you knock? You'll forgive me – it's such a blasted nuisance. Stone deaf in one ear and the other's packing up. If I don't hear you properly, all I can say is that I'm trying my best, and it will be a cold day in hell before I invest in an ear trumpet.'

McAvoy, who has gone the long way round, comes to a halt behind Pharaoh. He looks first at the cover of the book. *De Mulieribus Claris* by Giovanni Boccaccio. It's not a title he recognizes. He notices her following his gaze. She is giving a little mocking smile, as if he were a dog showing an unexpected interest in classical music. When she raises her hand again, McAvoy notices the way it hangs limp, the cigarette gripped between twisted swollen fingers.

'A blood clot,' she says, nodding at the appendage. 'I collapsed you see. Lay on this arm for an age before my husband found me. A little useless now. Dead, in fact. I just can't get used to smoking with my other hand. Silly, how these little things matter, isn't it?'

Pharaoh retrieves one of her own cigarettes from her inside pocket. Takes her time lighting up.

'We did rather wonder when you would be knocking on the door,' says the woman in the chair, brightly. 'I understand there's something rather jolly happening beyond our boundary line. None of our business, of course, but some portly young gentleman put your card through our letterbox inviting one to call, and one would no doubt have found the time. Still, you're here now.'

Pharaoh breathes out a plume of smoke. 'It's Mrs Dodds-Wynne, yes? Or Professor? Calpurnia, so I'm told.'

'Just call me Cally,' she says, shuffling her book around in her lap as if preparing to offer a hand. Pharaoh shakes her head, indicating she doesn't need to worry about formalities.

'Cally,' muses Pharaoh. 'I'm Trish. Detective superintendent, as it goes. This gentleman is Detective Sergeant McAvoy. You can call him Hector.'

'You look as if you have a touch of the Celtic in you,' says Cally, warmly. '"They are tall in stature, with rippling muscles under clear white skin, they look like wood demons." Diodorus Siculus, I believe, though my memory isn't all it was. And quite the hulking specimen, if you don't mind me saying so. Hector, eh? The noble warrior fated to die another man's death. You have something of the look of my husband, actually. Isaac's around here somewhere. Probably in the workshop, tinkering away. He tends to wear his headphones.'

'That'll be it,' says Pharaoh, breezily, taking a seat on the brick wall. 'Diodorus Siculus, eh? Played centre-back for Rotherham, if I recall, though my memory isn't what it was . . . Christ but this wall's cold on the backside.'

There's another deckchair folded up behind Cally, but she doesn't offer its use. The two women look at one another for a moment. McAvoy feels horribly out of his depth: mute witness as the two size each other up through a haze of smoke.

'We've found a body under your ash tree, Cally,' says Pharaoh, cigarette between her lips and her mouth in a tight line. 'Just down there. Five hundred yards away. Young man, nineteen years old, in fact. It's been on the news and everything.'

Cally lowers her book. Plucks the smouldering cigarette butt from her withered hand and drops it into a plant pot beneath her chair. 'A body?' she asks. 'Recent? Gosh. Well, I did see quite the commotion when I got back last night but I rather fancied it was something to do with the storm. We do get ramblers, you see. Out in all weathers. If I thought about it at all I rather assumed somebody might have hurt themselves. Gosh. A body, you say?'

McAvoy stays silent. Cally's reaction seems genuine enough but he likes to believe the best of people. Pharaoh, in contrast, presumes that everybody is lying – most frequently to themselves.

'Ian Musson,' says Pharaoh, flicking her sunglasses down over her eyes. 'A former pupil of Professor Bromley. Same course as your son. It's possible they were classmates?'

'Bradford boy, is he?' asks Cally, playing with her necklace and considering. 'Goodness. I can't say I know the name. Musson. No, nothing. Magnus did have one or two chums but I don't recall an Ian. A German fellow came to stay for a weekend – a German name, at least. Ian? Were they classmates? Magnus wasn't there until graduation, I'm afraid. Had his heart broken and rather went to pieces, though he's picked himself up since. Doing rather well now, though I can't say it's a world I really understand.'

'You're a Classics scholar, is that right?' asks Pharaoh.

Cally laughs: an unpleasant, scorn-filled sound. She glares at her haughtily, clearly unsure where to begin in educating this dreadful commoner who has blundered in to her landscaped garden. 'I simply call myself a historian,' she says, her nostrils briefly taking on the appearance of an out-of-breath stallion. 'My new work would be complete if not for this blasted hand. Rather slows one down.'

'That must be a right pisser for one,' says Pharaoh, nodding. She turns to McAvoy. 'Hector, could you just pull out that spreadsheet with the yes/no question on it. It's got "Murder" written on the top – underlined in red pen. Jot down that Cally here doesn't know anything. Then we can be off.'

Cally twitches a smile. 'Of course, of course – I know you have a job to do. But, look, that old tree isn't on our property. It's beyond the old boundary and I can say that for absolute certain as I've lived here my whole life. My ancestors are buried in the family crypt, just beyond the treeline. I am very much at home here, so I do rather know about such things. As for the poor unfortunate gentleman in the ground, well . . . that really is a tremendous pity, but one does hear about so many young people losing their lives that one's well of compassion does rather run dry. You are, of course, going to do whatever you please, I'm quite sure of that, but I would urge a note of caution before coming stomping in with bloodhounds and constables. I am, as you can see, not exactly the murdering sort.'

'That's a new one,' says McAvoy, unable to help himself. 'Murder doesn't respect postcodes, Professor Dodds-Wynne.'

'Oh, what a delightful accent,' says Cally, eyes shining. 'Say something else, do.'

'I think I'm going to have to push you for an address for your son,' says Pharaoh, with a sigh. 'I might enjoy a chat with your husband should he decide to appear from the woods. He's the outdoorsy sort, from what I hear.'

Cally gives Pharaoh her full attention. 'Trish,' she says, rolling the word around as if tasting a wine. 'Something of a hairdresser name, don't you think? I can see it on a shop sign – perhaps with the apostrophe in the wrong place.'

'That's funny, Calpurnia,' says Pharaoh, smiling. 'I'll be sure to remember that one.'

'You don't look half as funny standing there as you did skulking in the woods,' says Cally, shifting her gaze to McAvoy. 'You did look a little silly, a big man like you. I can forward you the security footage, if you're short of entertainment.'

McAvoy blushes scarlet. 'So you know what I saw . . .' he begins.

'A man in his garden,' says Cally, with a dry chuckle. 'A man drying animal skin, as he is more than within his rights to do. I really didn't wish for this little interlude to be so spiky, I do hope you know that, but there's something within me that prickles at authority and given that I have nothing of interest to tell you or any wish to continue this discussion, I shall ask that you be about your business. If you wish to speak to me further I shall require the family solicitor.'

Pharaoh runs her tongue around the inside of her mouth. Watches as Calpurnia Dodds-Wynne returns her attention to her book. Petulant, sweat beading her forehead, she drops her cigarette and grinds it out at her feet, looking down and noticing the different colours of the hard-to-fathom design. It's a mosaic, but the spectator would need to be fifty feet in the air to make out the picture.

'I'd rather you took that with you,' says Cally, as Pharaoh

stands up. 'A lot of time and money was spent on this garden. We're not animals.'

McAvoy steps forward scooping up the butt before Pharaoh has the chance to reply. She flashes him a hateful look. Looks, for a moment, as though she is about to command him to drop it again, and then the moment is gone, and they are heading back down the path towards the gates. As they go, McAvoy hears a faint muttering as Cally gives her attention back to the text.

'*Magna est veritas, est praevalet*,' she says, her tone close to prayer.

McAvoy stops. Turns. Walks back up the path.

'Great is truth,' he translates. 'And it prevails.' He lowers his voice. Jerks his head towards Pharaoh and makes sure he has her full attention before he speaks. '*Fronti nulla fides*.'

For the first time, Cally's eyes seem to register surprise. They hold one another's gaze. McAvoy sees the intelligence within. Sees his own self, huge and foolish, on the lapis pools of her irises. She beams suddenly, as if a previously docile dog had suddenly performed a backflip on the lawn. Then it is gone, concealed behind the mocking half smile and the bright blue eyes.

'What does that mean?' asks Pharaoh, grinding her teeth, as McAvoy strides past her, anger in the set of his shoulders. 'What did you say to her?'

'Never judge a book by a cover.'

FOURTEEN

McAvoy stays silent while Pharaoh knocks back the first glass of red wine. He knows from experience that, right now, she needs their conversation to be a monologue rather than a dialogue. She's good at ranting and it does at least seem to have a positive impact on her emotional wellbeing. He thinks of her as a vigorously shaken bottle of ginger beer. The ranting is akin to slowly taking the top off: letting the fury hiss out in tiny increments. The action serves to gradually dissipate the strength from the eventual explosion.

'. . . not somebody who likes confrontation, Hector, you know that, and yeah, I may have the reputation for being this hard-faced bitch but what the hell else am I meant to do to level the playing field at work, I mean if people can't see what's underneath then that's their bloody fault, isn't it, but for that snotty bitch to basically look at me and decide, to my fucking face, that I'm some silly cow who isn't even worth getting out of her chair to speak to, it's worse than being scorned by a bloke, because blokes don't know any bloody better, but she's a woman, and a successful one at that, and she looks at me as if I've got shit on me forehead and – another one of those please, love, and an orange juice and lemonade for the big lad – and now I can't even make my mind up if I really think she's hiding something or whether I just want a good reason to stick the cuffs on her and when I think of the way she looked at me, and at you! I mean for fuck's sake, Hector, it wouldn't have done you any harm to speak up for yourself, would it? And where's my bloody chips, I asked for them ages ago . . .'

McAvoy watches as the colour gradually returns to her face. On the drive down from Lepidus House she has gone a worrying slate grey colour but the pinkness is slowly seeping back into her cheeks – albeit with the help of a full-bodied Shiraz. They have made their way to the Triton Inn, on the outskirts of Brantingham, and no more than a couple of miles from the crime scene. McAvoy has quietly seen off a portion of sticky toffee pudding and custard. Pharaoh has devoured a chilli baked potato, though her extra chips have yet to arrive. She is an old-school dietician, believing that nothing qualifies as a main meal unless there is some potato-based accompaniment. McAvoy has witnessed many an uncomfortable scene in nice Italian restaurants: waiters and chefs audibly arguing about whether or not mash can be provided for the lady with the angry eyes and the inadequate squid-ink fusilli.

'At least we've made contact,' says McAvoy, leaning forward and crossing his arms on the varnished grain of the table. They've taken up residency in a little booth near the bar, watching as the unreasonably young waitresses and bar staff deal with the various requirements of the group of elderly ladies at the long table in the dining area, and the three old boys holding court at the bar. On a Sunday, the place is heaving. Midweek at a little after two p.m., it's almost deserted.

'Fat lot of good it did us,' growls Pharaoh, snatching her fresh glass of red from the barmaid's tray and swallowing two inches in one bite. 'No sign of her partner – not a flash of anything in her eyes. I mean, that's weird, isn't it? I'm no academic but even proper eccentrics react with a little incredulity when they hear there's a dead body in the garden.'

'She was very keen to tell us that it wasn't her garden,' points out McAvoy, rubbing his hand over his beard and idly wondering whether he should have had a main before embarking on the pudding. 'I don't know, I feel a bit deflated – like I had half a theory and it's fallen flat.'

'It wasn't even half a theory,' mutters Pharaoh. 'But it was a start. I don't know – you see the tails of a few coincidences and it's human instinct to plait them together.'

'You didn't mention the other remains,' says McAvoy, skin prickling as he thinks again upon those tiny white bones; the delicate skulls beneath the black earth.

'I don't want that getting out yet,' says Pharaoh. 'We'll keep that in reserve for now. As things stand there's not much national press interest and that's a blessing, but if we start talking about dead babies under an ash tree, the pressure goes through the roof.'

McAvoy nods, understanding. He has the beginnings of a headache kneading away at his temples and there's a tightness across his chest that is making his breathing a little laboured. He knows he's rundown. He's due some holiday time but doesn't have a clue when he will find opportunity to take it. He always feels a little guilty booking a day off, especially given how many convalescence days he has required over the past few years. He would love to head to the family croft for a few days of fresh air, but it's a nine-hour drive and he suspects that Roisin, even with her gentle spirit and boundless patience, might well kill one or both of the children if forced to endure such a journey.

'You look a bit off-colour,' says Pharaoh, narrowing her eyes and examining him properly. 'She's feeding you, isn't she? Say the word and I'll message her – tell her I've caught you snaffling leftover pasty crusts out of the work bin. Please, do, say the word . . .'

'I'm fine,' says McAvoy, with a little smile. 'I'm not sleeping much.'

'Fin?' asks Pharaoh, with genuine concern.

'We'll get there,' says McAvoy, with a sigh. 'Wherever "there" is.'

'It's hard,' says Pharaoh. 'Too hard sometimes. Being a parent – it's fucking exhausting. Throw in being a copper. How do you prepare them for the life we know is out there waiting for them? I've always thought I've done my best and I think the girls are pretty damn awesome, but who am I to judge? Sophia's scraping by on some art commissions and is raising her baby on her own. Two at university doing "ologies" they couldn't give a shit about. And Olivia staying with her mate's family so she can finish college while her mum moves over to Hull for work! I mean, it's all compromise, isn't it? But when you can see the negative consequences of your every action – how do we not go mad?'

McAvoy licks his lips. 'I hate it when you're not certain about things,' he mutters. 'It worries me when you're in two minds. Self-doubt is not what we associate you with.'

She laughs, finishing her wine. Shakes her head and huffs out a sigh. 'You must be rubbing off on me.' She grins at that, sensing an opportunity to make her sergeant blush, but she has barely started teasing when McAvoy looks past her and narrows his eyes.

'That looks familiar,' he says, under his breath. He's noticed an old black-and-white photograph on the wall. The Triton is decorated in a style designed to please anybody with a fondness for the quintessential country pub, but who likes enough light to read the menu by. It's bright and airy, with polished wooden floors and an abundance of brown leather. There are real ales, guest ales and at least two types of pie. The little wall space given over to artwork is tastefully presented – old monochrome photographs of local rural scenes: hunters, farmers, haystacks; maids in caps and pinafores; men with shirtsleeves and serious beards.

McAvoy eases himself out of his chair and crosses to the display. He crouches down and looks at the faded picture of the mausoleum. In this image the trees seem more spare and the words chiselled into the brickwork are easier to make out. There's nobody in the picture but the date in the bottom right-hand corner shows August, 1938. McAvoy turns to find Pharaoh at his side, still holding her empty wine glass.

'This is the family plot?' she asks.

McAvoy nods. 'I don't know how I'd feel about having my relatives buried in the garden,' he says, thoughtfully.

'I'd be fine with it,' says Pharaoh with a shrug. 'Mam's plot is a right state but it's such an arse-ache getting over to tidy it up. I'd be delighted if she was planted in the yard, though I doubt the neighbours would be. Communal gardens – the rules and regs are a nightmare.'

McAvoy pulls his phone from his pocket and takes a snap of the picture. He notices a missed call from Neilsen and looks enquiringly at Pharaoh. She waves a hand, clearly thinking about something else. She's looking past him, to the old boys at the bar. She gives him a nod and a wink and he makes his way outside, taking up a position in the doorway. Neilsen answers him within three rings.

'Sarge,' says Neilsen, with his pure Hessle Road accent. 'Y'know, that's not going to work much longer, is it? What with me a sergeant and you as, well, an inspector or something, so . . .'

'I'll take Hector,' says McAvoy. 'It doesn't matter.'

'I could try it the proper way,' muses Neilsen. 'With the rattle.'

'Don't worry for now, eh?' says McAvoy, as patiently as he can. He leans against the doorframe and stares out into the mostly empty car park. There are some ugly grey clouds rolling in from the higher ground. McAvoy fancies they haven't seen the last of the storm.

'Couple of useful tickles,' says Neilsen, and McAvoy hears his voice become briefly muffled as he tucks the phone under his chin to tap away at the keyboard in front of him. 'Not many calls to the incident room but two mentioned the same chap by name. Dieter Maxsted, if I'm saying that right . . .'

'I know that name,' says McAvoy, quickly. 'Professor Bromley mentioned him to me. Was he in his cohort at university?'

'Departmental assistant cum research fellow,' reads Neilsen from his notes. 'Not a student but very much a part of the department and certainly known to Ian Musson.'

'Go on,' says McAvoy, realizing he would be better served to just let him talk.

'One anonymous call gave nothing more than his name as a person of interest. Male caller doing a piss-poor accent. Why do they do that, eh? He sounded more Welsh than Indian, or more Indian than Welsh, depending on what he was going for. But he literally said that with regards to the body beneath the ash tree, we needed to look at Dieter Maxsted. Went to the trouble of spelling it out.'

'That's good of him,' says McAvoy, thoughtfully.

'So that went in the book along with all the other sods named by vengeful ex partners or slighted workmates eager to cause some trouble. But when the second call came in it rose a flag. She was with Heritage England, you see.'

'The conservation people?'

'The same. Gave her name as Trudy Wade and asked for Trish by name after reading the newspaper article this morning. She lives just outside of York but good news travels fast, eh? Anyway, she was quite agitated and really wanted the boss, but eventually settled for Sophie. Wants somebody to call her back but as an act of good faith she gave us the two names that tweaked my interest. Asked if the body was Dieter Maxsted, and whether we knew anything about Ian Musson. I was going to ring straight back but I thought you and Trish might have other ideas.'

'Thanks, Ben,' says McAvoy, watching as two crows fight over something dead on the road beyond the car park. 'Can you ping the number through?'

'Already done,' says Neilsen. 'And she might be giving us a decent steer with the name. I've run him through the PNC and HOLMES and he's got a good bit of form. Trespass, assault, possession, a suspended sentence for a breach of the Ancient Treasures Act, a couple for dishonesty. Armed robbery case nearly went to trial but the CPS ballsed up . . .'

'Ancient Treasures Act?'

'Handling artefacts,' explains Neilsen. 'A fifth-century crystal pendant and two Viking coins. He was a minor player in a bigger case against two metal detectors in 2014.'

'Detectorists,' mutters McAvoy, distractedly. 'What's he up to now?'

'Last came to our attention in 2017 when he was questioned by police, and by the Heritage England investigations unit, after his name came up in a robbery investigation carried out by West Mercia. Gave a "no comment" interview, albeit quite apologetically and was released without charge but the file suggests he had arranged a buyer for two golden Elizabethan groats stolen from a private collector in Tunbridge Wells. No charges brought. Trudy Wade came up on a Google search . . . LinkedIn profile mentions Bradford University, most recently appeared in the papers as a spokeswoman warning about the activities of nighthawks. Illegal metal detectors.'

'Detectorists,' repeats McAvoy, pulling at the coarse triangle of hair beneath his lower lip. 'Righto, send it all over. We have an address for Maxsted?'

'Living at a property in St Ann's, Nottingham, as of 2017. No other occupants. No phone number listed for the property and last year's census had a Polish couple living at that address. I've put a call in to the caretaker to enquire if he still lives there, but nothing yet.'

'Good work,' says McAvoy, turning around as a door bangs

open behind him and a small, blue-eyed woman gives him an awkward smile and jerks a thumb over her shoulder to where Pharaoh is sitting with two elderly men and waving him over. 'I'll tell her.'

'How did you get on with the homeowners?' asks Neilsen, conversationally. 'Were they there?'

'Spoke to Mrs Dodds-Wynne,' replies McAvoy, without emotion. 'Bit of a clash of personalities with Trish, but we've made contact. I'll go back before we release the news about the other remains. Perhaps she'll appreciate the courtesy.'

'Pathologist, Dr Salmond – she's got news on that front. Full briefing on the way over but she can confirm that she has found the remains of two other persons: both full-term pregnancies. Impossible to say at present whether they were stillborn. The materials are so degraded she isn't sure what she'll get but the DNA is a match. The two children were related.'

McAvoy breathes out slowly, gathering himself. Gives a soft grunt of thanks and hangs up. He feels bone-weary; gritty behind his eyelids and suddenly cold to his bones. He wonders if he's just getting old, or whether he really is coming down with something nasty. Perhaps, at last, the weight of the world is becoming too much to carry.

'This is Keith,' says Pharaoh, loudly, as McAvoy returns to the warmth of the bar. She's gesturing at a plump man in a pale-blue V-neck cardigan and neat polyester trousers, sitting somewhat precariously on a bar stool and wrapping a fat fist around the last dregs of a pint of bitter. 'Keith's my new friend. He's a very interesting man. You could learn much from him.'

McAvoy considers Keith. Broken blood vessels pattern his fleshy cheeks and there's a glaze of greasy sweat coating his completely bald head. He has unpleasantly wet lips: scarlet slugs that look a little chapped as if he has been eating chips with too much vinegar. As he smiles a greeting and gives a slightly effeminate wave, his pink tongue twice darts out of his mouth to moisten his lips, followed immediately after by a wet gulping sound, like a cat lapping at a bowl of water.

'You're a big fellow,' says Keith, looking him up and down. 'A fiery redhead, eh? Gosh, Patricia – how do you keep your hands off him?'

'I don't,' says Pharaoh with a shrug. 'Most of those scars are thanks to me.'

McAvoy stands awkwardly between them, unsure if he is expected to do anything more than provide them with something to talk about. He glances at Pharaoh and notices the almost imperceptible little wink she flashes as she raises a glass of something clear and sparkly to her mouth. He knows the signal. It encourages him to play along.

'You're a local man, Keith?' asks McAvoy, pulling up a bar stool and trying to fit himself onto it without taking a tumble.

'Victoria Dock, as it happens,' says Keith, making a little fluttering gesture at the distance with his fingers. 'But I'm a keen walker and it's no hardship to take a taxi out to the neighbourhoods of the slightly more rich and shameless.'

McAvoy looks at Keith's shoes. He's wearing patent leather brogues and some ugly, harlequin patterned socks, pulled up high. He hasn't walked in any dirt, that much is clear. He doesn't look as if he's walked anywhere but the bar and back for quite some time.

'Keith was telling me a story about the picture of the mausoleum that we were taking a look at,' says Pharaoh, all innocence. She's tucked her lanyard away. Right now she's being an attractive middle-aged woman rather than a police officer. It often has more effect.

'Ah yes, the transient skulls,' smiles Keith, and there's a certain raspiness to his voice that suggests daytime drinking isn't his only vice. 'Honestly, I think those heads spent more time at the police station than they did in their final resting place, back in the days when a boy could still have an adventure and get nothing more than a clip around the ear for his trouble.'

McAvoy slips into the familiar role. He's clueless. He's intrigued. He'd love to hear this barroom raconteur embellish his story and he's got all the time in the world to hear him tell it.

'Rite of passage, it was,' says Keith. 'The thing was built some time in the early nineteenth century by the family that used to own the big old house out near Cottingham. They had no shortage of money and it was quite the sophisticated thing to do at the time. The bit you can see – the dome and the column and the steps – that's the headstone really. Inside it there's a passageway that leads down into the depths. That's the family plot. Half a dozen lead caskets laid out side by side. Two of them are so small they'd break your heart. The original Dodds was a bit of a victim of hubris. I'm sure there's an old saying about not getting too big for your boots. Build yourself a grand old mausoleum and you might just attract Death's icy glance, eh?'

'Another for Keith,' says Pharaoh, her cheek cupped in her flat palm. She's looking at him as if he's endlessly fascinating. 'Tell Hector here about when you were a whippersnapper.'

'Rite of passage, as I said,' grins Keith, showing off unnaturally bright and neatly spaced teeth. 'I think it was wartime when some of the local kids found the loose bricks and dared one another to go wriggling into the darkness. God knows who was the first person to do it but by the time I had the courage to go wriggling down with my pal, the skulls had been in and out of that place a dozen times. They were found down by Hessle Foreshore a couple of times and the local coroner had to go through the whole rigmarole of declaring that they'd been dead nigh-on a hundred years. Didn't stop us going back in after them though. I feel a bit of a cad for it now, but it's one of those things, isn't it? When you're a child you like to prove yourself.'

'You've been inside?' asks McAvoy. 'That must have been something.'

'Black as the inside of a pig,' grins Keith. 'Must have been the late sixties, I reckon. We were both thinking of going trawling like most of the young lads round our way and it was one of those things we'd dared ourselves to do. I don't think I ever thought we would do it but Isaac's not the sort to take no for an answer. Of course, it was Muggins here who ended up going in. Isaac was too big to get through the hole, as the actress said to the bishop. I swear, it gave me nightmares for bloody years. But it was just like I'd been told. Little dark passage, then these stairs down into the ground. There was some graffiti on the walls and there were chains around the lead coffins, but it just took a bit of a wiggle to get the lid off. I only did it because I'd already gone so far it would have been stupid to turn back.

I swear, I can still feel the shape of it in my hand. No different to a sheep skull in terms of the texture. I think if my torch had died on me I'd have had a heart attack on the spot. Of course, I hadn't noticed that Isaac wasn't whispering down into the darkness any more. I was breathing so heavy that I wouldn't have heard a brass band. But as soon as I wriggled out and landed back on the grass, there he was having this stand-up row with the bloody owner of the house! Turned out he was only a bloody descendant of the woman whose skull I was holding in my hands. If Isaac hadn't been such a big lad I reckon the bloke would have gone for him, but Isaac wasn't the sort to get much trouble. Me, on the other hand – I'm a magnet for it. I didn't even notice the lass until she was slapping me about the head and going for my bloody eyes.'

McAvoy flashes a look at Pharaoh. She gives the slightest nod of her head.

'Did you get in bother?' asks McAvoy.

'I think I would have done if I was there on my own,' laughs Keith, shaking his head. 'As it was, I dropped the skull and scarpered. I figured Isaac was behind me all the way but he didn't even take a step after me. Had his eye on the lass, didn't he? Right out of our league, I thought, but Isaac was smitten just from one look at her. Told me later that he went into the whole "wounded bear" mode and told her dad it was all my idea and that he was only there to make sure I didn't get into any trouble. Offered to brick the opening shut and put the railings around it and do whatever he could to make amends. Worked out pretty well for him.'

'Yeah?'

'Aye, been together the best part of fifty years. Still smitten or so he tells me. He went away to sea but not in the way we'd thought. I was on oil rigs for a lot of my life. Spent years in Saudi, which isn't much fun for a drinking man. Still pals though. Christmas cards, weddings and funerals, that sort of thing. I'm pretty sure I was the last lad inside the place before he bricked it up. They haven't had much trouble since. Like I say, when you see Isaac, your bottle goes a bit.'

Pharaoh takes a sip of her drink. Shakes her head, as if astounded by the yarn. 'Glad we found you, Keith,' she says with a grin. 'Bloody local oracle, aren't you? You might know what's with all the police vehicles up the road a way. We got turned back by a right officious prick in a yellow jacket.'

'Bloody awful to-do,' says Keith, stifling a belch after slurping at his pint. 'I only heard about it myself this morning. Body found in the woods, right near Isaac and Cally's place. That's why I popped up, if I'm honest. He's a bugger for staying in touch but I phoned him this morning and got no reply so I thought I'd tell him I'd be in Triton for a couple if he wanted a natter. I don't reckon he's coming, but I'm trying to be a mate.'

'Cally,' says Pharaoh, running the name around her mouth. 'I've got a new granddaughter on the way, as it happens. Lovely name, isn't it?'

'Calpurnia, as it goes. Suits her, if I'm honest. I'd never say it to my pal but she's never really thawed. Even years later she still thinks I'm the arsehole who talked Isaac into nabbing her great great grandma's skull! That sort of thing can sour a friendship.'

'Calpurnia's a Roman name, isn't it?' asks McAvoy. 'Did I hear there's an excavation going on around here?'

'I figured we'd hear that the body was Roman,' laughs Keith. 'Bit of a shock to find it's not. They'll be hating having the coppers up there. Like their privacy, if you know what I mean.'

'Kids?' asks Pharaoh, still just making conversation.

'Just the boy. Magnus. That's a name to label a kid with, eh? Not much of his dad in him, that one. Runny eyes and knock-knees, though his mother would tell you he's part angel and part god. Never had any brats myself. Never had much luck with the ladies, though it's taken me three wives to find that out.' He stops talking and takes a gulp of his drink. Looks to Pharaoh and then at his glass. Back to McAvoy, wrinkling his brow. 'What brings you two to this part of the world, anyway?'

Pharaoh finishes her drink. Smacks her lips together. Leans back and fishes her lanyard out of her cleavage and dangles it in front of Keith's face as if trying to hypnotize him. He squints at the name and rank. His face falls.

'Same as you, Keith,' she smiles. 'Just looking for skulls.'

FIFTEEN

McAvoy plays with the car radio. Tries to find something to mumble along to. Stumbles onto a discussion show on Radio Four and within minutes is growling dark curses at the high-born voice dribbling out of the speakers. Some debate about anti-social behaviour policies. Ways to teach youngsters some respect. Usual drivel about national service and inclusion. He wants to put his foot through the dashboard. Would like to drag them to any street corner in Hull and point their eyes in the direction of reality. To show them there are no absolutes. No hoodies and baddies. Just people, with all their terrible inconsistencies and hidden elegances; their moments of grace and fleeting desperate acts of ill will.

He carries on up the dial. Finds something classical. Listens for five minutes and then swears when his slowly calming nerves are assailed by the grating tones of a voiceover artist trying to sell him an insurance policy over the codetta of Schubert's 'Danse Macabre'.

Switches over to the news in disgust.

Switches off.

At just after four p.m. he pulls in at the truck-stop café on the road between Howden and Goole. It has one or two bad memories for him, but he's willing to endure them in order to save himself another twenty miles of motorway, and to avail himself of a sausage butty the size of the *Oxford English Dictionary*.

He parks the fleet car between a camper van and a little blue Kia, sitting for a moment and listening to the rain and the wind hit the metal and glass. The café is properly old-school, with Formica tables, bolted-down plastic chairs, and sauce decanted into bottles the shape of a tomato. The tea comes in big white mugs or polystyrene beakers, and anybody not wearing dirty overalls is looked upon with suspicion. McAvoy, in his designer suit and long cashmere overcoat, looks as though he's either a copper, a gangster or both.

A trio of workmen are sat around empty, sauce-stained plates of food at a table by the big window. The woman seated near the till looks a little out of place in her roll-neck black sweater and patterned cardigan but if she feels uncomfortable she isn't letting it put her off her sausage, chips and fried egg. She half rises as she sees McAvoy, wiping her face with the back of her hand. McAvoy waves her back down and encourages her to finish her meal. He orders a tea and sausage sandwich from the small, harassed-looking woman in the pink tabard then sits himself down opposite Trudy Wade.

'Was that everything it appeared to be?' asks McAvoy, gesturing at the empty plate.

'It was,' confirms Trudy, taking a swig of tea. 'I was a little strung out when I arrived. I eat when I'm anxious, and as you can tell, I'm anxious a lot.'

McAvoy declines to offer an opinion. Trudy is certainly a sturdy-looking woman. He'd put her at perhaps mid-forties. She wears no make-up and her skin is the pink of somebody who spends a lot of time outdoors. She wears no rings and the skin of her hands is a little chapped and sore. Her front two teeth are slightly crooked and the overlap coupled with the unkempt hair and circular glasses conspire to give her a slightly eccentric appearance. McAvoy knows better than to make any assumptions about her character based on how she looks, but he would be willing to bet that she reads vampire books and knows the rules of Dungeons and Dragons.

'I really appreciate you coming out of your way on my account,' says McAvoy, as the waitress bangs down his sandwich and gives him some approximation of a smile. 'I wouldn't have got through York traffic before bedtime if not.'

'No problem,' says Trudy, looking at his sandwich with some degree of longing. She puts her hands beneath the table, perhaps to stop herself from jittering nervously or picking at the scabs on her fingertips and nail-beds. 'I wanted to help. I mean, I don't know if I am, of course. Help, I mean. But, well, you're here and I'm here and, well, maybe . . .'

'It's OK,' says McAvoy, in the tone of voice he uses on nervous horses. 'I'm already grateful to you just for the chance to get away from the investigation for a couple of hours. Even if nothing comes of this, you've done me a favour as well as doing your duty as a decent person. So you've got credit in the bank with me. Just tell me what you think I need to know.'

Trudy gives him an anxious grin, reaching for her cup and putting it back down on the table without a sip. Her bottom lip is trembling. McAvoy tries to catch her eye; to tell her that she's safe, she needn't worry, but before he's able to find the right words she's spun in her seat and started pulling out papers from the battered satchel that hangs over the back of the chair.

'Dieter Maxsted,' she says, and the name comes out in a rush of breath. 'I've investigated him umpteen times. He's got away with far more than we've ever got him for and I can tell you for a fact that he's a nuisance, a rascal and a right pain for anybody with an interest in heritage and history. But he's a likeable sod. He treats it like a game, you see? He's trying to make money and we're trying to catch him. There's no reprisal when we catch him and no gloating when we don't. So there's no bad blood there. In fact, if anything I've really rather grown fond of him. Is that awful?'

McAvoy pushes the sandwich away, painfully aware that taking a bite would not set the right mood. He nods his head. 'In my job you find out early on that some of the people you like most are the ones you're trying to lock up. Same in reverse – some of the people in uniform or setting the rules are terrible people who've never put another soul first in their lives. It's hard. It took me a long time to make sense of it and even then it wasn't so much that I came to a conclusion – just that all I could do was be somebody I felt OK about and judge each situation on its own merits. It doesn't always work. I get into trouble a lot. But I know that I'm trying my best, and that matters.'

Trudy stares past him. The rain is coming down heavier now. She looks as though she'd like to pull the door open and sprint out in the cold wet air.

'I'm an investigations officer with Heritage England – I said that to the nice lady on the phone,' says Trudy, holding her papers in her fist. 'I do a lot of work with the police but resources being what they are, well . . . not many police forces have got the time or the personnel to deal with breaches of the Ancient

Treasures Act or dealing in illegally sourced artefacts. That's a bloody shame, because it's a crime that affects all of us. We lose so much of our heritage to these unscrupulous private collectors who won't allow legitimate finds to go on public display in museums but would rather they were on the mantelpiece of their palatial study where they can admire them over a decanter of brandy, or whatever kind of glass posh people drink out of. It's a bloody scandal and nobody cares. We do our bit but we get so few chances to prosecute. Mostly I spend my time writing press releases asking for financial aid, or trying to persuade farmers to work with us and not against us.'

McAvoy urges her to slow down, trying to make sense of the tumble of words. 'Dieter Maxsted,' he says, softly. 'He has a colourful record.'

'He's a colourful man,' says Trudy quickly. 'I don't remember that much from before, but I remember he was always making people laugh and coming up with mad plans and making the most inappropriate jokes. I don't think I even knew his real name back then but when I started looking into him a few years back I recognized him at once. Lost some weight and gained some wrinkles but still the rascal who was always winding up the straight A students and running fiddles with phone cards and electric meters and whatnot. Obviously I thought he'd have gone into field archaeology but I found out during the investigation that he'd ditched his job at Bradford not long after I quit the course and that he'd spent years as a bit of a drifter, doing a bit of work at any dig that would have him. He had a reputation though. That's how he came to our attention in the first place. Things would go missing from the digs he worked on. He'd be given a job overseeing some volunteers or students going through a spoils heap or digging a trench and a week later he wouldn't need the job any more, he'd have cash in his pocket and questions were getting asked about smudged paperwork or finds that had been photographed but not checked in for assessment. It didn't take a genius to figure out that he was flogging stuff on to private collectors and his name came up more than once when we leant on a couple of metal detectorists who'd made some decent finds on the quiet and wanted to know whether they should play by the rules and get a fraction of a legitimate price, or put it to the black market and make a killing.'

'I know a wee bit about nighthawks,' says McAvoy, when Trudy pauses for breath. 'Illegal detectorists slipping onto private land in the dead of night – often places that have been legitimately identified as being of cultural or historic significance.'

Trudy nods, shaking her rolled-up papers at him for emphasis. 'We caught a couple of lads digging at Hadrian's Wall in 2015,' she continues. 'Brunton Turret, at Corbridge. Sophisticated equipment, real experts on their history. Made a mess of the site the previous time they'd been there so we arranged a good old-fashioned surveillance. Nabbed them in the act of digging up a decorative cuff and a small fertility idol. Really good finds. Maybe eight grand on the legit market and who bloody knows what they expected to get if done under the table. They broke easily enough and pinpointed Maxsted as their fence for whatever they found. Turned out he was the go-to guy for a lot of hawks. The police – well, I'm sorry to say, they barely gave a toss, so we did the legwork ourselves. I got to interview him twice on that occasion and, like I say, he was very much a charmer. Recognized me, of course, though I didn't think I was ever on his radar.'

McAvoy takes a sip of his cooling tea. Realizes he's missed something and mentally backtracks. 'You were at Bradford?' he asks, at last.

'One year and one term,' she says, regretfully. 'Found myself unexpectedly pregnant in my second year and promised myself I'd go back to my studies after the little one had come along. Never really happened, though I did do an Open University degree in my thirties and that put me in the running for the job I do now.'

'What can you tell me about the other students on your course?' asks McAvoy, trying not to make it seem too crucial a question. 'Universities can be dreadful for cliques. I didn't quite manage two years of my degree either. It's not for everyone – just like parenting.'

'I was pretty quiet,' says Trudy. 'I had it in my mind I was going to go and live these three years of drinking and pulling and going to festivals and stuff. Turns out that when you arrive at university you bring your own personality along with you. I made friends, of course, though I think I cried for the first few days. I was in halls. D Floor. A nice bunch – some nerds, some sporty people. I'd never heard so many accents or smelled such weird food! We spent most of our time drinking fizzy pop in one another's rooms and watching loud movies. We went out now and again but mostly we were just a little bunch of mates that didn't cause anybody any harm. I didn't even smoke a joint until second year.'

McAvoy sees a sudden flash of panic cross Trudy's face, as if she has just registered what she has told a police officer and is expecting a team of drug enforcement agents to smash in through the window. 'Me neither,' says McAvoy, with a smile.

Trudy pushes her hand through her hair, causing it to stick up wildly at the front. There's a real sheen of perspiration at her temples and McAvoy, taking the opportunity to glance at her hands, notices the bleeding cuticles around her nails. With the quick eyes and the jerky little movements, she seems more than simply a bit jittery to be spending time with a detective.

'Tell me about Dieter,' says McAvoy, gently. 'I know there's something you want to get off your chest. Why not just blurt it out and then we can deal with it together?'

Trudy gives a jerky nod. She reaches out and grabs the salt cellar and starts to play with it, staring at nothing. Beneath the table, her feet are jiggling up and down. When she finally looks up her eyes are glassy with unspilled tears.

'Dieter found us the house,' she says, quickly. 'In the department he was the guy you went to for most things. He always had a friend of a friend who could sort out the things you wanted. We'd all made the decision to get a house for our second year – me and my little gang. Eliska, the Sarahs, Julie and her boyfriend, then Ian. There were others who seemed to live there but weren't official. Dieter would come for a drink with us every once in a while and he said he had a mate whose dad rented out nice houses. He could do us a deal. He was as good as his word too. It wasn't a palace but we got this great big terrace with high ceilings and nearly enough bathrooms and we were paying less than we were in halls. I was always being teased for being the tidy one, which would be a laugh for anybody who knows me now. I'm a bit all over the place, to be honest. Anyway the downside was that we got an extra housemate. Nephew or second cousin or somesuch, I can't even remember, but he was family to the landlord and he kind of came with the house. He was friends with Dieter, that was the link. And because Dieter would come to see him from time to time, we sort of got Dieter into the bargain. He was always sleeping on the sofa or begging a top-and-tail with one of us.'

'You're doing great,' says McAvoy, draining his tea. 'I think I caught most of the names you said. Was there an Ian?'

Trudy nods, though offers little in the way of reaction. 'He left around the same time as I did but yeah, we were on the same course. He was nice enough. Not much of a drinker, and I wasn't in those days either so we'd often be the sober ones at parties, sitting in the corner and talking about books. He spent most of his time in his room or at the sports hall. He jogged a lot with that friend of his. He got on better with Mo than the rest of us.'

'Mo was the relative of the landlord?'

Trudy nods. 'He smoked a lot of weed. Dealt it too. It wasn't really my sort of thing. Ian liked a smoke so that's how he and Mo and Dieter became this little clique, sitting up until the early hours watching kung-fu movies and getting high. That's the way I always pictured Dieter until years later when I was investigating him. It's funny how life has a plan, isn't it?'

McAvoy takes a bite of his sausage sandwich. It's gone cold. He pushes it away, taking a napkin and wiping his mouth. He wonders whether he really is here for any purpose. Wonders whether, in his absence, Ben has already identified a suspect and locked them up.

'I hate to be indelicate, but can I presume the pregnancy was a bit of a shock?' asks McAvoy, willing himself not to blush.

Trudy gives an unexpected explosion of laughter. 'You know those adverts telling you that it's probably a good idea to use a condom? I should probably have listened. I had two one-nighters at university. Got caught out the second time.'

'Brave of you to proceed,' says McAvoy.

'Was it?' asks Trudy, looking up. 'Wasn't an easy decision.

Horrible shock, of course, but I sort of knew from the start I was going to keep him. I don't really like the idea that you can pick and choose when you're ready for things. Terminations are right for some people, but inconvenience wasn't a good enough reason not to go through with it, and university was very good. He's a lovely man, you know. Ran me ragged in his teens but he's turned out right. Reads a lot, likes the outdoors – calls me every couple of days. He's got a flat as part of his job so he's pretty set up.'

McAvoy nods, waiting for more. When nothing comes he prompts her, allowing a little impatience to enter his voice. 'Those full names would be helpful,' he says, glancing up at the clock. It's pushing five p.m. He needs to be back for the briefing. Needs to know what he's missed. He pulls out his notebook and makes a show of clicking the button on his ball-point pen. 'Trudy, you still haven't told me why you contacted us. Why you mentioned Dieter Maxsted to my colleague. What is it you suspect?'

Trudy chews her lower lip, hands clasped as if in prayer. 'Mo,' she whispers. 'Mo Laghera. The landlord's nephew. When I started investigating Dieter, he and Mo were still in contact with one another. Mo had, well . . . he'd kind of gone the way we suspected he might. A bit of a bad lad, I suppose you'd call him. We got the impression he was a middle-man for a lot of the fencing that we initially attributed to Dieter. Mo had lots of contacts, you see, but he was being investigated for other stuff – probably what you would class as more serious stuff – so the CPS weren't really interested in pursuing him for his involvement in some stolen artefacts. That's why we went for Dieter.'

'Right,' says McAvoy. 'And how does that get us here?'

'As I said, Dieter hasn't really been on anybody's radar for a while. I worry. I've always been a worrier. I'm still in touch with the Sarahs from D floor and we can chat until the sun comes up, and we were reminiscing a few months back about university and all the stuff people got up to and our different memories and stuff. It got me thinking about Dieter and Sarah P said that she remembered him and Mo having a falling out, but I'd already left by that point so it was news to me. And I told them I'd seen the pair of them a couple of times over the years and they seemed to be pals again . . . sorry, I'm gabbling, just stop me if you need to . . .'

'I need to,' says McAvoy, raising his hands. He drops his pen. Decides to take over. 'Trudy, do you think something bad has happened to Dieter Maxsted?'

'I think so,' she says, quietly.

'Do you think that he's the body we've found in the woods?'

Trudy lays her hands flat, fingers stretched out, as if taking part in a séance. 'I can't find him anywhere. No record. The coin dealership he was running – the phone number on the website isn't connected any more.'

'But why would you associate him with this crime scene? What's the connection?'

'Mo,' she hisses. She closes her eyes, suddenly looking weary. 'A couple of years ago, maybe a little more . . . I was trying to contact Dieter, you see. I wanted to put my mind at ease, and I thought maybe Mo would have an address. I swear I wasn't thinking the worst at this point. I just sent him a message through Facebook and asked him if he wanted to come to a reunion party I was thinking of putting on and whether or not he still had contact details for any of the old crowd. Of course, I'd hoped he wouldn't put two and two together and realize I was now an investigations officer with Heritage England, but he saw through that in a flash. Thought I was trying to set him up. He Googled me, just as I'd Googled him. He lost his temper. Called me up and started roaring and ranting at me and saying he wasn't going to let me put him back inside and that he'd done his time and didn't need me digging up the past. I hung up on him, a bit scared about it all. But I couldn't leave it.'

'You contacted the uncle?'

'I had to,' says Trudy. 'I just had this awful feeling. And he must have told Mo because Mo turned up at my house. It was late and I was home alone and he came in through the back door. Came and sat himself down in my armchair while I was laid on the sofa in my pyjamas. Walked in like he owned the place. He was very calm with what he said, but he told me to stop looking for Dieter, to stop digging up the past. He said that it might have taken nigh-on thirty years, but that what had happened in the woods near Hull had finally caught up with him and that if I kept coming after him, he'd make sure that not even an archaeologist would ever find me. I was too scared to say anything.'

McAvoy sits back in his chair. 'He said that? The body in the woods near Hull? And that's what made the alarm bells ring when you read the newspaper article?'

Trudy nods. Glances off towards the door and back again. Gives him a nervous smile, eager-to-please. Relief is coming off her in waves. She's got to the end of this unpleasant task and damn well wants to go home. 'I've done my bit now, haven't I? Can I just email you anything else? It's all kind of . . . I don't know – it's stirred things up . . .'

McAvoy rubs his hand across his jaw. 'Mo Laghera,' he says. 'You have a full name? Other details?' He stops, waiting until he can catch her eye. He gives her a nod of thanks. 'You were brave to come forward. It sounds like this Mo is a very nasty piece of work. It can't have been easy with his threats hanging over you.'

Trudy gives a weak smile. 'What can he do from where he is? I'm beyond his reach.'

McAvoy spreads his hands, not comprehending. 'Beyond his reach?'

'He's inside, isn't he,' says Trudy, with a smile. 'Sorry, I kind of assumed you would just know that, given what you do. Yeah. He's in prison. Attempted murder.'

McAvoy screws up his face as a cold ember of memory starts to smoulder. 'Bradford?' he asks. 'Turf war? Torture trial . . .'

Trudy nods. 'He admitted to it. What he did to those two young men – and he'd been there, in my house, bold as brass . . . no trace of who he'd been before. He had evil in him, I swear.'

McAvoy feels his heart start to thud in his chest. Recalls the detail that had made headlines a year before.

'Whips,' he says, as the pieces come together. 'He tore the skin from their backs. That's the man who you shared a house with? The man who was best friends with Dieter Maxsted?'

Trudy nods. Sniffs. A silence descends and McAvoy lets it stretch. Only when he feels she's composed herself does he lean forward.

'Your housemate, Ian. He left university at the same time as you? Have you had any contact since?'

Trudy shakes her head. When she speaks her words sound rehearsed. Sound like stock answers to a question she has been asked a lot. 'Disappearing Man, that's what the Sarahs call him. Probably did what he always wanted to do. Travelling, y'know? He probably left to get away from Mo. He was getting into the weed in a big way. Why? Are you looking for background on Dieter, because I can give you the numbers of all the others . . .'

McAvoy shakes his head. 'I'm sorry, Trudy. The body in the woods has been positively identified as Ian Musson. We think he's been there since around the time you left university.'

Trudy jerks back in her chair as if slapped. Screws her face up. 'No,' she says. Laughs: loud and shrill. Stops short, shaking her head. 'No, that's not possible. No, wherever he is, he's doing fine. He made his choices but he's done more than many people would.'

'I'm sorry?'

She's muttering to herself, scratching at the skin around her nails, nibbling a little strip of excavated skin – sucking at a spot of bright blood. When she speaks it's still there on her tongue: a smudge of crimson that turns pink as the tears reach her mouth. 'He's never forgotten a single birthday. Once a year, regular as clockwork. It goes straight in to Felix's account. Even when he turned eighteen. And nobody else could be doing it, could they? Why would they? He can't be. You're wrong. It's Dieter. It has to be Dieter, and Mo did it, and Ian's fine; he's happy, I told him he didn't need to provide – he just did it because he's decent . . .'

And McAvoy sits in silence as he watches a carefully constructed world fall apart.

SIXTEEN

Zeebrugge, Belgium
October 16th, 2009

The big man walks swiftly along the flat vastness of the beach, squinting into a low orange sun and scowling as a haze of windblown sand rattles painfully across his bare legs. It's far too cold to be out in just vest and shorts, but the man gets little chance to expose his scarred skin to the elements and is willing to tolerate such discomfort for the pleasure of letting air kiss flesh. He fancies himself unobserved. He knows from past experience that he is unlikely to see anybody this far from the little strip of pubs and restaurants that passes for the tourist trail. He has already made his way past the old lighthouse and though he can see the distant oblong of the port from which he will depart a few hours hence, he fancies he is beyond the glare of prying eyes. This is a bleak, sandblasted landscape: all dried grasses and ruffled dunes; great streaks of oil and seaweed writing indecipherable hieroglyphs along the distant water line.

He relishes times like these. Such moments are the closest he gets to liberty. He does not have to watch himself here. He does not have to camouflage himself within shyness; stillness – blend into nothing so as not to appear remarkable. He is a giant of a man, and yet the space he takes up in the memory is negligible. He moves as if trying not to disturb anybody. Moves like smoke. People struggle to remember whether they have been in his company or not. Such is his lot. He has had to make sacrifices to safeguard that which matters to him. He has had to make allowances. All is not as he would wish it, that much he cannot deny. He has to conceal himself, hurt himself; swallow down great chunks of the person he used to be so as not to appear ungrateful or dissatisfied with that which he has been so graciously permitted to enjoy.

He rubs the hem of his vest across his face. Looks down at the smudge upon the grimy white cotton. For a moment he sees his own face leering back up at himself. Thinks for a moment about the most revered shroud of all. His beloved had insisted he visit and venerate the sanctified relic at her side. Wonders, again, whether it mattered if the item was genuine, or whether faith could turn base objects into something spiritual through some benign form of spiritual alchemy.

He looks up. Sees a shape not far ahead: a little smudge of arms and legs, far out beyond the dunes. He fancies he should turn back lest he is forced into conversation. His Dutch is passable but he would rather not have to endure the stares of those who fate permits to look upon him. He knows his skin to be both hideous and fascinating. His flesh has been patterned with endless strikes of the studded, nail-garlanded flagrum. There are few inches of his naked form that are not whorled and twisted with lash marks. His skin is a fingerprint beneath a microscope: every scrap of epidermis pulverized until in places he seems to shine. He does not have much sensation left in his nerve endings. His hands, feet and head are all unscathed and he revels in their every gesture and caress. But the rest of him has been beaten insensible: every lash killing him off in fleeting increments.

The figure seems to be getting closer. The big man wonders whether this meeting has been somehow preordained. Such things are not beyond the will of the gods. And the gods know him to be their willing agent. He has done much in their name. The scars that adorn him are just a fraction of the sacrifice he has borne in honour of the gods who gave him that which his beloved sought beyond the point of madness.

The cold breeze dances across the sand, casting new pictures in the little dunes, as if a serpent is slithering across the surface. He wonders whether there is meaning to the act; whether the breeze was sent as a symbol; a warning to stop lying to himself; to speak with the forked tongue. He bites down on his cheek, his hands in fists, shoulders hunched. Wishes that he could still genuflect in such moments; to reaffirm his faith with a gesture of true belief. His religion does not permit such action. Constantine may have adopted the Christ as his standard-bearer in the dying days of the empire, but the big man knows that it is the old gods, those whom were worshipped during the days of Empire, who have answered his prayers and rewarded his sacrifice.

For a moment, the big man's head seems to fill with a great surge of colour and fire and noise. For a moment he sees that which he has committed in the name of duty. He sees the dead boy, in the ground, atop the two frail skeletons, impossibly fragile and porcelain white amid the hard darkness of the earth beneath the tree. He feels again the rush of hot blood upon his hands as he draws the blade across the taught neck of the struggling goat. Feels the kiss of the serrated leather cord as they tear into his skin; iron nails and animal bones rupturing flesh down to the bone. He thinks of the indignities suffered by his beloved; the terrible things she has permitted in order to be blessed by those above. And blessed they have been. The child with the golden hair; the dazzling eyes; the child they have earned with their devotions, their sufferings, their willingness to shed blood.

'*Goedenmiddag.*'

The big man stops. A few paces away stands a smallish old man: bald, save for a few wisps of hair around his ears, and dressed up sensibly in a blue raincoat and polyester trousers. He is smiling widely, hands upon his hips. There are binoculars sticking out of the pocket of his raincoat.

'*Goedenmiddag*,' says the man, without a smile.

'Ay, you're *Americann*,' says the small man, his face breaking into a smile. 'I speak some English. You catch ferry? Ferry to Hull always fun. You enjoy . . .'

The big man did not know he was angry until the cheerful little stranger started talking to him. Then the rage rushes up and out of him with such ferocity that he feels as if he is choking. His eyes bulge and water; tears streaming painfully over chapped cheeks.

The little man looks at his scarred skin. His face twists. Contorts; morphing into something that is part compassion, part fear.

'My friend, you have been burned? I am so very sorry – forgive me for staring, it was rude to have . . .'

The big man feels as though there are fingers within his throat, pushing down into his gullet like the head of a python. He thinks upon the incident in Palermo. Nero's Torches – that was what he had written upon the scroll as he described the brutality inflicted upon the fence who had tried to fool him with counterfeit gold. The big man had warned him of the consequences of dishonesty. He was not the sort to be crossed. He represented serious people, with serious wealth. To try and dupe him was to invite the full rage of Rome. For a moment he thinks again of the little Turk, his hands bound to a wooden stake, his body daubed in resin, screaming and simpering as the flames engulfed him and the fire burned red and gold; illuminating the little woodland where the big man's employer watched, impassively, before returning his attention to the priceless little curio he held in his hands, reading the inscription by the light of the burning man.

'My friend, I have offended you, please, may I walk beside you . . .'

The big man knows that tonight he will be back on board ship. He will be back within the shadows, blending in, hiding himself away, keeping himself unremarkable, unnoticed, keeping his secrets, taking whatever indignities he must in order to ensure that the golden-haired boy is unharmed, unprosecuted, unbound. He will suffer this, and more, to honour the gods who finally permitted his beloved that which she desired.

Here, now, he has the freedom to express himself as he truly is. Here, now, he can allow himself to rage. He can do bloody violence in the name of whichever god it so pleases, and he can regain a tiny fraction of his dignity with each blow he rains down.

The big man wonders if this is how it will always be. Whether he will have to steal moments of release, in order to continue being that which his beloved demands. He accepts that she needs her lovers. Needs to feel every extreme. Knows that she permits that which he, once, would have found abhorrent.

He takes the flagrum from the waist of his shorts. Squeezes the blood from its twisted leather tails. Hands it to the stranger and falls to his knees.

'Please,' he begs. 'Please.'

Only when the little man refuses does he allow his temper to truly explode. Only as he whips the clothes from his skin and the skin from his own unworthy bones, does he enjoy a moment's peace from the voice within his head – the voice that tells him, again and again, that his sacrifice has brought forth a monster.

Then there is just the blood upon the sand, and the sting of sea water upon flesh.

SEVENTEEN

Clough Road Police Station, Hull,
9.04 p.m.

'This is Dieter Maxsted,' says McAvoy, quietly, and clicks the 'return' key on the laptop. Behind him, the pull-down projection screen fills with a watery picture of a handsome man in his early forties. Some of the lower reaches of the photograph are cast upon McAvoy's face and dark jacket as he is caught by the iridescent glare of the projector. He raises his hand to shield his eyes and turns in his seat, joining the dozen other officers in staring intently at the picture. It's a police mugshot, but Maxsted looks as if he's posing for a vanity snap. There's a baffled little half smile on his face, as if he's enjoying a joke that nobody else is finding funny. He's got pale eyes and slightly weather-beaten skin; his longish curly hair bleached by the elements to a pleasing caramel-brown. His crumpled, collarless shirt is open to reveal a chunky pendant on a leather thong. His lips are parted just enough to show slightly overlong canines and his facial hair is perhaps two days away from becoming a beard.

'Handsome devil,' says Pharaoh, leaning against the wall by the window with her arms folded across her chest. She's taken her boots off and wrapped a cardigan around herself to try and cover up the shivers that keep running from the back of her neck to the tips of her toes. It's pushing nine p.m. and she hasn't had any opportunity to eat since the session in the Triton Inn. She's onto her third can of Dr Pepper. The ibuprofen and codeine mix is succeeding in keeping the headache at bay, but to McAvoy's eyes she looks genuinely ill. She's pale, washed out; her usual ebullience noticeable by its absence. There's a greenish tinge to her skin and she keeps massaging a sore spot at the nape of her neck; hair hanging forward as if she were dangling from a noose.

McAvoy clears his throat, drawing all eyes back to him. 'Dieter here was on staff at Bradford University when Ian Musson was a student there. There was a friendship of sorts between them and they were occasional housemates, along with numerous other students from the university.'

McAvoy clicks the key again. The image disappears and is replaced by the stern countenance of a fierce-looking Asian man. He's thick-set, dark-eyed: chestnut-brown irises staring broodingly up from beneath chunky black eyebrows. There's a gold chain at his neck, winking out from below his neat black beard. Time and money has been spent maintaining his thick crop of ink-dark hair. Muscles bulge beneath his tight T-shirt; complex scrollwork tattooed on both biceps.

'Mo Laghera,' says McAvoy. He hears a few rumbled expletives and exhalations from the team. Some of them recognize the image. Others are excited just at the idea that the sarge has identified somebody who looks so very much like a decent suspect.

'Mohammed Feazan Lagheram to be precise. Born March 1973. Housemate of Ian Musson, friend and sometime business associate of Dieter Maxsted.'

McAvoy clicks the keyboard a third time. The screen fills with crime scene photographs. Yellow evidence markers stand up in pools of dried blood. Chains hang from a hook in the damp grey ceiling of an empty lock-up. A bloodstained leather belt, studded with nails, lays coiled like a sleeping serpent on a workbench. The image changes again and the team wince in unison as they stare at the ripped and ruined flesh projected onto the screen.

'This is the upper torso of one Suleman Shafiz,' continues McAvoy, softly. 'In January 2020, Suleman, aged just nineteen, was lured to this lock-up on a promise of some knock-off designer gear. The message came from another youth he had thought of as a friend. In truth, the message had been sent by the criminal network with which Laghera was associated. Shafiz, a young man who had never been involved in any kind of criminality, was rumoured to have been making overtures towards the ex girlfriend of another, mid-rank member of the crime gang. A gentleman by the name of Junaid Khan, associate Stephen Chivers, and our man Laghera proceeded to imprison

Shafiz, strip him, and subject him to what the trial judge referred to as "acts beyond imagination – a despicable orgy of cruelty". For six hours they beat him, cut him, held flames to his skin, and lashed him with a belt studded with nails. He survived but not before begging to die. That recording was shown during the trial. In it, Chivers is seen as the ringleader. Indeed Shafiz testified that Laghera did not actually do any more than assist in tying his arms and hooking him to the ceiling. That's why he only got twenty-one months, while the other two each got sent down for sixteen years.'

Neilsen counts on his fingers. 'So, he's . . .'

'Out,' says Andy Daniells, who has spent the afternoon compiling the dossier which McAvoy holds in his lap. 'Model inmate, apparently. Sailed through his first hearing. Released to an address in Manningham, Bradford, in September of last year. Only served a fraction of his sentence.'

'Tie it together for the hard of thinking,' says Pharaoh, waving at the assembled officers and massaging her temples. 'Pretty picture wrapped with a pink bow.'

'Dieter Maxsted has been investigated by Heritage England for dealing in stolen or illegally sourced historical artefacts,' says McAvoy, closing the laptop and blinking as the overhead lights flicker back into life. 'During those investigations, conducted by an old friend from university, Mo Laghera was referenced as a possible business partner. No charges were brought against Laghera as he was already in the frame for more serious acts of criminality, but the investigating officer kept something of a watchful eye on Maxsted. When he vanished from her radar, she tried to track him down through Laghera, who responded with threats of violence and made reference to Maxsted being buried in the woods near Hull, and referenced an incident that occurred nearly thirty years before. Our informant believed the threats but when she heard about the discoveries at Brantingham, knowing that Laghera was locked up out of harm's way, she felt able to come forward with information. It will come as a nasty surprise to learn that he has in fact been free for several months.'

'She thought it was Maxsted?' asks Sophie Kirkland, taking a sip of lukewarm coffee and grimacing.

'She did,' confirms McAvoy. 'She didn't know how long the body had been in the ground and given her fear of Laghera, it made sense to her that he could perhaps have killed Dieter and dumped him there, as per his threats to her, and what she knew of the violence he was capable of inflicting having followed his criminal trial.'

'And Ian Musson?' asks Neilsen. 'What was his connection to any of the named players?'

'Musson was another housemate,' chimes in Pharaoh, from her perch by the wall. 'Friendly with Maxsted and Laghera. He was also the father of our informant's child.'

McAvoy watches as members of the team start drawing lines in their minds, filling in gaps and working up scenarios that might make sense of the complicated picture.

'Our informant left university after one term of her second year – just like Ian Musson. She confirmed to me that he was aware she was going to have his baby and that she didn't want anything from him. Despite that, she has received significant sums at least once a year for the whole of their son's life, helping confirm her belief that he has been very much alive all this time, rather than dead beneath an ash tree in Brantingham Woods.'

'Fuck,' says Sophie Kirkland. 'Somebody's gone to a lot of trouble.'

'How does any of this chime with the other two skeletons?' asks Daniells, as tactfully as he can. 'Why that site? Why does any of it drift over to this patch when it all sounds as though West Yorkshire's at the centre of it all.'

'That's what we're working on,' says Pharaoh, drily. 'Anybody know where we could find some detectives who might be able to find shit like this out?'

'You're seeing Laghera?' asks Neilsen, directing the question to Pharaoh.

'I'll leave that to Hector,' she says. 'I'm having a bit of a rummage around in the background of the homeowners. Calpurnia Dodds-Wynne, if you'll forgive the bloody stupid name. And if you mention that Patricia Pharaoh isn't exactly a belter, I will kick your fucking kneecaps off.'

'She was very rude,' explains McAvoy, diplomatically, as all eyes turn to him for explanation. 'Unnecessarily rude. It got a little heated.'

Pharaoh grinds her teeth, chewing on a thought. Glances at the clock and makes a decision. 'Home time, I think,' she says, clapping her hands together. 'A good day's work, or thereabouts. Both Maxsted and Laghera look like potential suspects and the deputy chief made very encouraging noises when I briefed him. Of course it was over the phone and he might have been sitting there trouser-less and enjoying some "me" time, but he certainly sounded pleased.'

The meeting breaks up in high spirits. McAvoy hears Daniells suggest an adjournment to the pub, Neilsen declining in favour of a jog along the waterfront, pumping out some endorphins before a protein shake and bed. Nobody asks McAvoy, so as to spare him the embarrassment of declining. All he wants is to go home to his family. It's all he ever wants.

Pharaoh appears at McAvoy's side as the meeting room clears. She smells of perfume, cigarettes, wine. There's a mustiness in there too, a suggestion of sleeping in damp sheets and yesterday's clothes. 'Drop me off?' she asks and puts her hand on his arm. He's horrified to feel that her iron-grip trembles slightly, as if she is coming down with a fever.

'You don't look well,' he says, bending down to look into her eyes. He reaches out without thinking and pulls at her cheek, gently tugging down her eyelid. 'You're a bit anaemic,' he says, frowning. He puts the back of his hand on her forehead. 'Clammy.'

Pharaoh shakes her head. 'You realize you just assaulted my eyelid, yes? You just went all paternal on a detective superintendent ten years your senior. And you called me clammy. Fuck off. You're the clammy one.'

McAvoy straightens up. 'Sorry. Instinct.'

'It's appreciated,' says Pharaoh, and as she breathes out there's a nasty rattling sound in her chest. 'Jesus, I feel fifty shades of shite.'

McAvoy knows that he should take her back to her place and let her get some rest. She needs a decent meal and lots of water; some quiet time and some paracetamol to help stop the fever getting worse. But he knows that she will open the vodka and order a takeaway, and fall unconscious at four a.m. talking inarticulate nonsense to her Icelandic friend and sending passive-aggressive messages to her increasingly absent daughters. He knows that Roisin needs some time with him. Fin needs normality and routine. Lilah will demand some remuneration for his unacceptably lengthy absences from the dinner table and the sofa these past two days.

'Come back to ours,' says McAvoy, before he can stop himself. 'The bed in the caravan's made up out the back. It's nice and warm. Roisin won't mind.'

Pharaoh bursts out laughing. Coughs again and looks up at him through glassy eyes. 'Don't mother me,' she mutters. 'Go home. Be you. Let me be me.'

'I worry about you,' he says, abruptly. Realizes how much he means it. 'With that woman today – you barely fought back. And the deputy chief's talking about you as if you're on your way out. That cough – Trish, you need to take care of yourself.'

'I'm not a bloody child,' mutters Pharaoh, though her resolve seems to be weakening.

'I won't even listen while you call whatshisname. I just want to know you're getting looked after.'

Pharaoh smiles. 'Whatshisname?' she asks. 'Why Hector McAvoy, that sounds positively discriminatory. You know very well he's Thor.'

'Yeah?' asks McAvoy, fastening his coat. He glances around to make sure nobody is listening before he permits himself the freedom to crack a joke. 'Roisin might have an ointment for that.'

EIGHTEEN

A little sprint of pain, almost like a zipper being pulled up, runs the length of Serena Menzies' thigh as she lifts her right leg and angles it across the left, fashioning a crude triangle with her limbs.

That's new, she thinks. Then, for emphasis: *Ow*.

She leans forward on the swivel chair and pulls the limb a little closer. The pain is there again. She sighs.

Bloody hell.

At forty-eight, her suppleness has always been the source of some pride, and despite being an optimistic size sixteen, she takes great pleasure in still being able to show off at parties by falling into a splits or backwards into a crab.

Getting old, she thinks. Then: Fuck.

She reaches down into her handbag and pulls out her black nail polish. Her fingernails are already patterned with an expensive amber veneer, and in deference to her boyfriend's football allegiances, she has decided to paint her toenails in Hull City's home colours. She's decided he deserves a treat. She's been feeling bad for hours. As she left the house she had made what she thought to be a jokey comment, but which, upon reflection, may well have been mean. He's ten years younger than her, and when they met he was tall and skinny, with gelled, fashionable hair and a wardrobe full of London labels. She had told him then that she liked her men with a bit of meat on their bones and set about feeding him up. He had responded enthusiastically, to the tune of around four stone. He shaved his head for her, too, when she told him that it was upsetting to be with a man who spent more time doing his hair than she did. And now, nearly sixty pounds heavier and with a head like a football, she has begun to realize that she preferred him gelled and slender. This morning he had popped downstairs to give her a kiss before she set off for work. Freshly shaved and wearing a flesh-coloured, round-neck T-shirt, she had told him, before she was able to stop herself, that in the half light, he looked a little like an erect penis. He had laughed it off, and given her the kiss he had intended, but on the drive to work she had replayed it in her head and realized that she had probably gone too far. He's texted her to this effect half a dozen times this afternoon, playing along with the joke and sending her funny pictures of animated members. Even so, she senses he deserves a conciliatory treat of some kind. Although he'll be asleep when she gets home, she's decided to wake him up in the manner that men fantasize about.

That'll be a test for the thighs, she thinks.

She looks up, briefly, from applying the first coat of varnish to her pretty toes, and looks at the monitor next to her desk. She's been a security guard for Hull Council for almost four years now and would be hard-pressed to describe the job as exciting. She came on shift at five p.m. and will work through until the morning. It's a little before ten now and so far, none of the exhibits at any of the city's museums or art galleries have come alive and started causing mayhem. She finds it dispiriting how little is actually demanded of her during a night shift. The Hull and East Riding Museum has a huge woolly mammoth in the entranceway and a whole family of hairy Neolithic artisans and she has passed many a shift imagining herself saving the day and embroiling herself in a fist-fight against an angry cavewoman in ill-fitting furs. Thus far, no such luck. All she needs do is sit in the control room and keep an eye on the monitors. In the event that Henry VIII's old siege cannon unexpectedly blows a hole in the wall, she has to fill in a form and jot down the details in the incident log. Other than that, her time is her own.

She reaches across the desk and plays with the joystick next to the first of the half dozen screens that sit in front of the large, curtainless windows which stare out from the admin block. She flicks between cameras. Wilberforce House. The Ferens Art Gallery. The Streetlife Museum. All empty. All dark.

She exhales, and returns her attention to her toenails. She could use a quiet shift. Her son, just a few weeks into his first year at Hull College, is thinking about quitting his course to take a job in a bait and tackle shop that belongs to an uncle of some new friend she has yet to meet. She and her son are butting heads on the issue, arguing at all hours, in a semi-detached house off James Reckitt Avenue that has begun to resound to the sound of slamming doors and 'hate yous'.

Serena pulls her leg a little closer and blows on the wet nails. She has done a good job, and hopes her man will approve, even if she does expect a little ribbing for having the kind of job that allows her to spend her shifts applying make-up and polish. She'll laugh along at that. She has no illusions about her job.

Reaching into her bag for her perfume, Serena feels the twinge of pain in her thigh again. *Bloody hell.* She fears she's going to have to start working out. She's tempted to use her late shifts to do some sit-ups and stretches, but there's something about the grey polyester slacks and scratchy black jumper that suggests to her she doesn't want to work up a sweat while in uniform.

She looks up at the screen again. Puts both feet flat on the floor and looks around for her socks and shoes. The security cameras are on a timer: the display changing every few seconds. Each museum has its own screen. In the event of an alarm going off she's expected to call her supervisor.

It happens thirty minutes later. One moment the screen is full-colour checkerboard displaying different rooms and displays within the museum. The next it is static and fuzz. Serena lets out a little growl. She taps a couple of keys on her keyboard. Wiggles the wires in the back of the first monitor. Checks the plug. Glances at her mobile to check that the Wi-Fi hasn't dropped out, then sighs all the way from the bottom of her soul. She's in the process of picking up the radio to report the malfunction to her supervisor when the static clears and the picture returns to normal. She pulls a face, irritated to have had her time wasted by a machine when she was doing perfectly well wasting it on her own. She sits back in the swivel chair, feet up on the desk. Looks at her toes. Looks past them. Sees the colourful image in the top right-hand corner of the screen.

Slowly, Serena leans forward, the pain in her leg forgotten. She takes hold of the joystick and zooms in, turning the image to full-screen display. This is the Roman Quarter: a recreation of Petuaria as it was seventeen centuries earlier. Displays of pottery, glass, oil lamps and brooches are mounted in shop windows around the town square; a tax collector's office and mosaic maker's workshop. The mosaic itself, in a lavish room adjacent to a replica bathhouse, is always a hit with visitors. It dates back to the mid-fourth century and the experts believe it depicts some forgotten deity: a figure donning a crown surrounded by adoring cup-bearers.

Serena knows the view as well as her own reflection.

The items in the centre of the floor are entirely new. She wonders which exhibit has been disassembled and moved. Wonders, briefly, whether her colleagues are playing a trick.

She doesn't recognize the objects from any of the locked display cases. Doesn't know whether they belong to a caveman, a Viking or a Victorian.

They're good, though. Gruesome, but well made. They look real. Uncannily real.

She flicks her eyes to the right. On her desk, a red light is flashing on the radio. On the screen a trio of bright dots suggest a tripped wire.

She looks again at the items in the Roman bathhouse. Feels a sudden tingling in her sinuses as she begins to realize what she is looking at.

Pushes the joystick until her whole screen is filled with one gory, grainy image.

Two hands. Yellowed flesh, dirty nails, claw-like fingers open in a rictus of agony. A head.

Ragged flesh dangling from the livid red neck. Gaunt features: holes punched in the parchment skin.

The glint of nail-heads. The dull sheen of ancient coins.

NINETEEN

'I tried to call, I just couldn't get a moment . . .'

'Aector, my love, it's fine, I swear. She's our friend. More to the point, she looks like twenty stone of shite in a fourteen-stone bag and there's nobody else to steer her right.'

'I'm not going mad, am I? She looks poorly. More poorly than usual – like the fight's gone out of her. The person of interest out at Brantingham – it was very much fifty-fifty and to Trish, that's a defeat.'

'We'll set her right, Aector, or damn well do our best. She's a good patient, right enough. Doesn't complain, though you can see in the set of her face that she's in pain. Just like you – a brave soldier.'

McAvoy smiles like a child who had been expecting a telling off and has instead been given ice cream. Relief floods through him. He and his wife are huddled together out the back of their little house, sandwiched in the gap between the back door and the colossal mobile home that takes up the entirety of their yard, along with a little of the wilderness beyond the boundary line. The family lived in the caravan for a time while the builders were repairing the main body of the house. It was a cosy, comfortable time. Nobody wanted to see it go once they were finally permitted back inside their home. It's now a guest room, reading room, playroom and general outdoor store room, though Roisin still bristles slightly when the children refer to it as Auntie Trish's caravan. She is a frequent house guest, though her presence here causes less commotion than it used to. She and Roisin have a complex relationship that seems to have grown considerably warmer in the months since Roisin saved her from a very bad man in the aftermath of Fin's abduction. McAvoy doesn't like to press either woman for too much detail about what happened. On balance, he would rather remain ignorant than be horrified by the truth.

'You look tired too,' says Roisin, looking up at her husband.

She puts both of her hands on his cheeks, stroking her diamante-studded fingernails through his beard. 'It's one of the bad ones, yes? I can see the light around you – it's gone that colour it goes when you fear you're chasing somebody who did bad things for pleasure. I've seen it too many times.'

McAvoy slumps against the kitchen door. He has a mug of hot chocolate in one hand and he pulls Roisin closer to him with the other, folding her inside his embrace and kissing the top of her head. Fin and Lilah are both in the living room, up past their bedtime to be allowed to entertain Auntie Trish. She's on the sofa, dressed in one of McAvoy's old rugby shirts and a pair of Roisin's old maternity leggings. She's eaten a bowl of stew with a couple of heels of crusty bread but she hasn't attacked it with her usual gusto and has neither begged for a glass of wine nor popped outside to smoke since they walked through the door.

'Babies,' says McAvoy, into her ear. 'Newborn, and nearly full-term. Both in the same location as the student we found after the tree was blown down.'

Roisin crosses herself. Pushes herself closer to him as if trying to give him some of her warmth. 'On purpose?' she asks. Then, iron in her voice: 'Were they killed?'

'We don't know,' says McAvoy, swallowing. He and Roisin suffered multiple miscarriages before conceiving Lilah. They cannot think of dead infants without remembering those seemingly endless bereavements, and the tears that fell upon newly turned earth.

'Related to each other?' asks Roisin.

'Near impossible to get a DNA match from the remains but they did their damnedest and managed to prove the familial link. Siblings. Soil samples make it clear they were placed there before Ian Musson was. It was an existing burial site.'

'So the tree was blown down and somebody saw an opportunity to get rid of a body?' asks Roisin, disentangling her hair from her necklaces. 'Just bad luck that somebody had already laid their babies to rest in the self-same spot?'

McAvoy looks up at the yellow moon. Watches the clouds scudding briskly overhead. Gives a little growl – the noise he makes when he finds something unsatisfactory.

'I can't get on board with that,' he says, quietly. 'It feels very deliberate to me. What was done to Ian – the torture, the nails, the coins, the placement – it has a purpose, a significance. The babies in the same space? It feels as though the two things are connected – almost as if there's something nearly sacred about that spot.'

Roisin chews her lip, fiddling with her earrings. She pulls her dressing gown a little tighter around herself. 'The people who own the land – the academic lady and her big, bad husband. Tell me again.'

McAvoy permits himself a little smile. He has always involved his wife in his work – sometimes far more than he ever intended to. She has a keen, insightful mind and often sees things from a different perspective. He is reluctant to admit it, but he benefits from the fact that his wife has a fine criminal cognizance.

'She barely even looked up from her book,' says McAvoy. 'No interest in what was going on. Said the tree wasn't on their land and seemed as though she couldn't care less about any of it. The man we met in the pub said that her husband was a Hull lad who fell for her when they were up to no good – trying to nab a skull from the family crypt, which isn't much of a walk from the house where they now live, and where he's in the habit of skinning rabbits and leaving them dangling from the branches of a tree.'

'Children?' asks Roisin. If the fate of the rabbits troubles her, she doesn't show it. Roisin has spent great chunks of her life living off the land and has done things far more visceral than simply skin an animal and cure its flesh when food has been in short supply. She is not somebody who judges others harshly.

'One. A son. Magnus, according to Professor Bromley.'

'And what does he do?'

McAvoy closes an eye, thinking hard. Had Ben come back with an answer on that one? A current address? He plays back some of his conversation with Trudy Wade, chewing on his cheek as he realizes that he didn't put the name to her. He curses himself, genuinely sick to the stomach at the thought of not ticking off every item in his notebook. Of course, if Magnus was on the same course as Ian Musson he could easily have known Mo Laghera and Dieter Maxsted. He could even be the link between Bradford and Brantingham Woods.

'You've thought of something, I can tell,' says Roisin, grinning. 'And you look like you want to rip your shirt off and lash yourself. I'd encourage you not to, though I'm in two minds, if I'm honest.'

'The lady I met today – the one who investigated Dieter Maxsted for his part in the trading of stolen artefacts – she mentioned so many names. I think it was Ben who was following up on the son. Shit, I can't do this delegating stuff, Roisin – I need to keep it all in my head . . .'

'You're a sergeant at heart,' says Roisin. 'But you'll get the hang of it. You'll feed it all into that big computer on the top of your neck and whatever comes out will make sense. I know that. Everybody knows that, Aector.'

McAvoy slides his phone from his pocket. There's a rustle as he moves and he reaches to retrieve a sheaf of folded-up papers from the seat of his trousers. It's a couple of the pages Trudy Wade had provided for him in the truck-stop – pages he dropped and scooped up and didn't remember to fasten to the rest of the bundle before it was scanned and logged and entered onto the digital case file. He is coming to the conclusion that, on balance, he has not put in a good day's work.

'What's that?' asks Roisin, curious.

McAvoy runs his eyes over a social media conversation – half a dozen different names all contributing to a chat full of exclamation marks and emojis. He passes it to Roisin while he calls up a search engine on his phone and puts in a simple search for Magnus Dodds-Wynne. Gives a grunt of frustration when the screen fills with references to Calpurnia and Isaac's only son.

'Jesus, I should have been all over this,' mutters McAvoy. 'We barely even asked her about him. Out of date though. Hasn't been updated since 2011 . . .'

'They seem a nice bunch,' says Roisin, using the light from the kitchen window to read through the documents in her hand. 'D-Floor Posse.'

'Sorry?' asks McAvoy, distracted.

'That's what they call themselves – this group. All old friends from university. They were in halls together, look. This is a chat from 2018. Did you say the lady's name was Trudy? She's asking her old friends: Sarah A, Sarah P, Julie, Eliska – they're having a right old nostalgia fest.'

McAvoy's eyes flick across the screen in front of him, not quite paying attention to his wife as she starts reading out passages of conversation. He's found the home page for Magnus's business.

'". . . OMG, the size of the rats at the end of the road . . . like, no fear, big as dogs . . . all the looks we got walking past McRory's in our full Rocky Horror gear . . . remember you bouncing up and down on that bush outside halls, using it like a trampoline, and those girls who totally wanted to bang DT, 'cause they totally didn't get that he had his eyes on the weirdo with the beardo . . .'

Roisin stops reading for a moment. Looks at her husband, who's thoroughly engrossed in the article on his phone.

'Magnus Dodds-Wynne is a former chairman of the Numismatic Society and one of the world's leading dealers in rare and antique coins,' reads McAvoy, poring over the words that accompany a picture of a tall, broad-faced and distinctly self-satisfied man: florid red-wine cheeks and a mismatched, bristly goatee. 'He has been collecting coins since the age of five when he accompanied his mother to a dig at Herculaneum, near the better-known site of Pompeii, and was fortunate enough to be present when one of the archaeologists uncovered a simple coin that had not seen the light of day since being buried in volcanic ash. So began a lifelong passion . . . main areas of interest include Celtic coinage, Byzantine and Greek, and he is one of the foremost experts in Roman Republic and Imperial coinage, bronze, silver, gold . . .'

Roisin gives McAvoy a squeeze to shush him and picks up reading where she left off. 'This is Eliska talking here, whoever that is . . . "Remember when Mo borrowed his uncle's car so him and Musson and DT could go on one of their mad treasure hunts and DT crashed it and did his knee in and had to hobble around the department with a walking stick looking like somebody from the Gestapo? It was constant 'can you just get me this . . . and if you're going to the shops . . . and Mo, mate, can I crash again tonight' . . . funny choice of words, ha—".'

'Say that again,' interrupts McAvoy, hastily adding a deferential 'please'.

'All of it?' asks Roisin, looking up.

'DT,' says McAvoy. 'Dieter, DT? Leg injuries . . . a borrowed car . . . treasure hunts . . . all around the time Ian leaves university, and Trudy decides to disappear too.' He stops talking, shaking his head. 'It's all guesswork. I've got nothing. Not really.'

'What about this Mo chap?' asks Roisin. 'Sounds like a bad man.'

McAvoy sighs. 'Maybe he put him there to point the finger at Magnus. Maybe Dieter knew that spot and told Mo about it. They might not have known about the babies.'

'If you had a crypt on your land, you wouldn't put a body in the first hole you came across, would you?' asks Roisin. 'You're leaving yourself vulnerable every time there's a high wind. But a crypt? A family crypt?'

McAvoy calls up the image of Dieter Maxsted. Looks into the intelligent, slightly faraway eyes. Tries to imagine such a man tying up a student and lashing him bloody then nailing his eyes shut and enclosing him in the earth. He pulls up the photograph of Mo Laghera, accompanying the article about the tortured young man. Looks into his dark eyes and tries to make sense of it. Shakes his head, tension at his jawline and the nape of his neck.

'I'm going to go read to Lilah,' says Roisin squeezing his forearm. 'I'll leave Fin to you. It will feel a bit easier after some sleep, I'm sure.'

McAvoy feels her soft, glossed lips brush his. Feels a moment's heat and nearness, and then she is back inside the house, scooping up their daughter amid a chorus of complaints and saying her good nights. Moments later, McAvoy follows her. Pharaoh is already asleep on the sofa, her mouth open, snoring softly. From his angle by the door, McAvoy can make out the tracery of blue veins across her slightly exposed chest. In the armchair, reading a science-fiction novel, Fin gives his dad a little nod and a grin. They both look at Auntie Trish. Fin clambers out of the chair and opens the blanket box, pulling out a patchwork quilt and a multicoloured crocheted blanket.

He drapes one over Pharaoh, and wraps himself in the other, returning to the chair and picking up his book.

McAvoy doesn't move. Just gives the merest nod. Fin can sleep here. Can sleep near Pharaoh. Can be here where it's safe, instead of alone in his head, where anything and everything stalks him in his dreams.

'Good night son,' says McAvoy, softly, as he bends down and presses his forehead to the boy's. He'll be fourteen soon. He's pushing six foot tall. He's got a rugby player's build. But here, now, he still smells of bubble bath and hot chocolate, and he's still the same little boy that used to flap his arms like chicken wings while his father fed him forkfuls of chocolate cake; the same boy who called the ambulance when his mammy went into labour while McAvoy was hunting a killer; the same boy for whom McAvoy would have gladly died a thousand deaths and for whom he lives each day as a proud man.

'Love you, Dad,' says Fin. Then, quietly: 'Auntie Trish said you forgot to find out what Magnus does for a living. Not to worry, she's done it and the website hasn't been updated since 2011. Worth checking for a deed poll change. She can fill you in over French toast around six thirty.'

McAvoy chuckles and blushes at the same time. As he closes the door and heads upstairs he takes a last look at Pharaoh. She's got one eye open and is staring at him, a tear spilling down her cheek to puddle in her ear.

He pauses for a moment. Holds her gaze. Then she is rolling over in a riot of squeaking springs, and McAvoy is walking slowly upstairs to his wife, mind full of skulls and rabbits and coins.

TWENTY

Two a.m. The moon yellow as a smoker's teeth.

On Hessle Foreshore, beneath the concrete and steel of the Humber Bridge, a big man is sitting motionless, perched like a colossal gargoyle on the lip of a rusting outlet pipe. Beneath him is a strip of sludgy beach. To his rear, across the deserted road, a row of pretty, white-painted houses. Midway along, a spray of red flowers cascade down the side of a hanging basket, their petals slate grey in the darkness. There is a horse-shoe over the little porch, and a stained-glass amulet set into the teal-coloured wooden door.

The man has been here for some time. He is perfectly invisible; his bike leathers blending in with the pitch darkness. He can hear the slow suck and pull of the Humber slapping the stones. Occasionally a cargo ship slides slowly along the wide brown waterway towards the docks. From time to time he hears the slam of a car door or the shushing of the wind through the mass of trees that form the pleasant country park nearby.

The man has keen hearing. Keen eyesight too. He's huge. Bald. Bearded.

Soundlessly, he turns and glances up at the bedroom window at the middle house. There's a soft warm glow of illumination from within. A little while ago he made out the shape of a small, dark-haired woman, moving with a lazy lightness behind the blinds. He had made out the shape of the big man, too. Had seen the way they moved together: held one another – took comfort in one another's nearness and communion. It had reminded him of a different time; a better time, when he had been the softly-spoken giant wrapping his big arms around a delicate, beautiful woman.

He raises his hands to his face. Smells the meat and the smoke. Lowers them again, a growl in his belly.

From across the road, the muffled sound of a ringing phone. Muted voices. Lights in the living room blaring into life.

The big man permits himself a moment's satisfaction. He likes these moments of fulfilled prophesy. Has known for the past hour that none of the occupants of the little house will get to sleep until the dawn.

The front door opens. The small, roundish woman with the long hair sits on the step. She has a leather jacket around her shoulders and wears pyjama trousers that trail on the ground. She has her phone to her ear. A plume of smoke drifts from her mouth as she whispers, harshly, into a mobile phone.

He hears her swear. Cough. Swear again.

Five minutes later, she and the big man are spilling out of the house. She's pulling on a biker boot, grumbling at her companion, telling him to go back inside, to go back, to let her do what she's paid for. And the big man is ignoring her. Slipping behind the wheel of the silly silver car. They will be at the museum within twenty minutes. It will be morning before they identify the head and hands.

Silence descends as soon as the pair are gone. The quality of the air seems somehow altered by their absence; the darkness thicker; the sky above suddenly malignant as the clouds twist in on themselves and the moonlight vanishes like a candlewick snuffed with a licked forefinger and thumb.

The big man stays for a while longer. Watches the house. Watches as the pretty woman and the broad-faced teenage boy sit together on the step, holding one another, heads pressed together as if trying to read one another's thoughts. They stay this way for long, precious moments. Only when the woman shivers do they return to the warmth of the house: she showing a flash of tanned shin and thigh as she re-ties her zebra-striped dressing gown about herself.

He grieves for them. Weeps, inside himself, in the full and certain knowledge that their futures hold bereavement and pain.

When the moon emerges again, the man has gone.

So too the iron horseshoe. In its place, a skinned rabbit dangles bloodily from a crucifixion nail, guts and entrails dangling from the slit in its belly; eyes reflecting the water, the bridge, the yellow moon, and there is no sound save the movement of the water, and the slow drip of crimson blood upon red petals, and damp earth.

PART TWO

TWENTY-ONE

High Street, Hull,
Thursday, April 10th
6.14 a.m.

The storm has devoured itself overnight. The dawn arrives clear and cold and blue, carrying with it the silt and diesel whiff of the docklands, skimming across the waters at this place where two rivers meet.

McAvoy stands with his hands on the railings of the new footbridge, staring out towards the coffee-coloured sludge of the estuary. He relishes the feeling of the chill air upon his face; the sensation of grime and death being sloughed from his hands and brow. It's been a hard night. Too much bone. Too much darkness. Too ripe the stench of rotting flesh and singed hair. This is more escape than respite. He couldn't stay inside the crime scene perimeter a moment longer; couldn't stare into the unblinking silver eyes or look upon the rictus grin of the screaming skull. He's fled the maze behind the police: staggered here – 500 yards from the mouth of the river.

He breathes in the good air, trying to clear his head. He likes this place. Likes this quiet spot below the flyover, with its old warehouses and artsy offices, half-empty museums and cobbled, narrow streets. The mud at the river's edge is the consistency of chocolate mousse. Anybody falling in from the open walkway would disappear, leaving a perfect outline to be filled in at the next tide.

'I got you one, but I drank it.'

McAvoy smiles at the sound of Pharaoh's approach. Feels her slot into position at his side. She's given herself a blast of perfume but she still smells of stale cigarettes and yesterday's clothes.

'It might not be him,' she says, softly.

'It is though,' he replies. 'You know it.'

There is a moment's pressure on his forearm as she leans her head against him. He returns the gesture. Bends down a little to put his cheek against the crown of her head. In such moments they are not colleagues. Each needs a little something of the other.

'Getting complicated, isn't it?' says Pharaoh, and there is a note of exhaustion in her voice. She's due to brief the media in an hour and sounds much the way she looks. She moves away, leaning her back against the railings and squinting up at him. 'I was joking about the coffee, by the way. I didn't get you one at all.'

McAvoy grumbles an affirmation. He feels a surge of anxiety flood him, the sensation of it all being too much, too difficult, too big a responsibility. He feels an overwhelming urge to absolve himself of responsibility: is momentarily overcome by the absurdity of his position, his job, his duty. He breathes through it. Lets the feeling settle. He pushes his hair out of his face and scratches his head. His scalp feels painful beneath his nails and for an instant he imagines laying his head in Roisin's lap and having her work her dainty, bedazzling fingertips through his hair. She can put him to sleep just by kneading his temples; sometimes singing to him softly as if he were a child frightened by a nightmare. He tucks the image away, promising himself he will return to it when needed. Even at a remove she can soothe him.

'Yorrick's on his way up to Hull Royal,' says Pharaoh. 'We'll have it official pretty sharpish. If it's not Maxsted I'll stand in Hammonds window wearing nothing but a traffic cone. And the DCC can give me a load of shite about not jumping to conclusions, but given the coins nailed through his eyes, I'm going to link this to Ian Musson.'

McAvoy nods. They both feel certain that the head and hands deposited in the Roman quarter of the museum are those of Dieter Maxsted – their prime suspect for just a few pleasant hours. The gold tooth and the overlong canines were as good as a name-badge. Both had stifled groans as they looked upon the gruesome remains. They had half convinced themselves that Maxsted was the man they sought for Ian Musson's death. His own demise leaves them with more questions and even fewer answers.

'Laghera,' says McAvoy. 'First priority. I can be in Bradford by eleven. I'll try softly-softly. If that doesn't work, we'll go mob-handed.'

'If he knows nothing about any of this then we really haven't got very much of anything,' broods Pharaoh. 'Sometimes I miss the days when you could just punch a homeless person until they admitted murder.'

'No, you don't,' says McAvoy. 'Your problem's the same as mine. You want the truth.'

'I want a gin and tonic,' says Pharaoh, moodily. 'And a cold peshwari naan with Nutella.'

'I told you about that in confidence,' says McAvoy, sullenly. 'It's very nice.'

'Roisin would murder you if she found out you'd had that for breakfast while she was away. Literal murder.'

'I know.'

Pharaoh glares at two pigeons fighting over a scrap of chicken-wing at the water's edge. Kicks a stone in their general direction and gives an air-punch of satisfaction when they scatter amid a flutter of protests.

'I want to speak to Bromley again,' says McAvoy. 'He must have been able to give me more than he did when I saw him. I thought he was being helpful but maybe he was just being friendly. It's worth thinking about at least. I mean his office is ten minutes from here. He might know about security systems; CCTV . . .'

'It's Hull,' snorts Pharaoh. 'Everywhere is ten minutes from everywhere else. And I think you're grasping.'

'I really liked the look of him,' broods McAvoy. 'Dieter, I mean. I just sort of warmed to him, even while I was sizing up whether or not he might be our guy. He had that rascal look. We need to find the rest of him. We need cadaver dogs up at the woods first off. The locals aren't going to like it.'

'You mean the Dodds-Wynne clan,' growls Pharaoh, shielding her lighter from the wind and sparking up one of her black cigarillos. 'Aye, they find it bad enough dealing with the ramblers, so they're going to love our lads and a load of yelping dogs. But we need to put some pressure on there.'

'Magnus,' says McAvoy, dourly. 'I'd like to know if he

remembers Ian or Dieter or Mo Laghera. He's the connection, and we haven't ticked him off the list.'

'The coins are a bit bloody interesting, eh?' muses Pharaoh. 'I'll have Ben run a deep dive on the three of them. Anything and everything. Financials, Land Registry, every parking ticket they've ever had – the big man especially, after what our new mate told us in the Triton.'

'You've got a location for Magnus?' asks McAvoy, still feeling as though he may have overlooked something important when interviewing Trudy Wade.

'The phone number on the website isn't active but Mummy will know where he is.' She pulls a face, pissed off with herself. 'I should have pushed.'

'She was hard work,' says McAvoy, as tactfully as he can. 'And you're dealing with far too much for one human.'

'Says you,' snaps Pharaoh. 'She got under my skin, I know that much. I don't know what it was about her – just so bloody superior. I shouldn't have let her rattle me though.'

'And I should have pushed Trudy about Magnus,' says McAvoy, looking like a repentant Great Dane.

'All right, don't do the whole "I'm Spartacus" thing,' snaps Pharaoh. 'Suffice to say, we're both a little way off our best. But we're making some progress, I suppose. I mean, we only had one body a couple of days ago. Now we've got four. That's some going.'

McAvoy hangs his head. 'I think we should have them both in,' he says. 'Mum and Dad. Calpurnia and Isaac. See how superior she is when we're in an interview room.'

'Get you,' says Pharaoh, surprised. 'I thought you'd be worrying about whether or not she'd had a difficult childhood and offering to go polish her statues and rub her sore arm. Perhaps there's hope for you yet.'

McAvoy pulls his phone from his pocket and calls up the website that Roisin sent him the link to just as the sun was coming up. Intrigued and unable to sleep, she had trawled the internet looking for information on Calpurnia Dodds-Wynne and found an interview she had given to a Classics magazine in 2014. McAvoy skimmed over the dry, largely tedious article. He'd been about to close it down when he spotted her reply to a question about her own academic journey.

'Listen, you might like this,' says McAvoy, pulling his glasses from his inside pocket and slipping them on. 'So, the question is . . . where does your love of Classics come from, right? And she says: "My father was an almost irritatingly clever man – one of those people of easy intelligence. He could read a book and somehow turn the last page knowing even more than the author about the subject. He was also very much ahead of his time in terms of his view of gender roles. He wanted me to have every opportunity to be all that I could be and the irritant of my sex rarely came up. We were fortunate enough that he was able to supplement what he saw as the gaps in my education. We had money – not a fortune, but we were comfortably off – and he was always in-demand as an assessor of artefacts interspersed with bouts of pedagogy . . ."' McAvoy looks up, wondering if he need explain.

'Pedagogy . . . that's teaching, yes?' asks Pharaoh, enjoying the feel of the word in her mouth. 'Fuck, I hate posh people. Is this going anywhere?'

'". . . it was Father who read the Classics to me as bedtime stories. Some children fall asleep to Hans Christian Andersen. For me it was Plutarch – the speeches of Cicero, the biographies of the great lives: Caesar bleeding to death on the floor of the forum; Cleopatra holding the snake to her breast; Mark Antony's wife clutching Cicero's severed head and stabbing his accursed tongue while his hands were displayed on the rostrum. Those stories took root. Of course, I discovered that academia is not nearly so gender-blind. The entire subject seems predicated on misogyny and I have been endlessly thwarted in my attempts to change the status quo. While it's true that we have few examples of Latin literature by women from the ancient period, we do have funerary monuments, graffiti, letters and election slogans by women. Furthermore, teaching Late Latin is a key step in bringing more women writers into classrooms. My poor partner and my son, Magnus, have to listen to me talk about these matters endlessly around the dinner table, though thankfully it hasn't deterred Magnus from pursuing his own passions for the Classics, although he prefers to feel solid items with his fingertips than to spend his life within the pages of dusty textbooks. Perhaps more of my grandfather is present within him. He was one of the first metal detectorists and perhaps it's from him that Magnus inherited his love of treasure hunting."'

McAvoy stops, wetting his lips. Pharaoh is staring at him, waiting for more.

'Cicero,' he says, hoping he's explaining rather than mansplaining. 'Brilliant politician and public speaker and nemesis of Mark Antony. When Antony and Octavian overcame their previous differences and agreed to divide power with the rather feckless Lepidus, they made a list of their enemies and all were put to the sword. Cicero had previously been a supporter of Octavian but he was, well, rather hung out to dry. Soldiers were sent to find him and he was betrayed by one of his servants and executed. The head and hands were displayed for all to see and the story about the stabbing of the tongue – that's been doing the rounds for 2,000 years.'

Pharaoh pulls a face. 'If you're telling me we need to look for somebody wearing sandals and a toga I may have to hurt you.'

McAvoy shakes his head. 'No, I don't mean that. It's just, the Romans did justice very well. They didn't hold back with their punishments. Symbolism was very important. And look where we are. Somebody has gone to the trouble of breaking in to a museum – disabling the security feed, all to be able to deposit Dieter Maxsted's head and hands on the floor of the Roman quarter. A Roman quarter that owes a lot to Petuaria.' He pinches the bridge of his nose. 'Sometimes I wonder if I've spent too much time unconscious.'

Pharaoh looks past him as DC Fusek yells a boorish greeting from the back of the museum. He's wearing a two-tone suit and a knee-length parka. He's only a pair of John Lennon glasses away from outright copyright infringement.

'Your lift's here,' says Pharaoh, with a little grin. 'If opportunity presents itself, hit him, yeah?'

McAvoy groans. Puts on his best fake smile. Beside him, Pharaoh turns her back, attending to some business on her phone. McAvoy glances at the screen, unable to help himself. Sees the deputy chief constable's name and the word 'Urgent' and looks away before he gives himself too much to worry about.

'Heard we've got a head,' says Fusek, conversationally. 'Fuck, it's never dull in Hull.'

McAvoy can't help but agree.

TWENTY-TWO

Hessle Foreshore,
7.48 a.m.

'Go on, then. But if you get muddy, Lilah, I swear, I will shave the head of every dolly in that bedroom.'

Lilah, already pulling on her coat over her school uniform, gives her mother a pitying look. 'Mammy, these are very empty threats. You should keep them believable. Tell me you'll be cross. Maybe even disappointed. Then I know the real consequences of my actions. The bigger threats sound a little fanciful.'

Roisin bursts out laughing. Crosses to her seven-year-old daughter and fastens her coat for her. Hugs her and breathes her in. She's got that lovely childhood smell about her: warm sheets and toothpaste, cereal and wet grass. She kisses her cheek, leaving a smear of lip gloss on her skin.

'Look after her,' says Roisin, to Fin, who has been sitting on the floor reading a book and waiting for the two women in his life to decide what the near-future holds for him. He's already got his coat on, knowing from past experience that Lilah will always get her way. He envies his little sister, albeit without malice. She will talk to strangers without a moment's hesitation, and can run rings around most adults in conversation. She doesn't blush. Doesn't worry what people think of her. Always has a good reason if she doesn't win the race at sports day or has forgotten to carry out one of their mammy or daddy's occasional instructions. Fin can't do any of that. He's shy and clumsy and blushes all the way down to his toes if he catches himself behaving in a way that might be considered inappropriate or remarkable. But he does enjoy her company. Loves her, in the way of big brothers everywhere. She's a pest, but she's his pest, and she has enough self-confidence to be able to say thank you, or to tell him she loves him, without ever appearing embarrassed. As far as Fin is concerned, to be hero-worshipped by somebody already considerably better than him, is something to be proud of.

'If Daddy comes back on the telly will you record it, please?' asks Lilah, standing on tiptoes to check her reflection in the mirror above the fire. She licks her thumb and pinkie finger and smooths down her eyebrows. Slaps herself lightly on both cheeks, and blows her reflection a kiss. 'If he calls, tell him he looked handsome but was a bit squinty. Maybe he needs to start wearing the glasses all the time. Anyways, *ciao* for now. Love you.'

Roisin shakes her head, grinning. Feels the nearness of Fin as he lumbers to the door. Pulls him to her and kisses his head. Still a boy, she thinks. Terrible teens ahead, but he's not going to give them any trouble. He's such a good boy. Kind. Caring. Scared of his own shadow but with the courage to face down whatever panics him. She's always known that she didn't so much have a child with Aector, as a clone of him.

'Watch her,' she says, in his ear. 'Love you.'

Lilah opens the door. Steps out into the cold blue air. Something brushes her face. Something slimy. Furry. Something dead.

She jerks a little, some primal instinct telling her to move away from the glistening pink thing that dangles in the doorway.

'Mammy,' she says. 'Mammy, there's a thing . . .'

Fin is at her side in a moment. Looks at the slit carcass, entrails dangling down like purplish rope. Looks into the empty black eyes. Feels himself start to shake.

And then Mammy is behind them, arms around their shoulders, pulling them back into the house.

'Was that a bunny?' asks Lilah, and her face is flushed. 'That was a bunny with its tummy all cut out. Who did that? Why did they do that?'

Roisin stuffs her hands in the pockets of her robe, not wanting the children to see that the shock has caused her to tremble. She takes a moment to compose herself. When she speaks, there is a cold quiet rage within.

'Daddy's looking into something important,' she says. 'There's a man who does things like this. A silly joker of a man. He probably thinks this is all a big laugh. It's not though, is it? It's not funny at all, and Daddy will be super cross if he finds out about it. So Fin, you look after your sister for a little while and Mammy's going to go and take the rabbit back to the man and have a little chat with him. If Daddy calls, you've both got tummy aches, yes? And if Auntie Trish rings, tell her to stay the feck out of it.'

Fin looks at his mother. Her expression leaves no room for argument.

Five minutes later and she is unhooking the dead rabbit from the nail above the door and dropping the carcass in a carrier bag. Furious, white-faced, almost unrecognizable in jeans, baggy jacket and baseball cap, she is sitting behind the wheel of the little Kia and punching an address into the satnav.

She has business in Brantingham Woods.

TWENTY-THREE

The wet road hisses beneath the big fat tyres of the Subaru, throwing up a spray of dirt and slush and leaves. The rain turned to sleet for a spell some time after midnight and the citizens of Bradford woke to find the city looked both cleaner, and yet more down at heel. The tangle of cramped streets and blocky old buildings are all a couple of shades lighter than yesterday, but the gutters overflow and the kerbs are thick with all manner of gunge: takeaway boxes, mangled food – the contents of the ripped bin liners that sit by the over-full industrial dustbins. It may be mid-morning, but all of the vehicles on the slow-moving roads have their headlights on and the windows of the nearby vehicles are all a mess of steam and dribbles – drivers leaning forward to peer out myopically through smudged portholes.

'Shithole, isn't it?' says DC Fusek, for the umpteenth time, as they make their way slowly along one of the main arteries through the city. 'How can it be uphill in every direction? Makes no sense. Proper bobbins.'

McAvoy has managed to tune himself to a frequency that enables him to block out much of what Fusek has to say but occasionally something of his prattle manages to get through. He turns to the driver and glares at the side of his face.

'Nowhere looks pretty on a day like this,' he grumbles. 'We could be in Venice and it would still look dreadful in this kind of rain.'

'I've done Venice,' says Fusek, pursing his lips. 'Twelve euros for an espresso and a pigeon shat on my knee. Fucking liberty.'

McAvoy doesn't really know how to respond so returns his attention to the file on his phone. He can feel a dull ache at the nape of his neck and his position in the bucket seats are doing little to help – pushing his head forward so he feels as though he is being eaten by his own beard. He's working his way down the message that pinged through a few minutes ago: a brief summary of what Andy Daniells has managed to ascertain about the finances of the various players in the hour and a half since McAvoy briefed him. Daniells has already discovered that Calpurnia Dodds-Wynne has four separate bank accounts – three of which are consistently active. Her wages for speaking engagements, guest lectures and the proceeds of her book sales are all paid in to a high-interest savings account. The total has been between £40,000 and £50,000 over the past five years. From there, a monthly sum of £1,500 has been automatically transferred to a second account to deal with direct debits for council tax and various utilities. She pays nominal sums to three charities and an eye-watering amount in home insurance. The third account makes a monthly payment of £860 to an accountancy firm in Guernsey, slowly depleting an initial deposit of £40,000. The fourth account is mostly static: a business account set up in the name of Lupercal. A six-figure sum sits idly accumulating interest – the only outgoings a bi-annual payment of £8,000 to the Oxford university where she was once a student. The origins of the significant sums are not yet accounted for but Daniells has found no accounts in her partner's name or any financial records for Magnus. Mo Laghera, meanwhile, has just one building society account, processing the wages he receives from his role as an 'estate manager' for his uncle's property business. It pays £28,000 a year. McAvoy wonders how many other ex-convicts are bringing in such a healthy sum. He sends a message of thanks to Daniells and glances at the trio of missed calls from his home number. He sends a trio of kisses and a question mark to Roisin's mobile – a piece of 'holding' correspondence that lets her know he is a little busy, but is thinking of her, and will call back when he can.

'Here we go, Smokey-Joe,' says Fusek, brightly, as a gap appears in the traffic and he's able to follow the satnav's instructions to turn left. He spots a bit of open road and stamps on the accelerator, shooting forward and swinging around a roundabout at such a speed that McAvoy is briefly pressed against the steamy glass. He decides not to make a fuss. It would take extreme violence to make a dent in Fusek's cast-iron shell and McAvoy hasn't got the energy.

The Subaru slows as they bump over a constellation of

rain-filled potholes and onto a narrow street of slim terraced houses; a great block of brickwork and single-glazed windows; of lace curtains and satellite dishes, empty front yards and sole-scuffed front doors. To the rear are a collection of lock-up garages, tattooed with a skin of gaudy graffiti; the doors rusting, paint flaking, but the padlocks thick and well-maintained. An ice cream van sits on a swathe of cracked forecourt, a dark-haired man slouched at the wheel, mobile phone wedged between ear and chin.

'Reckon that fella sells more wraps of crack than he does Soleros,' mutters Fusek, jerking his head at the van. 'Who the fuck is going to be fancying an ice cream right about now?'

McAvoy ignores him. Decides that now would not be the right time to salve his sweet tooth and treat himself to a 99.

'This one,' says McAvoy, and Fusek noses in to a parking space between a Ford Fiesta and a small blue van. Fusek looks around nervously as he kills the engine. 'You think she'll be all right? The baby?'

McAvoy senses an opportunity. Pats the dashboard as if it were a good dog. 'I wouldn't risk it. You stay here and keep an eye out. I know what she means to you.'

Fusek gives him a grateful look. 'If he runs I'll be after him like a greyhound with its arse on fire, sir.'

McAvoy doesn't let his pleasure at being called 'sir' show in his face. He wonders whether it will ever sound normal – if he will get used to it the same way he eventually did to the word 'sarge'.

Bones aching, McAvoy disentangles himself from the vehicle and steps out into the cold, squally air. Breathes in a lungful of city air. Smells spice and petrol, exhaust fumes and hot metal. Catches the faintest trace of cannabis drifting down from an open window five or six houses downwind. He straightens his clothes and tries to comb his moustache and beard with his fingertips. He looks rumpled and exhausted: a big man getting smaller by the hour. He's busy rubbing his hands over his eyes when the back doors of the little van whisper open and a figure within subtly readjusts themselves. The door opens a sliver more.

McAvoy stops, one foot raised. There's a snail in the middle of the road. He bends down to retrieve it, as gently as he can, and then looks around for a patch of greenery to deposit the little creature. He settles on a privet hedge, then turns back to the house. DC Fusek is pulling a face at him, looking at him as if he's mad. His cheeks burn with embarrassment, his thoughts a jumble. He feels a little like he's going mad. He fancied, as he stooped to pick up the snail, that something had whistled past him; that for a moment he had heard a noise just like the wind blowing across the top of a glass bottle. He shakes it away. Tries to focus on the job at hand. Tries to be what the job needs.

He doesn't notice the crack in the brickwork at the last house on the row: a spiderweb of fresh cracks and splinters spreading out from a deep dark hole.

TWENTY-FOUR

It is not his fault. Not really. The big man has held onto this belief for as long as he can remember. Perhaps he could have made different decisions; perhaps there were opportunities when he could have stepped in and redirected some of the lessons that were taking them all in directions that would end in blood. For all that he is physically imposing and has a singularity of purpose that makes him dangerous, he knows himself to be weak. She tells him often. Tells him how the gods despise him. Tells him how he disappoints and displeases her; how she permits him to still be in their lives only through pity and bitter necessity. She has not been kind to him in a long time. Sometimes, he wonders if she ever treated him with anything other than utter disdain. He has vague memories of their initial courtship; the intensity of their couplings, the glut of new experiences – the unexpected delights of finding pleasure in pain. He had thought himself to be a worldly man; had known half a dozen lovers before he gave himself to her. But none made his flesh sing with exquisite fire. None lost themselves so completely in acts of brute physicality and hedonistic abandon. When she had bound his wrists he did not protest. When her teeth drew blood from his neck, his shoulders; when they left coin-shaped wounds in the flesh of his cheek, he found himself utterly transported. There was never any possibility of retreating. He belonged to her from the very beginning. He belongs to her still. Of course, she has long since lost interest in him. He fetches, carries, cleans where she will permit it. He serves her in the limited ways she will permit. Sometimes she still finds pleasure in the whip, but she lacks the strength to strike him in the way that either of them need and both are left feeling frustrated – remembering their youth and the way the blood would fall like rain.

He hopes that this last sacrifice will return him to her favour. He will not witness her delight, her gratitude – not in this realm, at least – but he has faith that the goddess will grant him one last mercy. He has been a good disciple. He has stuck to his vows. He has lived by the old codes; praised the old gods and scorned the new. He has praised Juno in blood and bone. In the name of love, he has buried infants. Through duty and devotion he has planted bodies in the earth; disposed of the wriggling, glistening meat that the ceremonies demanded. He has flayed the hides from squealing animals; read the future in their guts. He has taught himself to stay one step ahead – ever watchful for some new atrocity that will necessitate the kiss of the whip and the shedding of blood.

The big man looks again at the shimmering mound of entrails that steam in the ornate bowl. Crimson liver, purply little knuckles of severed cartilage and crunchy tuberous twists of intestine and gut. He reads the bowl of gleaming offal with the same ease he might once have read a book. He knows what she wants of him. Knows that his goddess demands another sacrifice if she is not to turn away from them. He has served his purpose; has maintained his side of the pact. They were granted that for which they prayed. They were granted a miracle. It would be sinful, blasphemous, to resent the imperfections in that most benevolent of gifts.

Naked, his skin snake-like in the guttering light of the candles, he wonders whether he should permit himself a goodbye. Whether he should tell her what he is going to do. He shakes away the impulse. To explain himself would be to cheapen the act itself. Their relationship has survived many years on shared, unspoken secrets. She will understand. She will, at the last, understand all that he has done to keep them safe. His momentary losses of control have been atoned for. The things he did to the poor little man on the beach in Zeebrugge still pain him all the way to the bone. His frustrations should never become action, he knows that. It is his lot to keep his agony inside. Bearing it is his payment for the happiness of his beloved.

He looks again at the dagger. Glances around himself and feels a sudden swelling wave of absolute sorrow. He is lonely. He has been lonely for a very long time.

He looks at the pale blue veins on his thick, ropey arms. Wonders whether he will see her. Whether it will hurt. Whether she will weep for him, or revel in the ecstasy of this valiant, selfless act.

Something flashes in the corner of his vision; a discordant note sounding amid the glorious symphony of the moment. Modernity intrudes into this ancient place.

Irritated, he picks up his telephone with bloodied hands. He has a dozen different cameras mounted in the woods; all providing twenty-four-hour feeds. He has watched the police with mild amusement. Has spent countless hours witnessing the happenings in the woods; the animal acts committed by those who think themselves unobserved. The system feeds back on a loop, providing twenty-second bursts of footage from each individual location. He can focus on one video at a time if something catches his attention. And something has.

A little car is reversing down the curve of road at the edge of the woodland. It has come to a halt just before it comes into sight of the police officers who guard the crime scene and who probe, white-suited and hapless, at the sacred earth.

He takes control of the camera. Zooms in for a better look at the driver. Permits a little smile of surprise as he sees the registration plate. Toggles the controls and makes out the dark hair of the driver.

He finds himself strangely relieved. He had hoped she would understand the message. Had hoped she, like he, would peer into the entrails of the stinking rabbit and understand that her husband risked great harm if he were to continue on his chosen path. He had tried, had he not? He had given her fair warning.

He looks again at the pretty young woman in the driver's seat. Looks again at the blade and the steaming pile of offal.

The decision is relatively easy to make.

As he makes this final offering, he will not be alone.

TWENTY-FIVE

Elloughton Dale, near Brantingham
10.46 a.m.

The rage wore off an hour ago. Now Roisin McAvoy is feeling slightly silly, under-dressed and ever so slightly ashamed of herself. She wonders if there is a word for this feeling, for this dissipation of fury and its replacement with embarrassment and regret. She has always had a temper. Most of the most interesting things that have happened in her life were a result of some loss of self-control. But she knows she shouldn't be here, on this empty curve of road: a slick black shoelace of rutted tarmac curving between two great walls of woodland. Shouldn't be here, in this damp green tunnel, in her silly little car, barefoot in dressing gown and jeans.

There are police a little way up ahead, just out of her line of sight. The road is open again but there are yellow signs on the grass verges urging any motorist who recalls an incident in 1996 to call the number at the bottom of the sign. Nobody saw her as she came to a halt and reversed back down the hill, pulling in at the edge of the road with two wheels up on the soggy grass verge. An officer in a dark-blue coat had been chatting with a woman in a hi-vis jacket and she had spied two big white vans half blocking the road. No Aector. No Trish. No Andy Daniells or Ben Neilsen or any familiar face who might let her sneak up to the big house and dump a dead rabbit back on the mat.

She's been parked here for what seems like an age, nibbling the crystals on her fingernails and trying to work out what to do, and who to be. She will always view the police with suspicion. As far as she's concerned, the few decent coppers are the exception to the norm and are entirely the result of their proximity to her husband. She believes, quite ardently, that people raise themselves up in his company. She's heard it said that he's a good detective but a poor police officer. She can't understand that. She just knows he's a good man.

She glances again at the dead rabbit on the passenger seat: dead eyes staring up at her from within the slick folds of the carrier bag. She has the windows down to let out the smell. She knows that reek: that iron tang of offal and pooling blood. She butchered animals when she was a child and has no compunction about picking up a freshly killed pheasant from the roadside and turning it into something delicious. But this is different. She briefly tried to persuade herself that the dead thing nailed to her front door was left as some form of kindly gesture: a gift for the pot, given by some misguided but well-intentioned neighbour. She hadn't been able to buy into the lie. She knows why the rabbit was left for them. She knows what it signifies. She knows who left it. McAvoy has always shared the details of his cases with her. It's the one rule he has never shown any misgivings about breaking. She is an asset, helping him see things more clearly; listening without scorn as he outlines outlandish theories or admits to having no bloody clue what is going on. She had been unnerved by what he told her about the big man at the Brantingham house and his tree of dead animals. She had known at once that her husband was getting involved with a case that had its roots more in her world than in his. She may content herself with hedgerow medicines and the odd bit of positive manifestation, but her family know that she carries inside her a soul that would have been more at home in a different century. She can read tarot cards, palms and tealeaves. She can feel the heat of a stranger's pain as they pass her in the street. She knows to her very bones that it has been her own charms that have kept Aector safe all these years. As soon as she learned of the body beneath the ash tree and heard about the giant man laying out the gutted rabbit nearby, she had known it for what it was. Known it as both sacrifice and offering.

'Pick a side, Ro,' she mutters to herself, still unsure what to do. 'Sitting here like a fecking eejit . . .'

She's called home and told the children that she's sorry she made such a sharp exit. Told them they should have a sofa day and eat cereal from the box and that she will be home as soon as she can with lots of lovely goodies. She wishes she could turn that promise into a real course of action. She doesn't know why she's still sitting here. With her fury gone, it's only stubbornness that is stopping her from retreat. She had it in her mind that she would bang on the door and throw the rabbit in the face of whoever answered, telling the occupant that she had just saved their life. She has no doubts that McAvoy's rare bursts of temper would all coalesce into one colossal explosion if he were to have seen the rabbit pinned to his own front door.

She drums her fingers on the steering wheel: the diamante crystals on her coloured nails sparkling in tandem with her rings. She smiles down at the engagement ring. It was her grandmother's once. It provides her with some reassurance about who she is. She loves her husband with a fierce and passionate loyalty but there are occasions when she yearns for the open spaces; the freedom of the road – the liberty of not having to always do what is best for every bugger else. It seems obscene that her husband is out investigating a murder committed in a different century, leaving his own home and hearth to probe the death of an unmourned dead man. And yet she knows it matters to him. Matters so much that he would risk his own life if it was the price of truth and justice. She finds it sweet and decent and would never ask him to be anything other than who he is. But sometimes she'd like him to quit and move them all to the Highlands; to run the family croft and swim in Loch Ewe and breathe in the good clean air of a place far from harm.

'Grow a pair of bollocks, Roisin, stop being a babby.'

She makes her decision. Puts the car in reverse and commits a near silent three-point turn. She decides she'll take the rabbit home and leave it outside. She'll tell Pharaoh and she can calm Aector down before he gets home. Then the police can deal with it. Do their tests, take their statements, mess around doing things properly. She doesn't think there's any need to tell him that she made this little excursion. She fancies it will be no real challenge to convince the children that they really are poorly and that she left the house for a couple of hours for no other reason than to buy medicines and snacks. The only thing that will eat away at her is the knowledge that she stopped herself from doing that which her bones told her to do. She understands that there has to be some sort of code for society; some kind of rule about what can be done and what cannot and a set of consequences laid out for infringement. But she also knows that somebody who nails a dead rabbit to a family's front door deserves a swift kick in the groin and a headbutt to the nose.

She puts her foot down. Watches the curve of road disappear in her rear-view mirror. Fiddles with the radio and jabs at the controls of her mobile, trying to get the Bluetooth to pick up and fill her head with some Shakira. She pulls a cigarette from the packet in her pocket and pushes in the lighter on the dashboard. She feels a little better; experiences the tension bleeding out of her as she puts some distance between herself and the house where the big man hung the dismembered animals. She allows herself to smile, feeling quite pleased, wondering whether she will be able to resist telling Aector after all. He'll be so pleased with her, she thinks. Maybe the nail in the doorframe will yield a fingerprint that allows him to catch the bad man. Maybe he'll be able to arrest him and jail him and then forget about it all; come home and be held and hold them all in return.

The man appears like a face in the fire. One moment there is just the narrow winding road, and then there is a figure in front of her, utterly motionless: staring straight at her – a silhouette against a backdrop of rain and trees and darkening sky.

'Jesus Fuck!'

She slams her foot on the brakes, her arms rigid against the wheel, teeth locked and spit hissing through her teeth as the car comes to a screeching, shuddering halt mere inches from where the man stands. He doesn't move. Stands there like a suit of armour.

Heart pounding, pain shooting up her forearms, Roisin lets out a stream of multi-lingual curses; adrenaline flooding her, tears tickling her eyes and cheeks; a mad crazed smile of relief splitting her features as she tells herself that it's OK, she didn't hit him, that everything's fine . . .

It takes a moment for her senses to realign themselves. Only then does she truly see him. He's huge. Bigger than her husband. He wears bike leathers: boots and gauntlets. His head is perfectly bald but shaggy grey hair dangles down from an inch or two above his ears, tangling with the coarse grey of his beard. He's got his head slightly on one side, as if listening out for approaching thunder. And he's staring at her. Staring through the glass, face utterly expressionless.

Roisin's temper dies beneath the wave of icy terror that floods her. Suddenly she has no wish to confront this mammoth man about the gift he left at their front door. Suddenly she feels small and cold and very afraid. She glances at the dead rabbit and sees only her own fragility reflected back: the brittleness of her bones; the insubstantiality of her flesh.

She fumbles with the gear stick. Tries to find reverse but the clutch is sticking. The cigarette lighter pops and she gives a shriek of fright, grabbing for it instinctively and then dropping it into the footwell. Cursing, gabbling, she grabs for her phone. It slides, inexorable, towards the opening of the carrier bag, disappearing into the mess of blood and guts and fur.

And then he is at her window, filling the glass with black leather. He tries the handle. She spins around frantically, checking that all the door locks on the old car are pressed down. Too late she hears the rear door open behind her.

'Don't you fucking touch me – don't you put a fucking hand on me or I swear to God he will pull your fucking arms off and beat you to bastard death . . .'

Then there is a gloved hand around her mouth, pinching her nostrils shut, holding her jaw shut and her world is all darkness and dancing stars and the thud-thud-thud of blood rushing inside her head.

When he pulls her from the vehicle and carries her into the woods, he takes care to recover the rabbit from the passenger seat. She did not heed his warning. She did not want his gift.

Now, like the others, she will have to pay the price.

TWENTY-SIX

Mo Laghera lives at number twenty-four. There's no gate on the hinges and the tiny rectangle of front yard holds nothing but a bed of grimy gravel. There are two wheelie bins by the front door, the lid to the nearest one slightly raised. McAvoy uses his elbow to lift the lid and peeks inside. Sees folded pizza boxes and an empty packet of washing powder, sitting atop a layer of folded cardboard containers, edges sodden, little flags of unstuck packing tape fluttering in ragged twists. McAvoy reaches in and rummages through the packages. The first two are addressed to M Laghera. The next, stuffed down the side of the bin, is addressed to D Maxsted. McAvoy pulls it free. The addresses match. D Maxsted's post has been correctly delivered to the address where Mo Laghera has been a resident since his release.

McAvoy takes a quick picture with his phone and lets the box slide back inside. Slowly closes the lid.

Three knocks on the uPVC door. He used to knock so respectfully that nobody inside took any notice. Now he uses his big hands like hammers. He needs any occupants to be in no doubt that he is going to stay here until he gets a response.

He counts to ten. Does it again in Gaelic. Begins in Latin, getting cross. Reaches *octo*, breathing in and out like a flogged horse.

Finally, a movement from within. A shadow rippling the frosted glass. A shout from behind the closed door.

'Yeah, who's that?'

'Police,' says McAvoy. 'Is that Mohammed Laghera?'

There's silence for a time. McAvoy fancies that he can hear the occupant muttering a few quiet curse words. Then the key turns in the lock and the door swings inwards to reveal a slim, slightly dishevelled looking man with thick dark hair and a greying beard. He's wearing a T-shirt and jogging trousers. He's barefoot: thick black hairs creeping out of the bottoms of his trousers to snake around his ankle. A gold necklace glitters at his throat. His arms are slim, with veins so risen and thick that they give him the appearance of a cyborg: blue wires snaking over his living skin.

'You sound Scottish,' says Laghera, wrinkling his nose and looking up at him with darkly attractive eyes. He rubs a hand through his hair and stretches theatrically. 'I was asleep. Did you have to come so early?'

'It's nearly eleven, sir,' says McAvoy, politely. 'I'd call that a reasonable hour.'

'Eleven? Is it? Fuck, I should probably get myself together a bit, eh?' He looks around him as if expecting to find instructions as to what he should do next. He gives McAvoy a strange lopsided smile, revealing a gap in his lower row of teeth. When the smile fades, McAvoy notices some swelling to his lower lip, almost concealed by the beard. He glances automatically at his hands and spots some scabbing to the knuckles before Laghera stuffs his hands in his pockets.

'Scottish, then, eh?' asks Laghera, again. 'Had a cellmate from Aberdeen for a little while. Couldn't understand a word.'

'I struggle with West Cumbrian,' admits McAvoy, making conversation. 'Always sounds like they're asking you a question, even when they're telling you the time.'

Laghera glances out at the street. Scowls at the weather. 'It's not the best of times,' says Laghera, ruefully. 'Could you maybe come back? Or we could pop out and get a coffee and you can tell me what you're after . . .'

'This is a murder enquiry, Mr Laghera,' says McAvoy, with an air of finality. 'It's a matter of utmost priority. Even so, I try to be reasonable. I prefer to have a wee chat rather than turn up mob-handed and embarrass you in front of the neighbours. I'd far rather we simply had a conversation.'

Laghera doesn't react to the word 'murder'. Just spreads his hands, looking distinctly put-upon – as if this is a bit of an inconvenience but he'll help if he can. He doesn't seem particularly concerned to be woken by a police officer. His manner is considerably more friendly than McAvoy is used to.

'I suppose you'd best come in then,' says Laghera, stretching again and cracking his knuckles. 'Sorry about the state of it.

Not really had a chance to sort it yet. I do work for my uncle, collecting rent, tarting up bathrooms, fixing gutters and stuff. Pays the bills, just about.'

McAvoy makes a show of wiping his feet on the hessian mat as he enters the small living room. He takes a quick glance around the room. It's sparsely decorated. A three-bar electric fire is built in to the nearest wall, framed by a cheap wooden mantelpiece. The walls are a migraine of flock wallpaper: haphazard swirls in cream and magnolia. A big TV spills over the edges of a Perspex stand – a leather pouch splayed open on the floor, full to bursting with CDs and DVDs. The sofa, pushed back against the far wall and taking up some of the entry to the little kitchen, is a saggy affair: green and gold Draylon with worn-down handrests. Above, the bright bulb is cocooned within a lopsided paper lantern. McAvoy's eye is drawn to the pile of books mounded up by the side of the sofa. He glances at the expanse of wall by the staircase and marvels at the absence of a single piece of art. No posters, no bland landscapes, no family snaps. He changes his position to make better use of the light. Spies two little copper nails protruding from the mazy wallpaper.

Laghera leans against the space by the fire. He closes the front door but doesn't turn the handle, leaving it slightly ajar. McAvoy notices another little nail in the wall beside the velour, plum-coloured curtains. Another picture has been hastily taken down.

'Have a seat, if you like,' says Laghera, waving him towards the sofa. 'Did you say this was something about murder?'

McAvoy sits down on the sofa, his back to the doorway to the kitchen. He gives a nod of thanks for the hospitality, then decides to dive straight in.

'I wanted to talk to you about your former housemates,' he says, keeping his eyes fixed on Laghera as he slithers into a crouch with his back against the wall. 'Ian. Trudy. The Sarahs. I believe your uncle owned the property. You shared with a group of students.'

Laghera nods, scratching at his stomach. He pulls his phone from his pocket. Checks it and puts it away again. 'Right bunch of try-hards,' he says with a smile. 'Sweet lot. Not exactly party animals but we had some laughs. Years ago, like. It was all Britpop and Tarantino. Ancient history.'

'Can you give me the names of your housemates? See if we're working from the same information?'

Laghera pulls a face. McAvoy is clearly asking a lot. 'Bloody hell, I've not even had a piss yet. I'm not up for a round of *Mastermind.* I've shared with loads of people. Overseen loads of houses for my uncle. As for which was which, you'll have to help me out.'

'Ian Musson,' says McAvoy, keeping his eyes on Laghera's. 'An archaeology student.'

Laghera doesn't react. His face remains perfectly neutral. He glances at his phone again, chewing his lip – a portrait of a man doing his very best but failing.

'I'm told you and Ian were friends,' says McAvoy, his manner still entirely amicable. 'There was another gentleman who was a frequent visitor to the property – a departmental assistant at the university. I understand you stayed in touch over the years.'

Laghera starts scratching at his arms again. McAvoy glances at his bare feet, wondering whether there might be needle marks between the toes. Laghera certainly looks like his system is missing something that it's grown to rely upon. He's finding his assumptions about Laghera to have been very wide of the mark. He's not the gangland enforcer that he had begun to imagine after reading about the torture trial. Laghera looks more like a victim than a violent criminal, though McAvoy knows, to his cost, that even the most mild-mannered of people sometimes house a beast within their skin.

'I've got a few mates,' replies Laghera with a shrug, picking at his fingernails. 'I'm popular. Who do you mean?'

'Dieter Maxsted,' says McAvoy. 'You were great friends, apparently.'

'DT?' asks Laghera, his voice unnaturally high and bright. 'God, there's a blast from the past. What's he up to these days? Aye, we got on well enough. Must be years since I saw him though. Went travelling, last I heard, but he was the sort to get into mischief in an empty room, y'know, so he's not the sort I'd expect to last to pension age.'

McAvoy doesn't speak for a moment, letting the dead air

become awkward. Laghera, still trying to be helpful, starts gabbling.

'He wasn't so much my mate as Ian's, y'know? Ian, yeah, he's the guy you spoke about, did I hear you? It's coming back now. He was the one who didn't stick around, yeah? Left after one year and a semester? Him and that lass he was always trying to flirt with, they both left round about the same time. I was smoking a bit back then so I don't know how much I can remember for sure. Ian was the clever one, wasn't he? Quiet lad. Geordie, I think, though I'm never sure with accents. I think I sent some of his stuff to his mum . . . was it his auntie, maybe? Honestly . . . was he the one who was into Coen brothers movies? Had a poster on his bedroom wall. *Raising Arizona*, I think. And the big *Pulp Fiction* poster too. Uma, with the dark hair. Yeah, he was a Dungeons and Dragons guy. Liked his PlayStation too. Was it Tekken? The game we were all a bit obsessed with. Bloody hell, you've opened the floodgates. There were two girls called Sarah, I think. A Julie? Eliska?'

'Trudy Wade,' says McAvoy, without expression.

Laghera's mouth twitches. 'Trudy? I'm not sure . . .'

'You are,' says McAvoy, softly. 'You know exactly who I mean. You paid her a visit a couple of years back when she was trying to find Dieter Maxsted. She works for Heritage England. She's given me the transcripts of the interviews you gave police when they were following up on some stolen artefacts that you and Dieter fenced to some of your contacts. Are the floodgates open now, Mr Laghera?'

Laghera sits forward, crossing his legs, rocking a little: a schoolboy desperate for a pee. 'Don't mate,' he says, his voice wheedling. 'Don't be starting on all this shit. I'm out. I'm doing my best . . .'

'Am I right?' asks McAvoy, gently. He feels a genuine surge of sympathy for the pitiful spectacle before him, even as he reminds himself that Mo Laghera could be responsible for the murder of two old friends. He is preprogrammed to feel compassion in the face of all other emotions.

'Trudy, yeah,' sniffs Laghera, glancing again at the blank screen of his phone. 'I was off my face, mate. I shouldn't have scared her like that. She were all right. She'd go to the shops and bring you back a Milky Way without you asking. She was that kind of girl. Nice. Ian was really into her. I shouldn't have said what I did but I was in a bad place, y'know. I've made stupid mistakes in life. You know what I got sent down for. That's not my world, I swear. I'm not a fucking gangster, I'm just a bloke who knows people who are. I was trying to be like them, that's all. Scare her off, show her who she's messing with. It was a dickhead move.'

'Do you know that she left university because she was pregnant with Ian's child?' asks McAvoy, sitting forward.

Laghera looks up, wrinkling his nose. Shrugs, folding in on himself, as if all residual fight is leaving him. 'I never bothered myself,' he says, quietly. 'We never spoke about him much. Not after that stupid fucking night.'

'Brantingham Woods?' asks McAvoy, inserting the location into the conversation like a blade.

Laghera doesn't react. Just nods. 'Did I tell her? Did I say where it happened? Fuck, I've got such a big mouth.'

'I think you should tell me everything, Mr Laghera,' says McAvoy, looking down upon Laghera with kindly eyes. 'You might not be aware, but human remains have been discovered at Brantingham Woods. And I believe you're not above using your knowledge of what happened there to help make your point. The silver coins. You certainly scared Trudy into silence.'

Laghera smears his hands across his face. There are no tears, but he's acting as if they are streaming down his face. 'It's Ian?' he asks.

McAvoy nods. 'We think he's been there since the winter of 1996. He died a bad death, Mr Laghera.'

'I didn't see it,' mutters Laghera, resting his head on his folded forearms. 'Dieter said Ian had done a runner. Got clear. We came back for him, I swear, but there was no sign of him. We couldn't hang about, it stank like somebody was having a barbecue so we knew we'd be seen if we started making a fuss. We thought he must have just lost his bottle and gone off for a quiet life somewhere. I wasn't his dad, was I? And Dieter needed to get his leg set, and then when he didn't come back for the new term – well, he must have gone home, eh? Or travelling, like he'd said. Dieter knew more, course he did, but what did I want to go opening that door for? I mean, he was lucky to get out, wasn't he? And he smoked as much dope as I did, so what he thought he saw – well, it had to be in his head didn't it?'

'Take a breath, Mr Laghera,' says McAvoy, pulling himself out of the chair and crossing to where the stricken man sits and rocks, fitfully. He puts his big hands on his bare forearms and insinuates himself into Laghera's gaze. He breathes slowly, calmly, helping Laghera find the right rhythm. 'In through the nose, out through the mouth. Slowly. Just breathe with me. You don't have to talk until you're ready . . .'

'He said it was easy money,' whispers Laghera, panting. 'Dieter owed. I owed. Ian needed money . . . fuck, he said it was for travelling, but it wasn't, was it – not if Trudy was having his kid . . . fuck, he needed it for the baby didn't he?'

'Easy money?' asks McAvoy.

'Dieter had had a bit of a thing with one of the third year students. Proper freak. Beard like a prophet. Dieter went to his place out in the countryside towards Hull. Half term it was. There weren't meant to be any parents there and Dieter and his mate were going to have a few days of luxury. The lad was a bit indiscreet. Showed him just what a fortune his family were sitting on. Dieter was only human, wasn't he? I mean, he was fond of him but it wasn't true love, was it? It fizzled out, course it did, but when Dieter found himself desperate for cash, well – it seemed too easy, yeah? We all had reason, and it was supposed to be no risk, high reward. Dieter already had buyers lined up. I was the driver. Ian was the littlest so he and Dieter were the ones who did the job. It was supposed to be simple. Then the lights exploded. Straight up, fucking exploded, and Dieter fell and mangled his leg and smashed his head, and Ian did the sane thing and started running for it. Dieter managed to haul himself out and climb back out. Got back to the car all sweat and blood and thought Ian must have already got back to us. I just floored it. Took off like it was the movies. It was only when Dieter had got a few pulls of weed in him that he told me what he'd seen . . .'

McAvoy puts his hand on Laghera's shoulder. Starts to haul

him up. The phone slides off his knee and lands on the carpet, face up.

There's an active call.

Laghera has been letting somebody listen in for the last twenty-six minutes.

'Bro, I'm sorry,' says Laghera, though whether it's to McAvoy or the person on the other end of the line, McAvoy can't be sure. He gets his answer when Laghera suddenly springs forward, smacking his head into the underside of McAvoy's jaw. For a moment McAvoy's world is all silver stars and swirling darkness and then he is staggering backwards, bleeding from the mouth where his teeth have mashed his tongue. Laghera throws himself at him again, smacking him in the face with the edge of the phone and McAvoy shoves him in the chest with enough force to send him reeling back across the room, thumping into the wall. McAvoy shakes his head, his ears ringing. He glances up groggily, trying to make sense of the ripped picture his eyes are feeding to his brain. Sees Laghera fumbling around behind him, his hand disappearing into a mess of ripped paper and broken plasterboard. And then there is something green and gold in his hand and he is coming at McAvoy with desperate fury writ in his dark eyes.

'No, Mr Laghera . . . Mo, we can . . .'

Laghera swings the metal statue as if chopping wood. McAvoy throws up an arm to defend himself and feels the bone crack as the metal base of the dust-spattered statue thuds against flesh. The pain shoots all the way up his arm, and for a second he feels sick and faint, sweat pouring instantly from every pore. From somewhere nearby he fancies he hears glass shatter. Hears muffled yells; a squeal of fright and the screech of tyres.

Laghera above him, arm raised, an executioner aiming an axe at an exposed neck . . .

McAvoy throws the punch out of sheer instinct. Laghera, the statue raised above his head, has no time to react. McAvoy's huge fist slams into the side of his head. The crack sounds like a bowling ball hitting a wall. For a moment Laghera just stands there, gulping and making little cawing sounds. Then his legs buckle. He collapses in on himself as if his strings have been snipped through, the statue falling to land on his outstretched wrist, his eyes shark-like as they roll back in his head.

McAvoy slithers to his knees. Holds his head in his hands, trying to still the clamouring of church bells and ice cream vans jangling in his head. Then Laghera starts to fit. Blood pours from his ear as he jerks, uncontrollably, shaking like a live fish on a hot plate.

McAvoy pushes his fingers into his mouth and grabs his tongue before it can slide back into the airway, then rolls him onto his side, fiery pain gripping his left arm. He manages to manoeuvre him into the recovery position. Shouts for Fusek. Shouts for anyone who can hear him. He grabs at his pockets, looking for his phone. Where the hell . . .? He looks around frantically and spots Laghera's own device. Snatches it up. The call is still active. Somebody is listening.

'Who is this?' he demands, panting desperately. 'Hello. This is the police . . .'

The sound of metal on metal; a squeal of rubber on wet road. The door handle rattling; a shape against the glass.

The door bursts open. DC Fusek stands in the doorway. Blood is pouring down his face, oozing from an ugly wound in the dead centre of his forehead. One eye seems to be static while the other flits around desperately. There's glass on the front of his jacket. Glass and blood.

He mumbles something incoherent. Looks down his own nose. Says something that sounds, for a moment, like '*madferit*'.

Fusek falls forward as if nailed to a board. Lands on his front amid the dust and plaster.

McAvoy ends the call. Dials 999 immediately. Scrambles towards Fusek and rolls him onto his back, feeling for a pulse in his neck. Starts heart compressions. Looks back to Laghera. He isn't breathing.

'Please,' he says, into the phone. 'Ambulance. Hurry, I can't save both of them . . .'

He pounds on Fusek's heart. Stares into the dying eyes of Mo Laghera. Feels his broken hand start to throb. Feels the bones in his arm splinter as he pushes again and again on Fusek's chest.

Counts, and prays, and counts and prays. Feels the pulse

flutter back into something like life. Crawls to Laghera and starts to pump at his chest.

Don't die, he pleads. If you die, I'm a killer. I'm not a killer. I'm not . . .

By the time he hears the sirens, he has broken every one of Mo Laghera's ribs, and twice restarted his heart.

TWENTY-SEVEN

Hull Royal Infirmary,
12.28 p.m.

Trish Pharaoh leans against the grey wall. Lights a black cigarette. Blows out a lungful of sepia smoke and watches it drift up to join the parchment-coloured sky. Sometimes she feels as though the city is bleeding: its vivid shades leaching into the earth like blood seeping from a wound.

She feels the tickle in her chest again. Tries to clear her throat without it becoming a cough and ends up with bright spots dancing in her vision and tears threatening to spill out from behind her sunglasses. She is no stranger to such encounters. Her body is frequently her enemy. She's small, curvy; size four feet and barmaid breasts. She's nobody's mental picture of a senior detective but she's never thought of size or stature as relevant to how much space a person takes up in the world. She's small, but mighty. Now even her innards seem to be working against her. Bits and pieces that were once team players have recently gone decidedly rogue. Sometimes she wakes up with swollen ankles or knee joints so stiff that she has to rub them for twenty minutes just to get the buggers to bend. Her teeth bleed for no satisfactory reason. She dropped a bottle of Zinfandel on the arch of her foot before Christmas and the bruise is only just starting to fade. There's a little hump at the top of her neck where her headaches begin. Even the masseur she allowed to pummel her with his big hands had asked whether she had ever suffered a serious neck injury. She fudged her answer. She doesn't know whether any one of her late husband's punches ever turned her head further than was good for it. The whole thing is pissing her off royally. Not only does the coughing make it awkward to smoke, but sometimes it causes her to spill her wine.

'I'm thinking of asking for a transfer,' says Dr Salmond,

without preamble, as she emerges from the dark grey door and takes a position beside Pharaoh. She glances up at the faded sky and the sleeting, sideways rain. 'Jesus, the wind's picking up again, isn't it? Can do without another hurricane, thanks. I still haven't got my wheelie bin back after the last one.'

Dr Salmond stuffs her hands in the pockets of her big Aztec-style coat. Snuggles down inside the rough, mazily-patterned collar; dangly earrings sticking straight upwards and disappearing into her tangled grey-brown hair.

'I need . . . I don't know what I bloody need . . .' begins Dr Salmond, shaking her head. She looks drained of energy. Looks a little green.

Wordlessly, Pharaoh offers her one of the cigarettes she keeps in the inside pocket of her jacket. These are for other people. Her own panatellas stay in their fancy case, indiscreetly tucked inside her bra.

'Dieter Maxsted,' breathes Dr Salmond, finally, and rests her head against the wall of the mortuary. 'Definitely. Matched the swab taken when he was arrested in connection with some stolen Grecian artefacts. The hands match the fingerprints too.'

Pharaoh turns her head. Sucks on her cheek for a moment. 'I know you, Sally. You're either auditioning for amateur dramatics and practising your pregnant pauses, or you're trying to find the right way to tell me something outlandish.'

'The matter we found in his teeth,' says Dr Salmond, wincing in advance and licking her dry lips. 'His own.'

'His own what?' asks Pharaoh. She rubs the lump at the nape of her neck. Shakes the embers out of her dark hair before they catch fire.

'His own skin,' says Dr Salmond, swallowing. 'The epidermis removed from the front canines yielded a DNA sample. So too the mulch compacted in the rear molar.'

Pharaoh pushes her sunglasses up on top of her head and turns to properly face the pathologist. 'He ate himself? Fuck off.'

Dr Salmond shrugs. 'I had a feeling you'd say that. Ran it through some of the data-sharing services; some of the universities in the US upload interesting cases to an intranet that other pathologists have access to. More cases than you'd expect.'

'I'd expect none,' says Pharaoh, dropping her cigarette and grinding it out. 'Why? How?'

'One or two instances of people with mental health issues consuming their own skin while in a state of paranoia. Drug addicts too, especially those on crystal meth and fentanyl. Hallucinations, delusions – cases where people have taken whole chunks out of their own limbs.'

'I was fancying chicken for lunch,' mutters Pharaoh. 'That's that fucked. Go on, tell me what you're itching to tell me.'

Dr Salmond glances at the back of her left hand: black biro scrawled as far as her wrist. 'Nicosia, Cyprus,' she says. Briskly. 'October 2013. Thirty-one-year-old Greek national by the name of Ionas Chrysostomou. His body was found in woodland. He was missing hunks of flesh from his thigh, flanks, chest and his left cheek. One finger had also been bitten off at the knuckle. Cause of death was a downwards strike with a bladed implement, inflicted while the victim kneeled, hands tied. The blade went in at the base of the neck and proceeded down to the heart. Quick and clean, but the suffering he endured prior to his end – it was biblical.'

'They found the same as our guy? His own organic material in his teeth?'

'In his stomach,' says Dr Salmond, looking at the tip of her cigarette and losing interest in returning the butt to her lips. 'The victim was a known drug dealer. Convictions for fraud, violence – and one particularly intriguing mark against his name.'

'Go on.'

'2012. He was arrested in the wake of a robbery at the Olympia museum in Greece. Three individuals overpowered a guard and smashed their way into dozens of display cases. Made off with artefacts of – and I quote – "incalculable" value. Statuettes, jewellery, coins. Cleaned the place out. Police arrested two of the suspects inside forty-eight hours. Found 4,000 gold coins stashed inside a false wall in his apartment. Chrysostomou's name came up in interview. Police raided his premises but he'd already cleared out. Bank and phone records showed that he was a major player and he had the connections to fence the items on. He also had the connections to get himself false documents and head overseas. They think he was in Tunisia for a few months before he turned up in Cyprus, and in Cyprus, he met the person who roasted his skin for him and made him eat it.'

'Roasted?' asks Pharaoh.

'It had been held in flames. Sliced off, held in a flame, and then held to his lips. Wounds to the cheekbone and ribs suggest he took quite a beating first.'

'They catch anyone?' asks Pharaoh, hopefully.

'Still active,' says Dr Salmond. 'Lots of resignations in the wake of it all, and damn little of the hoard was ever recovered. The best lead they had was a witness statement that placed the victim in a seafront bar two days before the discovery of his body. He was drinking with a tall, bearded man. Accent was hard to place. Locals thought he might have been Australian.'

Pharaoh flicks her hair behind her ears. 'Can't have been that many people on the island at that time,' she says. 'Passport search would surely have narrowed it down . . .'

Dr Salmond shrugs. 'The details were basic on the database but they might give you more. Either way, it's interesting. I can't say for a solitary moment that it's connected to Dieter Maxsted, but I want to get this out of my head and into somebody else's.'

'Cause of death?' asks Pharaoh, leaning back against the wall and feeling horribly tired. It feels as though there is a paving slab pressing down on her chest.

'I've only got his head and hands, Trish,' says Dr Salmond, with a wry smile. 'I've taken samples of the matter beneath the nails and sent them to our botanist. She's swamped but she's promised to bump us to near the top of the list – see what pollen and plant materials can tell us about where he may have been.'

'When was this done to him?' asks Pharaoh.

'He hasn't been frozen,' says Dr Salmond. 'But from the degradation of the skin tissue, it's more likely years than months, although it all depends on the environment he was stored in. There's no obvious sign of head trauma.'

'And the nails? The knife used to remove the head?'

'Post mortem, certainly,' says Dr Salmond. 'The nails are certainly of a similar age to those used on Ian Musson. Coins too. There's evidence of another puncture wound in the back of the right hand. Driven right through. It's not there any more.'

'Fuck.'

'Indeed. As for the type of weapon used to remove the head, it was two swipes with a long bladed implement. Very sharp. A cut to either side, and then swift removal. Expertly done.'

'I can't wait to tell Aector all this,' says Pharaoh, shaking her head.

'You got his name right,' said Dr Salmond with a smile.

'I've been able to say it since the day we met. I just like waiting for him to get sick of "Hector".'

'You're very cruel to him,' says Dr Salmond, teasing. 'If he had pigtails you'd pull them for fun.'

'It's good for him. Character building.'

'You might want to pick his brains about the last little thing.'

Pharaoh pulls a face. 'There's more?'

'Pinpricks to the tongue. Half a dozen of them, conducted post mortem. Somebody pulled his tongue out of his excised skull and pricked it with a sharp object.'

Pharaoh screws up her eyes. 'That sounds oddly familiar. Why do I have it in my head that somebody important suffered a similar fate?'

Dr Salmond pushes her hands through her shock of frizzy hair. 'Cicero,' she says. 'Perhaps Aector mentioned . . .'

Pharaoh nods, sighing from the soles of her boots. Her head is pounding suddenly. She needs to eat. Needs a strong coffee with something fortifying tipped in. Needs two hours asleep in the back of the car. Needs to make fun of Aector McAvoy for a little while and enjoy the unfathomable comfort of his nearness.

'Can you not hear that?' asks Dr Salmond, nodding towards Pharaoh's little car, parked up in a space reserved for consultants.

'Hear what?'

'You know your phone's gone off a dozen times, yes? Honestly, Trish, when are you due a medical?'

'A medal?' asks Pharaoh, pretending to mishear. 'Got more than my share. Bronze in the four-hundred-metre hurdles, Mexborough, 1982. They called me "Flash".'

'I'll send this all over to you in a jiffy,' says Dr Salmond, looking disconsolately towards the mortuary door. She shows no desire to return to the gleaming stainless steel of the autopsy room. Looks as though the things she has witnessed today may have caused her to ask some big questions of herself about whether she wants to still be doing this job a year from now.

'Thanks Sal,' says Pharaoh, and gives her friend a brusque hug. 'We'll open a bottle soon, yeah?'

Dr Salmond gives her a nod of affirmation, and then Pharaoh is moving quickly across the wet tarmac of the car park. She's four car lengths away from her little two-seater when she hears the insistent buzz of her mobile, ringing madly on the passenger seat. She yanks open the door and looks at the screen.

Her heart starts to pound as she takes in the list of missed calls. Three from the office, six from Andy Daniells' mobile, two more from the McAvoy house phone, and fourteen from a variety of unknown numbers.

She calls Aector's number immediately. It's answered on the second ring by an unfamiliar voice. 'Hello, is that Detective Superintendent Pharaoh? My name is Yvonne Trevelyan. I'm IOPC. We've been trying to get hold of you—'

'Is he alive?' demands Pharaoh, her mouth flooding with water, the skin on her arms turning a bloodless grey.

'Yes,' says Trevelyan, a note of caution in her voice. 'Yes he is. And by some miracle, so is his colleague. The witness too. But he's got a lot of questions to answer. I've only just arrived. Mr Laghera's address is now a crime scene and DS McAvoy has been removed to a secure location where he can help us better understand what happened.'

'Fusek?' asks Pharaoh. 'Fusek's hurt too?'

'We are led to believe he was attacked in his vehicle. A projectile of some sort smashed the windscreen and struck him with considerable force.'

'And what happened to Aector?'

'That's what we're trying to find out. It's a question of whether he did the right thing or the wrong thing. He was in a very difficult position, of course. Does one save the criminal or the colleague?'

Pharaoh pulls at her hair, hard enough to cause her scalp to sting. 'Has he got his solicitor? Federation rep?'

'He said he's willing to proceed without counsel,' says Trevelyan, her tone suggesting that this is not the course of action she advised. 'He says he has nothing to hide.'

Pharaoh closes her eyes. Shakes her head. 'I want him back on our patch immediately. I want him given access to legal advice. I want him checked over by our own force medical examiner. If you've bagged his clothes and put him in a perp suit, I swear . . .'

'I'm sorry, Detective Superintendent Pharaoh,' says Trevelyan. 'Until we understand what happened here, Detective Sergeant McAvoy is going nowhere. This was very nearly a double murder.'

'But I need him . . .' protests Pharaoh, weakly.

'I would learn to get used to being without him,' says Trevelyan, a little apologetically. 'Warn his family too. We've tried to contact his wife but there's no answer at his address. If you have a way to contact her, let her know he's not going to be home any time soon.'

Pharaoh glances at the phone. Sees the missed calls from the McAvoy house. Looks at Roisin's mobile number and wonders how the hell she is going to tell her. And then the phone is beeping to tell her she has another call: Roisin McAvoy's mobile.

'I'm coming over,' says Pharaoh, cold rage in her voice. 'You take advantage of his good nature and I swear I will fucking bury you.'

She hangs up on Trevelyan. Answers Roisin's call.

'Roisin, Christ, where do I start . . . are you . . .?'

There is silence from the other end of the line. A silence that gradually becomes patterned with a slow, rhythmic breathing. There is a sudden cry of pain, a slew of angry cursing. Then there is the crack of a whip, loud as a breaking branch, and the screech of somebody whose whole world has become a searing point of white-hot pain.

'Roisin,' whispers Trish. 'Roisin, please . . .'

The caller cuts her off. She's left listening to nothing but dead air, and her own pounding heart.

TWENTY-EIGHT

McAvoy tries not to let the pain show as the doctor squeezes the knuckles on his left hand. He looks up, surprise showing on his pleasant face; his expert fingers unearthing something noteworthy beneath the skin.

'Not exactly virgin territory here, sergeant,' says Dr Khan, with a note of admiration. 'You boxed?'

McAvoy nods. 'I wasn't very good.'

'More damage to your hands than your face,' says Dr Khan. 'Usually a sign of a fine pugilist.'

McAvoy looks confused. 'You can see my face, yes? My boss says I look like I've let Edward Scissorhands give me a facial.'

Dr Khan grins, pleased with the joke. He moves his hands up to McAvoy's wrist. This time McAvoy can't conceal the agony. He grimaces as the pain shoots up his broken forearm to the shoulder.

'He needs it setting,' says Dr Khan, to the air. 'That will be the fourth time I've told you this same piece of information, Yvonne. It's broken. The jaw is bruised but nothing more.'

'And the right hand?' asks Yvonne Trevelyan, leaning by the door of the medical room with her arms folded across her chest.

'Swollen but not broken, though that may be because it's been broken multiple times before. When you photograph him, could you send me a copy please – just for posterity. There may be a lecture in this.'

McAvoy sits on the leather examination table, legs dangling over the side. He stares at the floor as Dr Khan re-ties the sling in a neat knot behind his neck. 'Codeine and ibuprofen,' he says, conversationally. 'One or the other, or both. But that's about as much as we can give you. When you get to the infirmary they'll maybe offer morphine. I'd encourage you not to be interviewed while it's in your system.'

'That'll do, doc,' says Trevelyan, looking put upon. She's a tall, trim woman with short hair and jointy limbs; all elbows and knees and neck. She has bad posture, her shoulders a little hunched over; her face held permanently in an expression of stoic forbearance. She's been nothing but courteous since her arrival but there's an air of frayed patience about her and it's clear she's in the dark about her priorities. West Yorkshire Police called in the IOPC as soon as it was ascertained that two of the people at the crime scene were officers with Humberside Police. McAvoy had been removed from the scene by two uniformed officers and a timid-looking detective constable who kept telling him he was sorry, that this must be a nightmare, and that he wouldn't wish it on anybody. Then they took his clothes and bagged his hands and made frantic phone calls to superior officers while paramedics worked on keeping Fusek and Laghera alive. Everybody at the scene wanted to get McAvoy to a hospital but he refused to leave until he knew about the condition of the injured men. Eventually the order came through from on high that he was permitted to be kept in situ until the nearest IOPC investigator could be dispatched. It was an hour before Yvonne Trevelyan arrived. By then McAvoy was shivering with the pain of his broken arm: his sweat soaking through the white paper oversuit he'd been given by the science officer. Now, safely removed to Shipley Police station, he's a little more comfortable in grey jogging trousers and matching sweatshirt, but no shoes are big enough for him and he feels ridiculous in his white socks. He doesn't really know what he wants to happen next. He feels as though he has done everything right and is trying to put his faith in the system, but he also knows that there will be a huge amount of scrutiny coming his way now that the IOPC is involved and that his every decision will be pored over by people who don't have to make decisions in the heat of the moment.

'I spoke to your boss,' says Trevelyan, moving the doctor's chair on its casters with her foot. She has her hands in her pockets and there are elastic bands around her wrist. McAvoy knows them to be a tool used in the suppression of obsessive compulsive behaviour, or at the very least, incessant fiddling.

'To Trish?' asks McAvoy, as Dr Khan gives him a little pat

on the shoulder and a nod to both of them. He leaves the little medical room without a backwards glance.

'Your DCC,' explains Trevelyan. 'I spoke to Pharaoh as well but it was pretty swift. Quite the dynamo, isn't she? I saw her give a lecture once. Bloody hell she was funny and terrifying all at once. She's loyal to you, I saw that much. Threatened me with all sorts if I didn't treat you right.'

McAvoy manages a sad little smile. He's trying not to feel too sorry for himself but he's in a lot of pain, he fancies he's caused Pharaoh a headache she's in no state to contend with, and he's no idea whether he has caught a killer or let one get away.

'The DCC was considerably less concerned for your well-being,' says Trevelyan. 'Not much of a surprise. You have to be a certain kind of bastard to get to that rank, as you know.'

'Is that official IOPC guidelines, ma'am?' he asks.

'No idea,' she says with a shrug. 'I'm a bit over it, if I'm honest. Went into this side of the game so I could help get the warrant cards off the dodgy and the incompetent. Nine times out of ten it comes down to which headlines are the least objectionable to some senior officer or another. This mess you're in – I'm tired out before I start.'

McAvoy looks up, intrigued. 'Are you always this frank?'

Trevelyan snorts. It's a funny sound, like a horse demanding attention. 'I acquainted myself with your file on the way over,' she says, with a wry smile. 'I take no pleasure in seeing you sitting there like this.'

'You've got a job to do,' McAvoy says with a shrug.

'Are you always so bloody reasonable?' asks Trevelyan, scowling. 'Most officers look at me as if they'd gladly burn my bloody house down. I don't know whether that's a sign that you're guilty or innocent.'

'Are those the two options?' asks McAvoy, cradling his arm. He's trying not to talk too much. His jaw throbs every time he moves it. 'Guilty of what?'

Trevelyan shrugs, hands still in her pockets. 'Well, it comes down to whether you did things properly. And "properly" is a continuum, as you know.'

'Am I allowed to ask questions?' asks McAvoy, trying to

focus. His head is pounding. He feels as though somebody has reached into his brain and opened all the doors and windows. His neatly ordered mind is in chaos.

'We're just chatting, sergeant,' says Trevelyan. She has the manner of a teacher who finds herself having to discipline a pupil who is more used to receiving awards and medals. McAvoy feels a certain sympathy coming off her, as if she'd like to tell him that it doesn't matter just now and he should probably have a nice lie down until he feels better. He almost wishes she would give in to the urge. He's tired and he hurts and he's never been very good at knowing whether a truth or a lie will hurt more.

'Did you trace the call?' he asks, his eyes on hers.

Trevelyan lets out a sigh. Pulls a face or two. She can't seem to make up her mind. 'Unregistered,' she says, at last. 'It's literally only just come through from the provider but it used the same cell tower as Laghera's. The call was being listened to by somebody within a seventy-yard radius.'

'So they were outside and went for DC Fusek when they heard something they didn't like?'

Trevelyan removed her hands from her pockets long enough to open them wide and do a remarkable impression of a louche French waiter. 'Maybe.' She shrugs. 'The thing that came through the window – a flat stone with a hole in it. Curious choice of weapon. I doubt they were aiming to kill him. Probably just picked up the first thing that came to hand and hurled it at the glass. Poor sod took it between the eyes.'

'He was nice as pie until he noticed me looking at the phone in his hand,' broods McAvoy. 'Then he lost it. What was it he hit me with?'

'We've bagged a statue of a horseman with a spear. Hard marble base. One good crack and he'd have killed you.'

'I just swung,' says McAvoy. 'I didn't think. He just keeled over.'

'When we do this properly, you probably don't want to go in with that as an opener. You were terrified. In fear of your life. He stumbled forward as you swung out your hand and your first thought was to save him.'

McAvoy rubs his jaw, unsure what the hell is happening now.

'That's all true, just about,' he says, moving his jaw in circles and feeling the pain run to the top of his head. He screws up his face, trying to remember all the questions that had seemed so important an hour ago. 'The false wall – what else have you found?'

'West Yorkshire are working through it for now but there's a treasure trove,' says Trevelyan. 'Coins, jewels, medals. There's a couple of valuers on the database who we can ask to give a price on how much stuff he had stashed away in there and maybe when he wakes up he can tell us who he was planning to sell it to.'

'I think we'll be first in line,' says McAvoy straightening his back. 'I believed him about Ian Musson and Dieter Maxsted. Believed him right until the moment he tried to kill me. Now? He could well be our man.'

'Mobile data shows several trips to Nottingham in the past six months. You said Dieter Maxsted, yes? That's the name on a lot of the empty parcels in his bin.'

'He's also the skull and hands sitting at the mortuary in Hull,' says McAvoy, with a grimace. 'Dealer in stolen antiquities. Laghera was an old friend. They both knew Ian Musson, a student at Bradford Uni whose body was found in Brantingham Woods a few days ago.'

'Sounds like you know how to stir up trouble,' says Trevelyan, shaking her head. 'Helen was right about you.'

'Helen?' asks McAvoy, surprised to hear the name.

'National Crime Agency,' Trevelyan says with a smile. 'Friend of mine. Good judge of character too. She called me about twenty minutes ago. Said you taught her everything she knows and that the bits you didn't, she learned from Trish Pharaoh. Won't make any difference to many people, but it makes a difference to me.'

McAvoy drops his head. Wonders how many people are going to risk their reputations for him before he finishes blundering about and getting himself hurt.

'What do I do now?' asks McAvoy, feebly. 'Now you're involved, I mean. That's our evidence. The rock, the phone, the items behind the wall. It's all relevant to our murder enquiry.'

'I wouldn't worry for now,' says Trevelyan, as somebody

hurries down the corridor outside, footsteps echoing loudly against the bare walls. 'Dr Khan was right. You need to get to hospital and have that arm set. Then I would give yourself a couple of days of sick leave while Trish Pharaoh and I have a glass of wine and come to some sort of an understanding. Let's be honest here, you saved two men's lives. The fact that you punched one of them in the head hard enough to kill him, is probably something we can fudge.'

McAvoy shakes his head. 'Do things the right way,' he mutters. 'He has an uncle who'll want to know the truth.'

'His uncle's a member of an organized crime gang,' scoffs Trevelyan. 'Jesus, when Bradford CID heard what had happened they were all for sending you a fruit basket. Leaving that nasty bastard in a coma and sticking one to his uncle? That's a good day's work.'

'Nasty bastard?' asks McAvoy.

'You know why he was inside. He may not have wielded the whip but he was shouting on encouragement from the sidelines. More than that, it was his whip they used on the poor lad.'

McAvoy jerks his head up. 'His whip? How do you know that?'

'I've been acquainting myself with Laghera's case,' she says, tiredly. 'A lot more to it than you'll have read in the newspaper report. They found the whip in Laghera's car and decided to use it on their victim. Horrible thing. Leather, of course, but nails and bones and all sorts of nasty shit. Ripped the poor sod to pieces.'

'Ian Musson,' mumbles McAvoy. 'He had the same injuries. That's why I came to see Laghera . . .'

'The two lads who did the real torture – they were happy to tell the investigating officers that Mo wasn't really involved. They were willing to do the time. They said Mo wasn't much more than a chauffeur and that he didn't want to be involved. But then they found that in his car.'

'Was it antique? Was it produced for court?'

'One of the lads chucked it in the canal,' says Trevelyan, ruefully. 'Apparently Laghera was as upset about that as he was about witnessing a man's death. It had been a gift, apparently. Hell of a gift, eh? From what I can understand, he told one of the killers that he'd had it for years. Some old mate of his had given him it. Their dad made reproduction goods. Cuffs, sandals, thongs, you know the sort you see at folk festivals. I'd be surprised if it was hard to track them down but the investigating team already had enough.'

McAvoy leans back against the wall. The pain in his arm seems to have reached a zenith. There's just a cold numbness now. 'Can I have my phone?' he asks, softly. 'Please. I think I know where we should have been looking. And the stone . . . can I see the stone? Was there a hole in it? Did any of the witnesses hear a whistle . . .?'

Trevelyan pats at the air, telling him to slow down. From outside comes the sound of running feet. The door opens with a bang and a uniformed PC shoves her head inside the room. She glances at McAvoy, then her eyes find Trevelyan. She jerks her head. 'Phone, ma'am. Urgent.'

Trevelyan rolls her eyes and mooches outside, leaving the door slightly ajar. McAvoy hears mumbled voices. Hears a trio of barked exclamations and a swift goodbye, followed by another hurried conversation conducted in a more deferential tone.

McAvoy sits quietly. Feels the pieces move around in his mind. Remembers again the whistling sound as he had entered Laghera's house. Remembers the pile of hag stones outside Calpurnia's writing shed. Remembers the leather thong tied about the feet of the dead rabbit. And further. Deeper. Way back in his memory, something in a book from childhood. Slingshots. Slingshots and whistling stones and . . .

Trevelyan pushes back into the room. Her face is flushed, her lips pressed together as if she is fighting to hold in a song.

'What's happening?' asks McAvoy.

'There's been an incident near your crime scene,' she says, her words slow and considered. 'A car found abandoned. A call made to your phone. Another to Trish Pharaoh. There's some concern for the safety of—'

McAvoy jerks forward. Drops down from the bed and stands up straight, his whole face transformed as he glares down at Trevelyan. 'Whose car? Whose bloody phone?'

'I've spoken with Trish. She's told me to keep you as calm as I can. She's tracked the phone. They're putting together a team and will deploy as soon as it's been authorized—'

McAvoy steps into her space. 'Roisin,' he says, quietly. 'You're saying she's in danger.'

'I'm telling you as a courtesy, Aector – there have been developments – I strongly advise you to stay here and allow Pharaoh to—'

'Am I under arrest?' asks McAvoy, his voice cold as the grave.

Trevelyan shakes her head. 'You're free to leave.'

'I need transport,' he growls. 'My clothes. Is it him? Isaac Plummer? The big man? I swear, I saw. Saw it from the start . . .'

Trevelyan puts her hand on his chest and pushes him back, gently but with enough force to cause him to feel a surge of remorse for using his size. He glances down and sees the mobile in her hand. She raises it to her ear.

'See, I told you he was going to ignore you . . .'

McAvoy takes the phone from her. Holds it to his ear.

'Hector, thank fuck. Don't worry more than you have to. I know where she is. I swear, I'll get her back. He took her from the car but she's got her phone with her. We've traced her last location. Just stay put and I swear I'll call you as soon as she's safe . . .'

McAvoy feels the phone slip from his hand. Feels himself shutting down. His head is all static and crashing waves.

And then he is sinking to the floor, his good arm wrapped around his knees, staring at the floor as the tears flow, silently, down his face.

He barely hears Trevelyan as she retrieves the phone and gives in to pity. 'I'll drive him myself.'

TWENTY-NINE

Roisin wakes to darkness. She can taste blood and earth and her arms feel dead and rubbery. She screws up her face, feeling some form of soft fabric rubbing against her cheeks. She grabs at the fragments of memory, trying to work out what is truth and what is nightmare. She opens her mouth, unsure whether she is in her own bed, or a hospital, or somewhere dank and dark and terrifying. She tries to talk, to ask for water, for help, but her throat explodes into a fiery pain and her mouth floods with a bitter, numbing taste, as if she had gargled clove oil and battery acid.

'The pattern of your breathing has changed. You're awake under there, yes?'

Roisin freezes, pressing her arms against her ribs. Her senses return in a great surge of fear and temper. The dead rabbit. The police in the woods. The big man in the centre of the road. The sudden helplessness. She feels the bare skin of her forearms rub against the soft flesh of her ribs. Rubs her legs together, sweat and dirt and urine causing her thighs to adhere to one another as she tries to wriggle up. She feels her bare feet step on some soft material and realizes that she is not naked, but dressed in some unfathomable length of fabric. Her hands are behind her, bound at the wrist. She is laid out on a floor that feels at once fleecy and sheer: a carpet of lambswool and kid-skin.

'I should imagine your throat is very sore,' comes the voice, from nearby. 'I had to serve you a concoction from the herb garden. Your voice will return, given time, but I could not deal with interruption. I need company – not conversation.'

Roisin wriggles onto her knees, falling forward as if in supplication, trying to remove the blindfold from her eyes by rubbing it upon the fleece beneath her. She hears the whip crack before the pain comes. Senses the rushing of leather through still air and the log-snap smack of cord upon flesh. The pain engulfs her, shooting from her tailbone to the top of her head. She twists, desperately, and feels skin tear as the ragged tails of the flagrum cut seams through the tattoos upon her back. She folds into herself, foetal, pulling her legs in, hot tears spilling from her eyes as she screams, soundlessly, into the fleece.

'I take no pleasure in this,' comes the voice, closer now. 'I have never enjoyed causing pain. Some of the things I have been forced to do have truly sickened me. It has been an act of will and resolution to overcome my own distaste. I truly hope that what needs to be done can be performed without the need for further suffering.'

Roisin feels hot blood trickling from the open wounds on her back. Her rage is all hot snakes; slithering, uncoiling, in the cauldron of her gut. She tries to picture the man who had taken her. Remembers leathers. Gauntlets. The straggle of a huge beard. He had been immense; a colossal statue of a man. She had struggled but she was a kitten fighting a bear. She tries to pull at the ropes. Tries to pick at the threads with the tips of her nails. Fills her mind with the faces of those who will come for her. Sees Pharaoh. Had there been a phone call? Had she heard her voice? She remembers shouting her name and then the savage kiss of serrated leather against her back. She had screamed for Aector as the big man bound her and pressed the goblet to her lips, bursting her mouth like ripe fruit and filling her throat with flame. Had she dreamed what she saw? She has a vague, half-formed image in her mind; a blurry picture of skins hanging from iron hooks; of yellowed scrolls stacked up like firewood. She has a memory of patterned skin and a golden pendant on a black chain. She cannot remember his face – just the beard and the size and that smell of chopped wood and tanneries on warm days.

'Don't take it off,' he instructs her, his breath upon her face. 'It's made of lambswool. I made it myself – many years ago. To do things properly I should have insisted that the lamb be killed by a wolf, but we live in times when such an act would be considered barbaric. We are strange creatures, are we not? I sometimes envy the person I used to be – so ignorant, so blessedly oblivious. I sometimes wonder whether knowledge is a kindness.'

Roisin feels arms around her. Feels herself being tugged into a sitting position, pinioned between huge thick legs and with arms thick as her husband's folded across her chest. She tries to writhe in his grasp; stretching her fingers out behind her, trying to claw or scratch at the exposed flesh of the figure who holds her. He simply squeezes harder, pushing the breath out of her lungs. She falls limp, head lolling forward, and screams within herself, pitiful and impotent, as a huge hand strokes the hair back from her face and tips her head back, exposing her throat.

'You wear a cingulum about your eyes,' he says, quietly, his lips against her ear. 'She wore it around her belly for nine whole months. Held herself immobile. Slept, and prayed, and rubbed her swelling stomach with olive oil. She would not lose another. Twice she gave birth to a dead child. Twice she beseeched Vitumnus and Sentinus to accept her offering and grant just one child. She would raise him in their honour – raise him as a gift from the ancient Gods. She kept her promise, as I kept mine.'

Roisin gasps for breath. Throws her head back and connects with bone. It has no effect. She feels the arms tighten around her again. Feels blood coursing stickily down her stomach and puddling in her lap.

'How does one discipline a god?' asks the voice, quietly. There is a rasp, a breathlessness to its timbre now. 'How to raise a child that has been anointed by the same deities who chose Augustus? So much was given to receive this perfect, golden-haired child. So much blood and sacrifice . . .'

Roisin rubs her tongue against the roof of her mouth. Tries, desperately, to generate enough spit to swallow. Desperately, her throat in agony, she manages to croak a plea for mercy. 'Aector,' she rasps. 'He will . . .'

A cheek against hers, finger and thumb holding her jaw, tipping back her head, exposing her neck . . .

'Were it not for the blood we share, I would wish your husband all the blessings such a good and noble man deserves. I would wish him happiness and prosperity and applaud his righteous pursuit of he who has taken life. But I cannot make such a wish. To do so would be to curse my own flesh. All I can hope is that when this is over, people remember that I was more than just one thing. I was kind and determined, and I knew love. Knew it truly. Knew it in the old ways.'

She feels his grip loosen. Feels blood pulsing, pumping, across her skin.

'I had thought I would be alone. Myself, and my regrets and my wishes and my sorrow at what I lose. Truly, you were sent. You are my messenger. You will explain. You will tell those left behind that I took life after life to honour the gods who took her pain and soothed her mind and gave the golden-haired child . . .'

Roisin hears the voice fade. Feels the life leave the huge man who holds her. Feels his last breath tickle her ear and flow coldly over her cheek, and then the arms that hold her are falling away and she is squirming forward, sucking down air, skin sticky with her captor's spilled blood.

She stumbles. Pushes the blindfold against the mass of skins and fleeces. Blinks, tearfully, as she stares around at this unfamiliar space. Sees iron bars and a low roof, a workbench festooned with tools and rolled-up parchment; hinges and clasps and scraps of leather. Looks up and sees the skins hanging from the hooks in the ceiling. Looks again at the mounds of rolled-up paper, sealed and stoppered with wax. She looks back at where she had lain. Sees a floor of matted, bloodied sheepskin. Sees a huge man, back against the wall, staring sightlessly at the floor as the blood still leaks from the ragged gashes in his wrists. At his feet, an evil-looking whip: tassled leather ornamented with iron and bone. In his hand, an ancient, rusted blade; stained crimson at its dark, serrated tip.

She looks around for a way out. Stumbles forward and looks down at herself. She wears a white toga, red across the breast. She feels her own blood trickle down from the wounds upon her back. Sobs, her throat agony, as she totters forward, barefoot, to where a little light bleeds in from the gap between two black double doors. She presses her face to the wood. Forces her hand out through the space, feeling her skin tear at her wrist as she hisses in pain and grabs, desperately, at handfuls of cold, wet air.

And then she hears them. Hears the sirens and the shouts

and the screeching of tyres and the thrum of engines. She hears metal upon metal; hears dogs barking desperately. She presses her face to the gap. When her scream dies in her throat she starts kicking, barefoot, at the wood. Knees it over and over. Slams her head against the wood until her ears ring and her hairline is rich with blood.

'She's here . . . Boss, she's here . . .!'

Somebody grabs her hand. She feels a warm palm enfold hers, fingers interlace, thumbs snake about one another, and then the chain that holds the door is falling to the ground and the light is flooding in, and Roisin McAvoy is falling into the open arms of Trish Pharaoh, falling to the floor amid an army of police officers as the blades of the helicopter whir overhead; bending the branches and trunks of the trees.

'You're safe,' whispers Pharaoh, enfolding her in her coat and stroking her hair; face turning pale as she looks at the web of slashes to the dark skin upon her back. 'You're safe . . .'

A shape above her. Andy Daniells, face grey. 'Inside. The dad. Isaac. Cut his wrists, boss . . .'

Roisin finds her voice. Swallows, and whispers, her mouth against Pharaoh's ear.

'The children . . . Aector . . .'

Pharaoh glances behind her, back to the house where Calpurnia Dodds-Wynne turned to the old gods when the new betrayed her. A huge shape is lumbering through the mass of police officers, pushing aside the uniforms who briefly don't recognize him in his grey jogging trousers, grey jumper, sling around his neck and tears streaming from his wide, frightened eyes.

'Here,' says Pharaoh, disentangling herself from Roisin. 'She's OK. Hurt, but OK . . .'

And then McAvoy is tearing off the sling and scooping up Roisin; holding her against himself as his fingers find the gap in the rope that binds her hands and he pulls it apart as if it were paper. She reaches out for him, her hand in his beard, making desperate little fists and whispering, softly, that she is so sorry, she shouldn't have lost her temper, she shouldn't have left the children . . .

And then McAvoy has an arm around Pharaoh, pulling her

to him, pressing her to his chest, both women crushed against him.

'Thank you,' he whispers, again and again. 'Thank you . . .'

And just for a little while, the living are more important than the dead.

THIRTY

Roisin was discharged from hospital inside twenty-four hours. Her back needed fourteen stitches where a twist of barbed wire cut deep. The other lesions were cleaned, anointed with antiseptic, and held closed with steri-strips. The orange blossoms tattooed on her back will incorporate the new scar, given time. The little Chinese symbol at the nape of her neck has lost its hat. She declined the painkillers offered by the nurses. She doesn't like the fuzzy feeling they create in her head and would rather embrace the pain. She's endured worse than this. Fancies that she will endure worse still, before the end.

McAvoy was only absent from his wife's bedside for long enough to have his broken arm set in a cast. Nobody gave him any trouble about visiting hours. He wasn't any bother. Just sat beside her, holding her hand in his, staring into her as if trying to heal her wounds through sheer force of will. She dozed off from time to time, waking to find him still gazing into her with his big sad eyes: guilt and shame radiating off him like warm air above a deserted road. He didn't check his phone once. Didn't listen to the radio for updates. Barely acknowledged Pharaoh when she said that she and her eldest would take care of the kids and that nothing was as important as letting them heal. His whole life shrank down to one single point: an existence of blood and colour and dirt all spiralling down like paint into a plughole. All that mattered was Roisin.

It's now four days since Roisin felt Isaac Plummer's life bubble out wetly onto her skin. She cried just once, fierce and primal, on the first night home. It's out of her now. Whatever terrors she endured while locked away with a killer, she does not carry their ghosts within her. She won't let McAvoy coddle her. She keeps telling him that he has the worse injuries and that of the two of them, she is far better equipped to play the role of nursemaid. She's ordered a special outfit complete with wipe-clean apron, just to look the part. McAvoy can't laugh at her jokes yet. There's a numbness in his bones; a sense of having been smashed and then cackhandedly put back together again. The dangers of his job are coming too close to home. The litany of his failures is written in his mind's eye in big dark letters. He missed Lilah's birth while chasing a killer. Fin was taken captive by a madman bent on revenge. Now Roisin, permanently scarred by a giant of a man, intent on having some company as he left this world for whatever awaited him in the next.

It's early evening on a cold, squally Monday when Pharaoh and DS Neilsen arrive at the house to take a full statement and update their acting detective inspector on developments. Pharaoh brings petrol station flowers, two boxes of chocolates and some knock-off Polish cigarettes. Neilsen has brought a book for McAvoy to digest while he's recuperating; a weighty guide on meditation and kundalini yoga, and which will be just the right size to prop up the wobbly leg on the kitchen table. Roisin receives the gifts and guests with a genuine shriek of pleasure; a little girl receiving the bicycle she wanted for her birthday. McAvoy just mutters and broods, his spirit virtually absent. He doesn't speak as Pharaoh follows Roisin into the living room; all cigarette smoke and red wine, Issey Miyake and wet leather. Manages only a little nod as Neilsen gives him an awkward pat on the arm and tells him he's looking well. He makes the teas himself, allowing Roisin to sit on the sofa, the TV on pause, as she chats back and forth with their guests about how she's feeling and her hopes of getting a family holiday booked in for the first week of the summer holidays. McAvoy, operating with just one good arm, spills the hot water as he fills the teapot. His hands shake so much that the teaspoons jump from his fingers and clatter onto the cups and saucers. He has to keep stopping, taking deep breaths; sweat oozing out of him across his shoulders and forehead. He catches a glimpse of himself in the glass of the kitchen window and sees nothing but a great lumbering fool. He hasn't brushed his hair or his beard; has slept in the crumpled lumberjack shirt that he wears with jogging trousers and trainers. He doesn't look like the man he tries to be. Looks instead like the man he has always tried too hard not to become.

'You should have a trolley,' says Pharaoh, her tone overly jolly, as McAvoy brings in the drinks one at a time. She's sitting on the sofa beside Roisin; sunglasses, leather jacket, scuffed biker boots smudged with sand. Neilsen is sitting in McAvoy's armchair, trim and handsome in his neat grey suit. McAvoy doesn't know where to sit so just squats down by the fireplace, his back against the wall. He glances at Roisin, who gives him the look that tells him it's all going to be OK.

'There's no biscuits,' mutters McAvoy. 'I can pop to the shop.'

'Eat them all, did you? Thought I saw some Bourbon in your beard.'

McAvoy combs his fingers through his tangled red-grey hair. 'I haven't really wanted to go out,' he explains, blush flaring. 'I don't want to leave Roisin.'

'He's doing my head in,' says Roisin, lighting a cigarette. She looks at her husband and her face falls into an expression of absolute pity and love. 'He hasn't slept yet.'

'He's not dealing with it all particularly well then?' asks Pharaoh, directing the question to Roisin and leaving McAvoy feeling like a toddler whose mum is chatting with the neighbours about his habit of wetting the bed.

'Feels guilty, of course,' says Roisin, gently. She looks spectacular in her baggy cardigan, tight vest and ripped jeans; her make-up extravagant; every nail painted and with her hair falling in dark ringlets. 'He won't listen.'

Neilsen looks at McAvoy, embarrassed for his friend and boss. 'Nowt to feel guilty about, Aector,' he says, kindly. 'You were busy saving two lives, as far as I can tell. And look at Ro – more gorgeous than ever.'

McAvoy gives a little nod of thanks. Glares into his teacup. He doesn't want anybody to be nice to him. Wants this done with, his visitors gone. Wants to hammer planks of wood across every door and window and start digging them a subterranean panic room in the back garden.

'Fin slept through last night,' says Pharaoh, moving her sunglasses to the top of her head. 'Tonight we'll try it without the hammer.'

'The hammer?' asks McAvoy, groggily.

'Lilah's idea. He's scared in his sleep, isn't he? So she thought if he felt like he could handle anything that came for him, it might make a difference. Worked a bloody treat. Snores like his dad.'

McAvoy nods, his lips pressed together. 'I should have thought of that.'

'I can't wait to see the big eejit,' Roisin says with a grin, sipping her tea and giving a little grimace. 'Jaysus, Aector, that's weak as a nun's piss.'

'Sorry,' mumbles McAvoy. 'I'll do another . . .'

'Let's crack on, eh?' says Pharaoh, rummaging around in her bag and finding a sheaf of papers. She pulls her phone from her pocket and starts to record, making sure to announce all those present along with date and time. She'll use her own notes to write up the statement but she likes the security of having her own copies of all interviews, however informal.

She looks at McAvoy, her blue eyes hard and clear: sunlight on snow. 'You've been thinking about it, I know you have,' she says, in the voice she uses in interviews. 'You've got misgivings.'

McAvoy meets her stare. 'Doesn't matter, does it? It's gift-wrapped. Murderer kills himself – it's the neatest conclusion. No need to build a case, no need for a trial. We can just put a line through it. Problem solved.'

'You don't think that's who I am, do you?' asks Pharaoh, looking a little hurt. 'Christ, Hector, you're not the only copper fighting the good fight . . .'

'Not you,' says McAvoy. 'You neither, Ben. But I've seen what the top brass do. See how they tweak the narrative so that everybody's happy with the outcome.'

'You're not happy, I take it?'

'I don't understand it,' says McAvoy, his back teeth clamped together. 'How could he be in Bradford threatening Mo Laghera and firing a stone at DC Fusek at the same time as he was grabbing Ro?'

'There's no guarantee that the two incidents were linked,' says Neilsen, looking at the backs of his hands. 'Somebody threw a stone at DC Fusek, that's for certain. It struck him with considerable force, causing an immediate bleed on the brain.

He's still too mixed up to remember much, other than a vague sense that it came from the back of a van. But it could just have been a complete coincidence.'

'That's pish,' says McAvoy, his face twisting in scorn. 'The whistling stones – the ones the Romans used in battle. We saw a bloody pile of them outside Calpurnia Dodds-Wynne's writing room. I wasn't sure at first but I remember it now. One of the buggers flew past me as I was walking to Laghera's door.'

'Laghera's still unable to confirm your memory of events,' says Neilsen, quietly. 'He's out of the coma but he's not out of danger yet. As for the phone – whoever was listening in, we can't trace them. The mobile phone company has provided the information we asked for – whoever they were they were nearby, but the phone is unregistered and pretty much a dead end.'

'The change that came over him,' mutters McAvoy. 'As soon as he saw that I had clocked it, the mask slipped completely. He was a different person. He would have killed me.'

'That's not in doubt,' says Pharaoh. 'The investigation is still ongoing, as you can imagine, but I think you've made a new friend in Trevelyan. She can read between the lines.'

'He did them all, did he?' asks Roisin, dropping her cigarette stub into her teacup. 'The student under the tree? The head and hands at the museum?'

Pharaoh waits a moment, choosing her words carefully. 'He made a dying confession, did he not?'

Roisin pulls a face. 'He said a lot of things. He said he had done terrible things. He talked about the sacrifices he'd made. He spoke like somebody seeking forgiveness, I suppose. But specifics? The whole "I did it, guvnor"? No, not really. And don't forget I had my eyes covered and I wasn't in a great state for taking notes.'

'You don't have to think about it,' insists McAvoy, immediately. 'If it upsets you, don't—'

'I'm OK, my love,' she says, kindly. 'I want to help. I'm not somebody who ever imagined they'd be happy to speak to coppers, but on this occasion I feel pretty damn bulletproof. Wasn't my fault, was it?'

'There's some debate about that,' says Pharaoh, without expression. 'He left a note, you see. More than a note, in fact

– more a great bloody scroll. Working theory is that he was on his way to either confess or chuck himself off the bridge when he spotted you loitering down the road. He recognized you, of course. He wasn't in his right mind so we can't begin to know what he was thinking, but he clearly felt that you were there for some symbolic purpose. Maybe he thought you were a threat to his wife and that's why he took you – cobbled together a hasty last hurrah. The way he dressed you, the knife he used, the scourge. I think he saw a chance to die as he'd lived.'

'They really were his babbies under the tree?' asks Roisin.

'Stillborn,' says Pharaoh, looking away.

'It can make the best of people insane,' says Roisin, with genuine sympathy. 'All those children we lost, all those tiny bones without headstones. You can go mad trying to make sense of it; asking why, needing to know why some people have all these wonderful children and you can't even have one . . .'

McAvoy wraps his arms around his knees. Drops his head. 'How has she taken it?' asks McAvoy.

'Calpurnia? Doesn't really compute. She was giving a guest lecture at Durham when it all happened. She came home not long after you two got in the ambulance. She's confirmed his movements over recent days. She even gave us the "peculiar object" she'd found in his trousers when she was doing the laundry. High-powered laser, as it goes.'

'For knocking out CCTV?' asks McAvoy.

'His internet search history is fascinating,' says Pharaoh, with a hint of a smile.

'What does she have to say about the children?' asks Roisin.

'She was quite matter-of-fact about it. Pregnancies went wrong and she wanted to keep the babies close by. They buried them under her favourite tree, first one, then another. There's a third we haven't found yet but they were so small there may be nothing at all to find. The tree took on a meaning for them. Over time it became symbolic. They both went a little crazy trying to conceive a child. The house was full of books from her studies and her husband pored over them like they might contain treasure. They were willing to try literally anything.'

'Lupercalia,' says McAvoy, quietly.

Pharaoh nods. 'Pagan festival. Forerunner to our Valentine's Day. Ritual and sacrifice.'

'They did it all?' asks McAvoy. 'The goat?'

'She had the grace to look a little embarrassed,' says Pharaoh. 'But yes, her husband did the honours. Slit its throat and made leather thongs from its hide. She stripped and let him beat her. All very sacred and symbolic. Load of fucking nonsense, if you ask me, but nobody did.'

'It worked though, yeah?' asks Roisin, pointedly. 'Fertility rites matter. Rituals have power, whatever anybody says.'

'Magnus came along nine months later,' says Pharaoh. 'Golden-haired. Nine pounds eight ounces. As big and glorious a boy as you could ask for. A gift from the gods.'

Roisin looks to her husband as he raises his head. 'He spoke about that,' she says, quietly. 'Asked me how you raise a boy who has been sent from above.'

'Discipline seems to have been a little lacking,' says Neilsen, glancing at his phone and calling up a file. 'Spent most of his life as his mum's shadow. Home-schooled, you see. Tried mainstream education for a couple of years but he wasn't exactly a people person. Huge lad but his head was always elsewhere – nose in a book more often than not.'

'Sounds familiar,' smiles Pharaoh.

'Followed Mum on her lecture tours, up to his eyes in archaeological digs and fusty old libraries, forever getting on and off planes to go help his mother with her research for whatever publication or doctorate she was working on. Dad was away more often than not. I think it's fair to say she spoiled her boy a little.'

'Can't be easy for her,' says McAvoy. 'Him being on the far side of the world.'

'Apparently he visits when he can,' says Pharaoh. 'Got over the heartbreak at least. Very much a force to be reckoned with these days.'

'Heartbreak?' asks Roisin, intrigued.

'His mother told us why he didn't finish university. Reacted badly to a relationship going wrong.'

McAvoy pushes his hair back from his face, palm greasy with sweat. 'Did she give a name?'

'Referred to him as "some beastly chancer". That's a description that sticks, eh?'

'Dieter Maxsted,' says McAvoy. 'I read a social media chat – talking about DT being sweet on the bearded weirdo . . .'

'Self-same weirdo who fell head over heels in love with him,' confirms Pharaoh with a nod. 'Dieter broke his heart. But he only really paid attention when he tried to win him back. I bet he told him that the family had money. Dieter, in debt, trying to get ahead . . . he couldn't resist. Ian had his reasons too. And Mo.'

'An easy score,' says McAvoy, remembering what Laghera had told him. 'Musson, he needed money, you're right. He'd just found out he was going to be a dad. He was the third wheel, wasn't he? Friends with Laghera and Maxsted and got drawn in to a little bit of light criminality.'

'Passport office is unequivocal that Isaac was in Zeebrugge over the weekend when Musson disappeared,' says Neilsen. 'They also mentioned that he was questioned by Dutch police after a nasty assault on an old man back in 2009.'

'It's possible, isn't it?' muses Pharaoh. 'Slip on to a ferry to Hull, come home early to surprise the family – find an intruder in your house . . .'

'And whip him to death? Nail coins through his eyes?' McAvoy's voice is rising, incredulous.

'He might have recognized Maxsted,' suggests Pharaoh. 'Might have realized that the lad who broke his baby boy's heart had come back to steal the family silver. Maybe when he grabbed Musson he just went biblical on him.'

'And Maxsted?' asks McAvoy. 'Twenty years later he tracks him down and tortures him to death?'

'Stranger things have happened,' says Pharaoh, sounding suddenly tired. 'This is Hull, after all. Maybe their paths just happened to cross.'

'You hate "maybe",' says McAvoy.

'I've got my reservations too, of course, but he left a confession. He nailed a bloody rabbit to your front door, Hector.'

'He talked about its guts,' says Roisin, wrinkling her nose. 'Said he'd left it here so we would understand.'

'I think he should have bought himself a nice pack of notelets and a biro,' mutters Pharaoh. 'I tell you something – explaining this to the DCC is a bloody mission. I made a joke about Nero and he thought I was offering to get him a cappuccino.'

'Why the coins?' asks McAvoy, shaking his head. 'Why risk getting caught to deposit Maxsted's head at the museum? Wherever he'd been keeping the corpse for the past few years, we weren't about to find it . . .'

'Maybe we were,' says Pharaoh. 'We've been digging up the woods. Maybe we were getting closer.'

'Did you get the briefing note about the cases overseas?' asks Neilsen.

McAvoy shakes his head. 'Which cases?'

'Three executions as things stand – minor league thugs and burglars tortured to death for their part in various robberies of ancient artefacts. They bear all the same hallmarks. Scourged, beaten – roasted in two cases and forced to consume their own flesh . . .'

'Cicero,' says McAvoy, quickly. 'The slave who betrayed him. After Mark Antony had him killed, his head and hands were cut off and displayed in the forum. Cicero's slave was handed over to his sister-in-law, who made him eat parts of his own roasted flesh before she killed him.'

'Feck off,' says Roisin, aghast. 'That's fecking awesome.'

'The psychology of it all doesn't make sense,' muses McAvoy, glancing past Neilsen to where the swirling rain taps cold fingers on the glass. 'I could understand revenge of some sort, but are we thinking he was some sort of fence for stolen artefacts? Is that the coins? We must be able to pin down where he's been from his passport records. If these crimes are linked . . .' He looks up, narrowing his brows. 'What did the son say? Where was he when you told him? Is he coming back to support his mum . . .?'

Pharaoh looks across at Neilsen and gives a bright smile. 'Told you.'

'Told him what?' asks McAvoy.

'One Magnus Dodds-Wynne changed his name in 1997. He's been legally known as Lucius Benedict ever since. Passport in that name. Thrown out of America in 2015 after being arrested for his part in the robbery of two bronze figurines from a museum in Boston. He's been living back in the UK ever since, other than making a couple of trips to Cyprus, Sardinia, Hungary . . .'

McAvoy combs his beard with his fingers. 'His dad . . .'

'Knew what he was. Tried to hide it.'

Roisin looks from one to the other. 'The daddy tried to take the blame? To protect his perfect child?'

McAvoy looks across at Roisin and hauls himself to his feet. 'He did it to protect the woman he loved,' he says.

'So, where has he been? Where? How?' Roisin takes a sip of her cold tea, complete with floating cigarette butt. She doesn't react to the taste.

'That bloody mausoleum,' says McAvoy.

Neilsen sighs and reaches into his back pocket. Hands over a twenty-quid note to Pharaoh, who takes it with a grin. 'Get changed, then. You look like Shrek's your dad and your mother's a haystack.'

'You're going now?' asks McAvoy, glancing at his wife.

'Wouldn't be the same without you,' replies Pharaoh with a smile. 'Team are on standby.'

McAvoy looks again at Roisin. She nods her head. 'Go get the fecker,' she says. She looks to Pharaoh. 'Has he got time to make himself look like himself?'

Pharaoh nods. Lets a lascivious leer twist her features into something that is pure seductress. 'Only if I can scrub his back.'

'You can get to feck,' spits Roisin, turning gimlet eyes on Pharaoh. 'I'll have the eyes out of yer head before you touch my man.'

Pharaoh sighs. Tuts. Takes the twenty from her cleavage and gives it back to Neilsen.

'He knew you'd go for the eyes,' says Pharaoh with a shrug. 'Me, I'm all heart.'

THIRTY-ONE

Galen Court, London
March 11th, 2017
5.25 p.m.

The little courtyard hisses in the rain. Drops bounce off the glistening paving stones like coins.

Dieter Maxsted shivers as he waits for the door to open. The downpour has soaked him to the skin. He always has a somewhat bedraggled air but most of the time it is deliberate. He likes to look crumpled; a little unkempt. He can spend many a contented evening fraying the elbows of a sloppy woollen jumper or rubbing the collar of a thick cotton shirt against a rough stone. He can make a new pair of jeans look twenty-years-old with nothing more than a wire brush and a few drops of white wine vinegar. His power lies in persuading people that he is guileless. Naïve. Perhaps even a little eccentric. He has mastered the persona of the bookish bumpkin: all weather-beaten skin and patched-up clothes. It helps people to trust him. He sees it in their eyes: can read them even as they misread him. Sees them make their minute calculations, reassure themselves that this is not the look of a shyster; that no self-respecting con man would be seen thus.

Here, now, he fears that the rain risks spoiling his artfully prepared appearance. His old donkey jacket is heavy with rain and his swirl of thinning, expertly bedraggled hair is plastered to his face. His jeans cling to his legs and his sturdy boots, toecaps protruding through the battered leather, are three shades darker.

'Come on, come on,' he mutters, shivering. He's keen to get things over with. He's had some brushes with the law recently and never feels very comfortable in London. People are more suspicious here. People are streetwise. If people see through him, it's invariably here, in the city, where patience is limited and credulity in short supply.

He looks again at the wooden door. Snatches a look up into the teeming sky, running his gaze over the frontage of this old building, discreetly tucked away between a hair salon and the entrance to an office block. There are apartments upstairs, according to the research he carried out online when the address pinged through to his phone. They will at least be comfortable as they conduct their business. He may even feel sufficiently emboldened to ask for a towel.

Dieter feels the little tremble of excitement that he always experiences as he nears the conclusion of some shady undertaking. He is perhaps half an hour away from turning the items in his jacket pocket into a series of pleasing zeros on his bank statement. He does not want to jinx it with unduly positive thinking, but he fancies it will be a relatively easy transaction. The man he is meeting is said to be ultra-professional. There will be no chit-chat; no offers of refreshment or enquiries about his difficult journey down from the East Midlands. No, he will simply examine the goods, give his nod of approval, then authorize the transfer. He will take the items without thank you and then permit Dieter to be on his way. There will be no need for threats or warnings. The man's reputation is enough to ensure that Dieter would not dream of attempting to inflate the price or hint at extra costs incurred to buy his silence. He has heard the stories about Lucius Benedict. Everybody in his business has heard the rumours. Those who wrong him face a wrath that is unimaginable. He purchases goods for a very select clientele: men who are willing to pay whatever it takes to possess items of questionable provenance. The reputable dealers require proof of ownership; documents of provenance. The dealers cannot make a purchase or authorize an item for auction without endless bits of paper. But they can, on occasion, point men like Dieter in the direction of a third party – somebody with a less rigid code and deep, deep pockets.

Dieter winces as he presses the buzzer again. Hopes that he is not becoming tiresome. Shivers, hands in his pockets. Hears a wagon swish past on the wet road just beyond the entrance to the courtyard. He'd like to pull his phone from his pocket and double-check the address, but to do so would be the actions of a man who lacks confidence, and Dieter has spent many years becoming somebody who knows what he is doing and how to do it. In moments like these he occasionally permits himself a little nostalgia. He considers himself with an affectionate whimsy – pleased with the way he has managed to repeatedly turn misfortune to his advantage. He has been true to himself, that much is absolute. Convention and conformity are not in his nature. He took only the exams that he wished to take. Dropped out of three different university courses and started two apprenticeships before the age of twenty-three. He found some sense of belonging while briefly employed at the University of Bradford, but circumstances curtailed that brief attempt at leading a stable life. And yet those same circumstances helped lead him here. It was in Bradford that he met the man who was to become his closest friend and confidante. It was Bradford, too, where he met the strange, heavy-set young man with the blue eyes and the thick blonde beard and the curious air of somebody forever on the edge of things. He was friendless. Awkward. He wasn't exactly shy but he made no attempt to talk to the other students. He only came in for certain practical lessons, preferring to spend his time at home and fax across his essays to his tutors. They were very accommodating. He was an exceptionally bright student who could have gone to the university of his choosing if not for some unpleasantness on his personal record and some less than stellar grades in subjects that he had deemed unimportant.

Dieter finds himself smiling as he remembers their brief union. He is not a man to experience guilt and is well aware of his own failings. As such he makes no attempt to lie to himself about his motives for his actions. Dieter was attracted to him for no other reason than desire. He was a hulking specimen: broad-shouldered, brawny-armed. He was very much Dieter's type. And it didn't take long to catch his eye. A few clever little witticisms whispered in his ear; one or two compliments – a suggestive line scribbled in the margin of an essay. He was Dieter's plaything for a good chunk of the first year. Of course, Dieter was not the sort to commit to a relationship. To do so would be conventional; conformist. He did like him though. He didn't speak much but he listened with an intensity that Dieter found beguiling. He has fond memories of laying among sweat-stained sheets, his head upon his lover's broad chest, telling him things he did not know he even wanted to say. He remembers the big lad's fingers in his hair; the gentle way he touched him; the intensity in his eyes as they kissed. Dieter could have fallen in love with him, were he the sort. Instead he turned cold on him. Grew distant. Missed dates and didn't call and let it be known that he was seeing other people. It all bewildered his lover. He grew urgent; desperate. Made lavish gestures to try and win him back. Purchased him an antique pocket watch engraved with some saccharine Latin motto. Paid off some of the dealers who were starting to lose patience with Dieter and his friends. Dieter feels no guilt for what came next. The lad had money. He'd confessed as much as they lay nose to nose on a mattress in an empty house, sharing and touching and doing a damn good impression of falling in love. He'd sworn Dieter to secrecy, and taken him at his word when he promised never to tell a soul. Dieter has never blamed himself for his lover's poor judgment of character. It was his great grandfather who had made the discovery one day while digging out the thorny bushes that were strangling his wife's rose bushes at the edge of their little plot of garden. Something had glittered in the black earth as he turned the soil. He had rubbed the dirt from its surface and glimpsed the face of an emperor. It was the first raindrop in a deluge. In the days that followed, he dug up a hoard of buried coins, jewels and finery. They were Roman. Second century. And he didn't tell. Too afraid of discovery to seek expert advice, he taught himself Roman history. Learned the value of the items in his possession and the difficulty he would face in turning his good fortune into actual cash. There were boundary issues: some uncertainty over whether the items were on his land, or just over the ancient perimeter into land owned by the church. Instead, he made the contacts to sell off the items as and when he needed to. He hid the hoard in the family mausoleum and bricked up the entrance. Guarded it like a pirate safeguarding treasure. When the academics and the archaeologists started searching for some rumoured Roman villa somewhere in the vicinity, he did his damnedest to misdirect them – even going as far as to steal an entire mosaic pavement diligently exposed by a team of scholars.

He sold only a fraction of the items in his possession – enough to help his odd, bookish granddaughter go to the university of her choosing. He bought some rare texts from a black market dealer: scrolls and pamphlets centuries old, gifting them to his darling Calpurnia to help in her studies. She read them with the passion of a zealot.

The door suddenly buzzes and Dieter pushes it open, stepping into the chill of a wide, airy corridor. Goose pimples rise on his skin. He realizes he has been lost in memory, drifting in a little bubble of pleasant recollection. He's pleased the spell has been broken. To dwell upon it would be to invite painful thoughts to bubble up from the place he has trapped them. What came next was not his fault, but it was his idea. He needed money, that was the crux of it. So did his friend. So did the other poor bastard who lived in the student house and had knocked up that quiet girl at a drunken party. And it had gone wrong. He has a memory of exploding lights and a sudden terrible tumble into a dark hole in the outbuilding where his lover had told him they kept some of the family treasures. He'd heard his ankle snap and fire flash up to his hip. He'd seen the other lad running for his life, vanishing into the woods. In time, he'd heard screams. When they ceased, he had dragged himself back out through the broken glass and made his way back to the waiting car. They hadn't spoken about it very much in the days that followed. Weeks and months became years. From time to time Dieter prospered. He could identify valuable objects and find ways to purloin them for a minimal outlay. Sometimes he stole to order. He arranged meetings between interested parties: metal detectorists looking to profit from a find without alerting the authorities, and private collectors tired of having people meddle in private affairs. Some of what he does now is quite respectable. Some of the items he sells are actually worth what he pays for them. By accident, he occasionally conforms.

Dieter walks damply up the first flight of stairs and makes his way to the door at the end of the little corridor. He composes himself before he knocks. Tries to clear his head of the twisted memories. He does not wish to look too closely at the unanswered questions. He fancies that if he were to enquire about how his betrayal affected his lover, the answer would distress him.

Deliberately, professionally, Dieter Maxsted knocks on the door.

He doesn't recognize the man who answers at first. Is halfway through his glib opening line and extending a soggy palm when something deep within him makes the connection.

By the time Dieter has remembered why those eyes are so familiar, it is already too late. He is on the floor and bleeding from the mouth before he has a chance to blink.

Before the dawn, Dieter Maxsted will be forced to consume scraps of his own roasted flesh. It will not sate the hunger of the man who has spent these long years awaiting a chance to revenge himself upon the poor fool who betrayed him.

But it will be a start.

THIRTY-TWO

Calpurnia Dodds-Wynne refuses to come to the door when Pharaoh hammers her pudgy fist against the wood. She gives her a good minute to respond to her entreaties before she shrugs and moves aside. A uniformed sergeant steps forward with a battering ram and thuds it against the wood beneath the lock. It splinters at once. McAvoy is first inside, stepping out of the rain and the dark and shouldering the door aside. He stops at once, taken aback by the extraordinary visual spectacle within the long, wide hallway. Swathes of red cloth hang from golden standards along either wall: a series of blood-hued flags that trail upon a floor paved with a shimmering sea of small metal discs. Oil lamps flicker in a series of alcoves, casting orange and yellow light into the shadows and causing the floor to ripple and writhe as if it were the hide of a living serpent. McAvoy catches his breath, gagging for a moment as the scent of ammonia and meat fills his nostrils and tickles his throat. He looks up. The festering remains of dead animals hang from crucifixion nails; wraps of fresh herbs pinned here and there. Flies buzz in the air and feed in the corners of the room.

'Fucking hell,' mutters Pharaoh, holding back the uniformed officers and appearing at McAvoy's side. 'I thought my bedroom was bad.'

McAvoy makes his way down the corridor. Behind him, Pharaoh keeps shouting out, announcing their arrival, demanding Mrs Dodds-Wynne make herself known.

At the end of the long corridor McAvoy steps through an open doorway into a low-ceilinged living room. Presses the cuff of his coat across his mouth and nose as he smells the familiar rancid sweetness of dead flesh. The room is full to bursting with books and papers, mounded up in floor-to-ceiling piles of rotting mulch. Bags of rubbish, tied like balloons, are crammed into every possible alcove, nook and cranny. One wall is entirely made up of old textbooks; their pages damp and mildewed, coverings pressed so tightly together that they form one impenetrable mass of leather and paper. McAvoy looks down to the floor. Sees the edge of a mosaic peeking out from beneath a mountain of soiled clothing and half-empty food containers. He squats down. Uses his cuff to rub the grime from the filthy tiles.

'Yeah?' asks Pharaoh. She nods, pleased. 'That'll make somebody happy.'

The mound of papers conspires to dead the sounds and McAvoy's head is full of shouted orders and heavy footsteps in the hall. Even so, he hears the thrum of the cord as it whips in savage loops through the fetid air. Hears the whoosh and whisper as the stone leaves the slingshot. He grabs Pharaoh with his good arm and throws them both sideways into a teetering tower of rotting scrolls. The stone smashes into the wall by the doorway. Throwing a damp spray of plaster across the face of the nearest uniformed officer. He throws himself backwards, yelling 'gun, gun', screaming at his colleagues to leave him, to get out, to save themselves . . .

McAvoy picks himself up. Dusts the filth from his suit and coat. Pushes aside a wall of filth and refuse. And makes his way into the next room.

Magnus Dodds-Wynne is waiting for him. A length of hide dangles from his wrist. He is otherwise naked. He's not as imposing as his father, but he's a big man; statuesque – the hair on his well-muscled body slick with sweat and oil. He wears a golden torque around his neck and a pouch on a leather thong dangles down to just above his groin. In the light of the guttering candles he does, for a moment, look divine. His hair is the gold of fresh-cut hay and his blue eyes are as intimidating as the barrel of a gun.

McAvoy looks past him. The bedroom is all reds and golds, the walls painted with a series of erotic friezes: engorged organs; spread thighs; a diorama of ancient erotica.

In the bed, tangled up in thick white sheets, is Calpurnia Dodds-Wynne. Her hair is unpinned and flows out upon the silk pillows. She wears a matching torque. Her naked body is patterned with dark, sinewy brushstrokes. She too is glazed with sweat.

McAvoy steps forward. Stands like a statue, half a dozen paces from his foe.

'Magnus Dodds-Wynne, I am arresting you . . .'

The naked man smiles, showing perfect white teeth. He reaches behind him, eyes on McAvoy's, and grabs a flat white stone from the foot of the bed. He slips it into the slingshot with one swift, practised movement and whips the cord through the air fast as a whip.

McAvoy's good hand closes around his wrist. He feels sweat and oil and grime. Breathes in a whiff of olives and earth, red wine and cloves. Feels the strength in him. Locks eyes, for just a moment, nose to nose, eyes blurring, blending, smile becoming a leer, becoming a grimace, becoming a yelp of absolute pain, as McAvoy twists his wrist until it's about to snap and Trish Pharaoh surges forward and cracks him across the knee with her extendable baton. Then it is all shouts and footsteps and orders to get down, and McAvoy is being dragged away and Calpurnia is screaming, screaming until blood erupts from her mouth and she begins to fit, hideously, in the sweat-soaked sheets. Then her son, writhing beneath a mound of uniformed officers, spews up a torrent of black blood and his eyes begin to bleed and he, too, is dying in agony on the animal skins that cover the cold floor.

McAvoy holds the eyes of the divine child. Watches him gulp and gasp and buck with pain. Watches as he bites off his own tongue and rivulets of crimson run from his lips as if he were eating raw liver.

The uniforms pump on the dying man's chest, but he is wide-eyed and dead long before the paramedics stumble through the mound of filth and try to attach the defibrillator to his chest. He doesn't respond to the electric current. Greasy coils of singed hair spiral upwards in twists of dirty smoke.

And then Pharaoh is pushing him out of the room, dragging him back down the corridor. He glimpses gleaming skulls set in an alcove behind the wall of parchment scrolls. Sees something that might be Dieter Maxsted's torso skewered on a golden shaft of metal.

Then they are outside and the rain is slapping at their faces and it is all blue lights and white lights and long leaping shadows stretching off into the dancing darkness of the woods, illuminating the dead rabbits in the trees and the curved dome of the roof of the mausoleum.

McAvoy smells cigarette smoke. Looks to Pharaoh. She's sparked up one of her cheaper cigarettes and is scrubbing at her cheek with her cuff, pulling faces and fighting the urge to spit.

'Are you OK?' asks McAvoy, taking care to keep the tremble from his voice.

'You don't say anything, right?' spits Pharaoh. 'Not a word.'

McAvoy lets his confusion show. 'What did I miss?'

'He was naked, Aector. And I'm short. And when we all went down in a clatter . . .'

McAvoy folds his mouth into an inscrutable line. Gives a solemn nod. 'I'll never think about it again.'

McAvoy turns away. Makes sure nobody is looking and then permits himself a smile. Roisin is going to love this.

EPILOGUE

Rain falls upon full-fledged leaves: a pleasing rhythm – a rousing cheer of damply clapping hands. McAvoy sits with his back against a knobbled oak tree, arms wrapped around Roisin. She leans back against him, rain jewelling her dark skin. She gazes upwards, letting the droplets slide and slither through the branches and leaves to drop onto her bare brow, her blushing cheeks, her parted lips. This little copse of woodland is a special place for both of them. They have come a-maying – collecting bright flowers and interesting-looking sticks; a tradition that means a lot to Roisin and her ancestors. Bringing the outdoors indoors, co-existing with nature, rejoicing in the goodness of the meadows and the wood. They are traditions that border on the superstition. Superstition, in its turn, is not far from religious observance. McAvoy cannot help but wonder when routine becomes ritual; when belief becomes zeal.

McAvoy has his eyes closed. Fin is big enough to keep an eye on his little sister now. They are somewhere beyond the little slope, fashioning a den from fallen branches. McAvoy's world is sensuous and close. He can smell the soft honeyed aroma of the drooping bluebells; the rich pungency of the wild garlic. From time to time he hears the harmonies and discords of woodpecker, chaffinch, thrush. Were he to truly focus he might catch the lingering trace of fox; that fur and ammonia musk that lingers, low, amid the fern and the damp earth.

Eight days have passed since Magnus Dodds-Wynne ingested the hemlock that killed him. His mother still lives, stupefied, her brain starved of oxygen for so long that whatever of her remains would be a stranger to those who knew her. An elite team of the National Crime Agency has taken over the fall-out. McAvoy's unit didn't fight to be kept involved. There is something about the investigation that has made each of them feel somehow tainted by association. Each, in their own way, has felt as though there were elements at work that were beyond the understanding of any of them. Pharaoh is happiest catching killers. This has been an enquiry littered with gods and monsters, and neither she nor McAvoy know how to deal with either. They have both witnessed brutality before and have seen what people can do to one another when they feel vindicated or compelled. But the things that Magnus Dodds-Wynne did to Ian Musson, Dieter Maxsted and countless business associates across two-and-a-half decades, have seeped inside them and left a stain. Even the intriguing developments have left them cold. Ben Neilsen unearthed CCTV footage from a private residence near the museum in Hull's old town, showing Isaac Plummer shining a high-powered laser into the security camera outside the side door. He carried a leather bag with him, and it was empty when he came out. McAvoy has pieced together the movements of Dieter's corpse. Magnus brought it home for his mother to appreciate, and to desecrate in her own little way. It has been in the family vault for the past few years. Isaac retrieved the bits that mattered as he tried to draw the eye of the police away from his beloved wife and the boy who eventually replaced him in her bed. When the relationship began is a secret that has gone to the grave, but Pharaoh suspects that there has been incest within the family home since childhood. She doesn't excuse Magnus for the cruelties committed in adulthood, but does at least extend him some sympathy for being brought up in such an insane environment; sacrifice and ritual, pleasure and pain; dead rabbits in the trees and his many dead siblings hidden beneath the earth.

'You're humming,' says Roisin, snuggling back against him. 'Your thoughts – they're letting off a buzz.'

McAvoy opens his eyes. Blinks as the greenery floods his vision. 'I'm relaxing,' he says, softly. 'Just like you asked.'

'No, you're thinking, but somewhere new,' laughs Roisin, shaking her head. 'It's OK, my love. Just try not to let it eat you. Be here. Be with us.'

McAvoy grunts an affirmation. He has much to think about. Too much, in fact. He still doesn't know whether there will be any consequences for his career as a result of what happened in Bradford. DC Fusek is already on the mend and Mo Laghera has provided a statement filling in many of the gaps in the timeline of events. He's so grateful to McAvoy for saving his life and removing the threat of Magnus from his life that he has given them more than they actually expected and West Yorkshire Police has been able to close the file on several burglaries and one attempted murder. He'd always had his suspicions about what happened to Ian Musson but there had been no room for doubt when it came to his best friend. Dieter had gone to London to sell some gold coins and the black-market fence had turned out to be the man he had double-crossed at university a quarter of a century before. Magnus Dodds-Wynne had taken out many of his frustrations on Ian Musson when he caught him breaking in to the family home. In the wake of that horrific execution he had embraced what his mother called his 'glorious destiny'. He, the child bestowed upon her by the gods; the golden-haired, blue-eyed gift from Juno herself – he allowed her to guide his fate. He travelled. Drifted. Made contacts. Evolved. Changed his name and embraced his destiny. He made his mother proud. His father had known what he was from childhood. He'd seen the rotten thing that lived within him. But his beloved Calpurnia believed their boy to be special; magnificent, infallible. Even as he killed birds and flayed animals and bit at his mother's breast with his little sharp teeth, she knew him to be divine. His father had done what he had promised. He had protected them. He had cleaned up after his son. He had buried the mangled body of Ian Musson beneath the ash tree blown down by the storm, using a winch to raise it from the forest floor and packing the mighty roots across the dead man. It had pained him to see his own dead babies in the same grave. They had shifted from where he buried them, moving beneath the earth as if tunnelling their way to some better, more appropriate location. He had trusted in Juno. Trusted in Calpurnia. She never told him that she had helped her darling son exact revenge upon the young man who tried to rob them. Isaac didn't ask. He just set up the standing order, directing a portion of their income to the account of the young woman whom the dead man had impregnated and by whom he was attempting to do the right thing.

'Has she told you yet?' asks Roisin, picking a bluebell and twisting it in her fingers.

McAvoy shakes his head. 'She will.'

'Don't make it too easy for her,' says Roisin with a smile. 'I want to see how long it takes.'

McAvoy closes his eyes again. Pharaoh's eldest daughter, Sophia, has let slip that her mum has decided to retire. She has a full pension, and thirty years of service, and the powers-that-be have been pushing her to call it a day. They value her, but she's expensive. With her gone, they can cut, and cut, and reshuffle CID so that the unit becomes more streamlined, more efficient, and cheaper. A newly-promoted detective inspector will be given the reins. McAvoy isn't sure what he will say. He's starting to feel as though he might have had enough. He's struggling to work out what he really thinks about things any more. He fears the loss of his compassion; fears growing weary with excuses and mitigation. He can feel parts of himself shutting down – tired of the futility of it all; tired of pretending that society actually works. He'd like to slip away. Would like a small patch of land in a pretty little valley; his wife and his children and nobody trying to hurt him or anybody else.

He opens his eyes at the sound of shouts from his children. Realizes that they are laughing. Lets his gaze drift to the little muddy pond, reflecting back the bruised blue of the teeming sky. On its surface, mayflies live and dance and feed and die. None will live more than a day. He wonders whether a mayfly ever questions its purpose; whether mayflies ever question where death will come from; whether they have an expectation of living their allotted twenty-four hours and begrudge the beaks of birds or the sucking gulp of rising fish.

'What are you thinking about?' asks Roisin.

'Mayflies,' he replies. 'And fish. And if I tell you any more than that you'll think I'm insane.'

'You are insane,' says Roisin, sweetly. 'Pleasantly so.'

McAvoy suppresses the urge to scratch at his broken arm. It's itchy as hell beneath the plaster. He's had to wear his sleeves down over it at work after Roisin and the children decided to emblazon it with embarrassing messages. Roisin, in particular, had taken great pleasure in drawing two beady eyes and a stern warning to Trish Pharaoh about what would happen if she kept him past the end of his shift. She's working hard on protecting him at the moment. Can sense the changes in him. Is daring to hope that soon, perhaps, he will stop being a police officer, and concentrate instead on being hers.

McAvoy lays his head back against the tree. Holds his wife. Watches his children play. Breathes in the rich, fragrant air, and allows himself to think, for a moment, what life would be like without all the death.

'Daddy. Daddy, look!'

McAvoy looks up as his daughter comes running towards him across the bluebells. She's holding something in her hands, her eyes wide.

'Look, Daddy – I found it. There were bits of shell. Blood. It was on its own . . .'

McAvoy parts his daughter's clammy fingers. Looks at the tiny little chick held gently captive within. It is impossibly fragile. Big dark eyes and an open, hungry beak. It yearns to feed. Yearns to live.

'Can I keep it, Daddy? Can I?'

McAvoy catches Fin's eye as he approaches across the thicket. 'I think it was a fox, but I might just be guessing,' says Fin. 'It was a real mess. I don't know what happened. Do you want to see?'

McAvoy closes his daughter's hands around the bird. Squeezes Roisin and pulls himself up. He rubs Lilah's hair. 'Take care of it, my darling. Fin – let's see the crime scene, see if we can't find out what's gone on.'

He trudges behind his boy, Lilah at his side. Feels the good rain upon his skin and the caress of the damp grass against his bare legs. Glances, for a moment, at the buzz of mayflies. Focuses on one, for just a moment, and wishes it well.

'He's eating my finger! Daddy, he's biting my finger!'

McAvoy stops and pulls a tuft of grass from the earth. Grabs the tail of something pink and wriggling, and gently opens his daughter's hands. Drops the worm, live, into the open maw. Nods to himself, as if a decision has been made.

A Latin phrase, half remembered, bubbles up from nowhere.

Mortui vivos docent.

'The dead teach the living.'

And McAvoy knows, to his bones, there are countless more lessons to learn.